Readers love
JACOB Z. FLORES

Please Remember Me

"I really enjoyed *Please Remember Me…* There was a sweet romance at heart, with some sexy moments and a HEA…"
—On Top Down Under Reviews

"Moments and memories cling to me and I have no intention of letting them go. You don't have to worry about me forgetting Santi and Hank, I will always remember."
—Boys in Our Books

"Hank and Santi were an inspiring and sweet couple, and I am so glad to have experienced their story."
—Rainbow Gold Reviews

Being True

"I devoured this book in one sitting, unable to put it down once I'd started reading. It was emotional, engaging, romantic and passionate."
—MM Good Book Reviews

"So this story, you guys, I'm not sure I have enough words to tell you how truly fantastic it is."
—Joyfully Jay

The Gifted One

"I am glad to have discovered the work of author Jacob Z. Flores."
—Live Your Life, Buy the Book

By JACOB Z. FLORES

3
Being True
The Gifted One
Please Remember Me

THE WARLOCK BROTHERS OF HAVENBRIDGE
Spell Bound

PROVINCETOWN
When Love Takes Over
Chasing the Sun
When Love Gets Hairy
When Love Comes to Town

Published by DREAMSPINNER PRESS
http://www.dreamspinnerpress.com

SPELL BOUND

JACOB Z. FLORES

DREAMSPINNER PRESS

Published by
DREAMSPINNER PRESS

5032 Capital Circle SW, Suite 2, PMB# 279, Tallahassee, FL 32305-7886 USA
http://www.dreamspinnerpress.com/

Spell Bound
© 2015 Jacob Z. Flores.

Cover Art
© 2015 Paul Richmond.
http://www.paulrichmondstudio.com
Cover content is for illustrative purposes only and any person depicted on the cover is a model.

ISBN: 978-1-63476-123-9
Digital ISBN: 978-1-63476-124-6
Library of Congress Control Number: 2015905051
First Edition May 2015

Printed in the United States of America
♾
This paper meets the requirements of
ANSI/NISO Z39.48-1992 (Permanence of Paper).

For my mother, whose love has always been like magic to me.
Thank you for always supporting me in whatever I decided to do in life.

CHAPTER 1

AS USUAL, the cafeteria at Havenbridge High roared with conversation. My classmates busily gossiped with one another about the morning's events while stuffing themselves with what passed for food at our school. Not much could tear them away from their processed lunch and the nasty rumors they enjoyed gorging on.

At least until I entered the room.

From the moment I strolled through the double doors from the main hall, an eerie silence filled the room.

It happened every damn day, and it always made me grin.

Most of them were afraid of me. It wasn't like I was some jock who could bench-press twice his weight and had more muscle than common sense. I didn't have scary tattoos or weird piercings, and I didn't walk around in a trench coat that might be concealing a shotgun.

I was just your typical eighteen-year-old high school senior of average height and lean build.

Still, I terrified them. Their gazes rarely met mine, and whenever I passed, their voices dropped to whispers. Just the way I liked it.

They should be scared of me. I had more untapped potential in my pinky finger than they did in their entire bodies, and they could sense it. They just didn't know what it was they felt whenever they were around me. It had been that way ever since I was a kid.

If I told them why I had always made them so uneasy, they wouldn't believe me. My kind had been forced from this world and shoved into the obscurity of myth and legend. It had been necessary for survival.

And it pissed me off.

I was a warlock and damn proud of it. If I could have, I'd have shouted it from the tops of these tables, but that was forbidden. We had to live alongside those who had once hunted us and pretend to be like them. If we didn't, we'd face extinction once again.

"Mason!" someone shouted from the back of the cafeteria. "I got your lunch, man."

It was Brandon Priestly, one of the juvenile delinquents I called my friends. He snuck out of fourth period every day to buy my lunch. Since it was Friday, I'd sink my teeth into a wicked juicy hamburger from Barrelman's. They had the best eats in town.

I strolled over to where Brandon sat in the back with Simon Busby and Eddie Harmon, who made up the rest of my crew. These were the guys who dared to hang with me. Since they usually spent their days causing shit and teasing losers, they believed they were like me.

But I was nothing like them.

I didn't waste my time with petty crap like bullying someone who obviously couldn't defend himself. That was beneath me. Where was the challenge in that?

"Hey, Mason," Laura McBride said as I passed her table. She sat with the other girls who'd gone bad. She flipped her long dark hair away from the cleavage she proudly displayed, and she slipped her bright red fingernail into her mouth. She'd been trying to get me to nail her for two years now. "Can I see you this weekend?"

"Can't. Busy," I mumbled as I walked by, and I wasn't even lying this time. This was going to be a crazy, magical weekend, and my family had a lot to do. And even if we weren't all gathering for an important ritual, Laura and her slutty friends weren't for me.

My type tended to have lean muscles, a firm bubble butt, and a nice cock. Now someone like that would have my complete and undivided attention.

When I reached the table where my friends sat, Brandon took the burger out of the bag and moved my drink over to my usual spot. His chubby face twisted in apology; what had he gotten wrong with my lunch today? He was the largest of all my friends, but his mass wasn't due to being overweight and out of shape. Brandon was one of those guys who were just big, and he used his size to terrorize most everyone else. For me, though, he turned into a lapdog. "They were out of root beer," Brandon said as I sat down. "I got you Sprite instead."

Fuck. What was I going to do without my root beer fix? "That's the second time this month."

He gave me a small smile. "I spoke to the manager and told him he needed to get his shit together. He said they'd make sure to have some next week."

I took a sip of the Sprite and grimaced. It just didn't hit the spot. My lunch was ruined.

"But I did get you extra cheese and bacon on the burger," Brandon said.

Okay, so maybe it wasn't totally ruined after all. I patted him on the back. It was my way of saying "good job." The huge smile that broke across his face practically blinded me.

"We're gonna head over to Boston this weekend," Eddie said. His brother went to Boston College and had tons of access to alcohol. We'd occasionally use the connection to get our drink on. "You're coming, right?"

I shook my head. "Got plans."

"What?" Brandon asked. If he were any more disappointed, he'd be tearing up right now. "You've got to come."

"Yeah," Simon chimed in. He was more attractive than plump Brandon or acne-scarred Eddie, who enjoyed getting into fights. Simon had a good complexion and a nice set of full lips, but the boy had absolutely zero ass. It was so square and flat, he might as well be SpongeBob. "We're gonna stay the whole weekend. Get drunk, smoke some weed, and bang some sorority chicks."

I had to stifle a laugh. No college girl in her right mind would offer up her T or A to any of these guys. "You boys have fun. I've got plans," I repeated.

"Like what?"

My body tensed. Brandon knew better than that. I asked questions. I didn't answer them.

"Mind if I join ya?"

No one ever asked to sit with us at lunch. I was just about to tell the newcomer to fuck off when the sight of his big cornflower blue eyes stole the words from my lips. I'd never seen this dude before in my life, and I would certainly remember him if I had.

He was the hottest guy I'd ever seen.

A white V-neck T-shirt under a black vest covered his lean, muscular chest, and the arms that held his tray were smooth, creamy, and nicely defined. He obviously spent time in the gym. His shaggy blond hair blocked his vision, and he shook his head to the left to clear his view. When he could see again, he arched a big bushy eyebrow at us and said, "Uh, are y'all deaf or somethin'? 'Cause if this is the short-bus table, it don't bother me none."

What the hell did he just say?

"Are you calling us retards?" Brandon asked. I winced. I hated that word, but Brandon didn't notice. He stood and growled.

"Not really," he replied through clenched teeth. He clearly didn't like the word Brandon used any more than I did. "I'm just sayin' if y'all happen to be special needs, then that's no skin off my teeth."

Where the fuck was this guy from? His Southern accent meant he hadn't been born in Massachusetts, and he definitely wasn't from Havenbridge. Otherwise, he wouldn't be talking to us like this. No matter how hot he was, the kid needed to learn his place. My older brothers disrespected me enough; I wasn't going to let some country bumpkin insult me and get away with it.

I nodded at Eddie.

"This is our table, newbie," Eddie said. "Why don't you take your hillbilly ass somewhere else?"

"That's not very hospitable," he said as he slid onto the bench next to me. His body heat filled the space between us, and my cock sprang to life. What the fuck? How could this guy piss the shit out of me and turn me on at the same time? Thankfully, Brandon reacted the way he always did. His face turned redder than a clown's nose. He was about five seconds away from grabbing this guy by the throat and throwing him against the wall.

That didn't seem to bother the hot hick, though. He unfolded his napkin and placed it on his lap. This guy had balls. I had to give him that much.

"Maybe you're the retard." I snapped my attention to Simon as he leaned across the table. I was going to have a talk with these boys about their language. If someone said that word one more time, I was going to lose it. "'Cause I don't think you're hearing what we're saying."

"Oh, I hear you," he said, picking up his plastic spork. "I'm just choosin' to ignore you."

I'd had about enough of his attitude. I turned in my seat and glared at him. He didn't acknowledge my presence. He stared straight ahead as if he wasn't seconds away from a beat down. Or being turned into a fly that I would take great pleasure in swatting. "Is there a reason you've come over here to start trouble with us?" He seemed intent on picking some kind of fight, and he was prodding the wrong boy at this school.

He took a bite of his spaghetti casserole, grimaced, and spat it out into his napkin. He had balls and better taste in food than most people around here. "Not at all," he replied with a smile that was genuine and not forced. What was his deal? He offended us but then had the 'nads to pretend he'd done nothing wrong. "I was just being friendly, is all. It's your friends here who think intimidatin' me will make me run off with my tail 'tween my legs. I don't do that for no one."

"And we don't let 'no one' just sit at our table."

"Well, I guess I'm someone, then, ain't I? Because here I am, sittin' at your precious table."

If we weren't in the middle of the cafeteria, he'd be dead underneath a fly swatter. He was talking to me as if he had magical blood to back him up, but he was nothing more than an ignorant human.

"Well, well, if it isn't the bottom of the barrel."

As if lunch couldn't get any worse. The shrill, annoying voice told me Miranda Proctor had decided to grace us with her presence. Unlike most everyone else at school, she had no fear of me, and it wasn't just because she was a witch.

She knew my secret.

I glanced over my shoulder and sneered. Miranda stood behind me wearing a white button-down blouse and khaki-colored jeans. What was it with witches and white? Did the color have to be a part of every single fucking outfit? I sure as hell didn't wear black every damn day. "What did you say? I don't speak hag."

Eddie and Simon snickered while Brandon guffawed. The cafeteria, which had slowly resumed its natural hum after I took my seat, once again quieted down. They knew from experience that whenever Miranda and I crossed paths, fireworks weren't too far behind.

Her cotton-candy-colored lips twisted into a mocking sneer. "And not too good at Latin either, from what I hear."

I gripped the table until my knuckles turned white. No matter what I said or did, she always reminded me of what I tried to hide the most.

"Who fucking cares about Latin?" Brandon spat. "No one needs to know that shit."

She pressed her lips together to keep from laughing in my face. "Right," she said with a wink. "No one." She turned to the shaggy-headed fucker who still sat next to me. "You seem like a nice boy. Why are you sitting with these losers?"

"Well, thank you, ma'am. That's very kind of you to say," he said with a tip of an imaginary cowboy hat. "I was just hopin' to make some new friends, is all."

She surveyed our table and frowned. "Next time try my table. The only thing you'll get here is fleas."

I had to put a stop to this. Miranda was the only person at Havenbridge High who openly challenged me. I couldn't very well have her and this new buck, who was obviously looking to carve out a name for himself, become pals. "What the fuck do you want?" I asked Miranda.

"I have a message from Elliot."

"Speaking of retards," Brandon said with a sniff.

I pounded my fist on the table. "Don't any of you use that fucking word again!" That immediately shut them up. The boys glanced at one another before bowing their necks in submission while Miranda and the hick smiled in appreciation of my reply.

I might be a warlock, but that didn't mean I was an insensitive fuckwad, especially to someone like Elliot Stonewall. Most kids at our school teased him mercilessly because he was mute, but that didn't mean he couldn't communicate. Elliot was a wizard who used telepathy to speak when he needed to be heard. Usually the only people he did that with were his family, which consisted of his twin sister Edith, their younger siblings Kate and Keaton, who were also twins, and his parents.

Although our species weren't supposed to mingle, I'd always liked Elliot, and no one was going to call him a retard.

"What does he say?" I finally asked Miranda.

She'd bent down to whisper in my ear when someone suddenly burst into the cafeteria, screaming, "There's a dead body on the football field!"

We all exchanged glances. A curious grin cut a sideways path across my friends' expressions. Miranda mumbled under her breath, no doubt saying a blessing for the departed soul.

The new kid, though, stared out the window that faced the football field and then turned to me, his eyes wider than his O-shaped mouth. The news had rattled him. Where was that cocky motherfucker now?

PRETTY MUCH the entire school had poured out onto the football field by the time the boys and I made our way there. Our new "friend" thankfully got lost in the shuffle of anxious bodies exiting the cafeteria. Although the news of a corpse on our campus intrigued me, I had a rep to maintain. Getting excited about anything wasn't cool.

"Who do you think it is?" Brandon asked. He wet his lips and grinned. "Maybe it's Principal Skinner. I'd certainly lose no sleep over him. The fucking asswipe."

Simon and Eddie echoed his sentiment. My friends hated our principal, mostly because they spent more time in his office than they did in class. I didn't hate him at all. Principal Skinner had always been decent to me, especially since most teachers went out of their way *not* to help me. Just like the students they taught, the faculty feared me. Principal Skinner had seen how the adults reacted to me, and he'd always done his best to reach out to me because unlike Brandon, Simon, and Eddie, I didn't terrorize the school.

I hung out with the bad boys, but I didn't make a nuisance of myself. What was the point of that? Besides, most kids were scared of me already, and I'd never picked one fight, bullied someone, or gotten snarky with a teacher.

I didn't need to be an ass to be a badass, but it didn't mean that I could be pushed around. It had happened once, and both he and I lived to regret it. Since then, everyone had made sure I had plenty of room whenever I passed.

"That's a fucked-up thing to say," I told Brandon. "Death shouldn't be wished on anyone."

Brandon immediately apologized, and the boys grew quiet. As they all knew, death and I were well acquainted.

We reached the circle of kids who had gathered around the body. The crowd was at least ten people deep all around, and it prevented me from seeing who was lying in the middle of the field. I was about to work my way through the throng when Brandon ordered, "Move!"

The crowd immediately parted to let us pass. Brandon might be an insensitive dumbass, but knowing him had its advantages. Most kids did what he told them to do.

Before long, I stood within the circle where the body was clearly visible. It was a woman, probably in her midforties. Mud caked her long blonde hair and was smeared across her graying skin. She had obviously been in a struggle. Her clothes were ripped, and deep purple bruises spotted her forearms.

"Holy shit!" Eddie said at my side. "Look at her neck."

How could I not? It had been torn open on the left side. Flesh and muscle had been ripped right off her body.

"Shouldn't there be more blood?" Simon asked.

Yes, there should be. With such a deep wound, the area around her should be soaked in it, but there was no detectable red tinge to the grass or mud.

"Do you recognize her?"

I turned to find Miranda standing to my left. Brandon hissed behind me, but we both ignored him. She and I had business to conduct. I shook my head. "How about you?"

"I've never seen her before." Her dark brown hair fell in front of her downcast eyes. Death wasn't easy on anyone, but it affected witches the most. Their white magic made them far more susceptible to the loss of a life's energy. It hurt them deeply.

"That's good, then. It means we aren't needed," I said to her in a whisper.

She nodded, but the news didn't cheer her up.

I didn't know her either, a voice suddenly said in my head. It spoke so loudly, I grabbed my head in pain. What the fuck?

Sorry about that, it said. It sounded sincere, but every word it spoke was like a knife twisting in my brain.

"Mase, you okay?" Brandon asked. He gripped my arm as I tried to keep myself from stumbling and passing out. Miranda regarded me with stitched brows before turning her attention to the crowd.

Even though I wasn't, I told Brandon I was. *Who the fuck is this?*

Turn to your left.

My head hurt so much, my vision became blurry; all I saw was a cop car and an ambulance pulling into the school's parking lot.

Your other left, the voice said after a long sigh.

I found Elliot standing with his sister, Edith. They both had hair as black as their father's and skin as fair as their mother's. They were almost a perfect physical combination of their interracial parents.

Will you and Miranda get over here already?

I nudged Miranda and gestured to where Elliot and Edith stood. She nodded in understanding.

"I'll be back," I said to my friends.

"What? Why?" Brandon asked.

I locked gazes with him until he looked away. Simon and Eddie patted Brandon's back, turned him around, and proceeded to talk about the body. Brandon and Eddie laughed while an amused smirk danced across Simon's features. He'd no doubt said something crass about the dead woman. My friends were going to have to learn a lesson or two about respecting the dead and those different from us, and I might have to be the one who taught them.

AFTER MIRANDA and I crossed the field to Elliot and Edith, the four of us broke away from the crowd that had begun to be dispersed by the police and school administration.

"You two didn't know her either?" Edith asked. Unlike Miranda, who was still clearly upset, Edith and Elliot seemed unfazed. That was typical of wizards and their gray magic. As a species, they were more detached than witches and warlocks. Logic and intellect ruled their lives, and they saw the world through the veil of neutrality that defined their usually dull order.

"Nope," I replied. Miranda only shook her head. "She's not one of us, so there's not much we can do. It's up to human law enforcement to figure out." If she had been a warlock, witch, or wizard, then as members of the protector covens, it would have been our job to investigate what happened. The councils of our respective orders didn't handle magical laws broken here as they did in other cities.

Havenbridge was special. The source of all magic, which my kind called the Gate, was here, and it was our job to keep it safe. And if one of our kind turned up dead in our town, that usually meant the Gate was in trouble.

I noticed Brandon, Eddie, and Simon staring at me. They were no doubt wondering why I was talking to these three, and since we weren't needed, there was no sense in continuing this conversation. "Well, I'm gonna go now."

No, Elliot said in my head again. *Something's not right here. Didn't Miranda give you my message?*

I winced and rubbed my temples. "Will you stop that already, Elliot? That telepathy of yours is worse than a migraine."

"You get used to it," Edith said.

"Not really my idea of a good time," I said. "And no, Miranda didn't give me your message."

Miranda stood in silence, staring over at the body.

"My brother said he heard someone's angry thoughts this morning," Edith said.

I glanced at Elliot and shrugged. So what?

They were thinking about you.

"Does that surprise you?" I asked as I turned to face Elliot. He gripped my shoulders with trembling fingers that pleaded with me to take this seriously, but why? Most of the kids didn't like me, and as long as they kept their thoughts to themselves, who fucking cared? "You're getting yourself worked up over nothing."

"A woman is dead," Miranda said in a gruff whisper. "I wouldn't call that nothing."

I sighed. Why did she turn everything I said into an excuse for an argument? "That's not what I meant. This has nothing to do with us, and you know the rules. If none of our kind are involved, we stay out of human affairs."

Edith flinched and held her breath. Her brother was obviously speaking in her mind now. "Elliot seems to think that someone is trying to cover up their magic."

That didn't make any sense. We could sense other magical beings. That was how we knew who was a part of the "family" and who was just your run-of-the-mill human. "Is that even possible?"

Elliot shrugged and glanced between Miranda and Edith.

"I don't know," Edith said.

"They'd have to be extremely powerful." Miranda's voice was distant, as if she hadn't come all the way back from whatever emotional time-out she'd taken. "Even more so than our parents."

Elliot couldn't nod his head fast enough.

"I don't sense anything at all."

Miranda snorted. "Yes, well, your magic isn't exactly reliable, now is it?"

The white witch bitch was back. "Fuck you, Miranda."

She ignored me and began mumbling in Latin. It was the language we used to cast our spells. When she had stopped speaking, the air grew heavy as the energies Miranda had summoned swelled. An unseen wave flooded everything. It rippled outward in invisible, magical currents that rolled through the grass, crashed around the unsuspecting humans, and surged toward all life around us before it suddenly dispersed.

When her spell was complete, she gasped and stared at Elliot. "You might be right."

He sighed in relief, and a triumphant smile drew across his lips.

"Why? What did you sense?" I asked.

"Absolutely nothing," she replied.

I stared blankly at her and then at Edith and Elliot, who traded concerned glances. "And that's not good?"

They gaped at me as if I'd just spelled cat with a *K*.

"What do you think, doofus? I'm standing on a football field with a warlock, two wizards, a dead body, and a whole bunch of our classmates, and my spell sensed nothing." Miranda crossed her arms and stared at me.

That didn't make sense. She should have detected the fading echoes of death or, at the very least, our magical energies. "But that's not possible."

She pretended to ring an imaginary bell. "And we have a winner."

I flipped her off with a big smile. "So what does that mean? Is she one of us or not?"

"I can't say," Miranda answered as she glanced over her shoulder at the dead woman. "But magic is most definitely involved."

If that was true, then so were we.

CHAPTER 2

"DAD!" I yelled as soon I was through the front door of Blackmoor Manor. He needed to know what had happened at school; that way he could inform the Council of Black, who would then let the Conclave know what might be going on here in Havenbridge. Once our governing bodies had assessed the situation, we protector covens would get our orders.

I proceeded down the hallway decorated with the priceless art my father collected and turned into the living room. He wasn't there. "Dad!" I screamed again, this time at the top of my lungs. When I didn't get an annoyed reply, I figured he either wasn't home or was upstairs taking a shower and getting ready for this evening's events.

Just to make sure, I checked the library, which had bookcases filled with more books than I'd ever read, and then went into the kitchen before heading into the grand hall. This was my favorite room. It spanned the entire three stories of the house. Its huge windows looked out upon the expansive back property that made up our estate.

But he was nowhere to be found. "*Dad*!"

"Will you shut the fuck up already?"

I turned to see my older brother Pierce descending the staircase. As usual, he was shirtless. He loved showing off his muscular body even more than he enjoyed teasing me. Why he insisted on doing that around the house was beyond me. "When did you get home?" I asked. After graduating from college, Pierce had gone to work for our family's company, Blackmoor Enterprises, where Dad hired him as a vice president. He'd spent the past few months abroad, learning about the company's international holdings. It wasn't really what he wanted to do, but as the eldest, he didn't have a choice. One day the business would be his to run.

"A couple of hours ago," he replied.

Even though he was a pain in my ass, I'd missed him and the way we taunted each other. "So you come home and immediately go topless?" I pretended to throw up.

He snuffed. "When you look as good as me, why the hell not? Besides, I had to take a shower. I needed to wash off the skank I boned in the airplane bathroom."

"Classy," I replied. Pierce's libido had always been in hyperdrive. He fucked anyone, man or woman, who caught his eye. He didn't discriminate. He was an equal opportunity man slut.

"I take it you're still a virgin?" he asked after slamming his shoulder into mine on his way to the kitchen and sending me stumbling into the wall. He snickered and went to the refrigerator to drink directly from the milk carton.

"I take it you're still a disgusting slob?"

After he'd finished drinking, he let out one of his famous belches that shook the rafters. "I guess that's a yes for both of us."

"Have I told you how happy I am that you're home?" I asked with a smirk.

My teasing didn't fool Pierce. He missed me too. "I can tell you're about ready to piss the floor," he said with a lopsided grin.

The front door opened. "Dad?" I asked before backing into the hallway, but it wasn't our father. It was my other brother, Thad. He lived part-time in Salem, where he was finishing up his graduate studies at Southern Salem University. He was specializing in witchcraft and historical occult practices and was the resident know-it-all in the family.

"Just me," he said after placing the books he always seemed to carry with him everywhere on the foyer table and shrugging out of his backpack. Thad didn't have dark hair and baby blues like Pierce and me. He'd inherited our mother's strawberry blonde locks, hazel eyes, and fair skin.

Pierce stood next to me in the hall, eating a protein bar. "How's school, Brainiac?"

Thad scowled and arched his reddish eyebrows at our older brother. "Enlightening," he answered. "It's funny how much you can learn when you aren't fucking or drinking your way through college."

I couldn't help but smile. This was how the Blackmoor brothers hugged.

Pierce snorted. "You'd be surprised how much you can learn that way."

"Yes, I would," Thad replied.

It always surprised me how different the three of us were from one another. Pierce had always been the super-popular jock who partied his way through life, while Thad had always been more serious, as if he had something to prove. He was always studying and had no personal life that I had ever seen. I wasn't even sure he'd ever had a girlfriend or boyfriend. Hell, I didn't even know if he was gay like me, bi like Pierce, straight, or asexual.

But no matter how dissimilar they were, my brothers had one thing in common. They were powerful warlocks in their own right. They weren't nearly as strong in their magic as our father, but they had both tapped into their active powers. That was one thing that separated them from me.

I had yet to come into mine.

"So how go the spells?" Thad asked me. He and Pierce stood side by side. They clearly hoped I'd finally learned to master my magic.

"Um, they're coming along just fine?"

Pierce slowly shook his head and went back into the kitchen. Thad crossed his arms. "You're not practicing, are you?"

"Every chance I get."

"Liar!" Pierce accused from the kitchen.

"Bite me!"

"Um, that's just gross."

"Will you two stop it already?" Thad asked. His narrowed eyes told me to get ready for a lecture. Thad launched into a speech about how important it was for me to study my magic and all the other blah blah blah he always spouted. It wasn't that I didn't realize everything he said. I just wasn't good at it. My spells either didn't work or backfired, as everyone knew, including that pain in the ass Miranda Proctor.

Maybe that was why I projected my badass persona at school, to make me feel less like the loser I really was. And everyone at school had bought the act. They sensed the power within me even though I didn't know what to do with it.

But here at home or around Miranda, I was reminded that it was all just that: an act.

I suddenly noticed that Thad had stopped talking and tapped his foot on the wood flooring. Pierce had returned. He leaned against the doorframe, eating a banana.

"You didn't hear a word I said, did you?" Thad asked.

"Why would I? You say the same damn thing all the time. I'm sick of it."

"Well, if you'd listen, I'd stop."

"Why don't you just stop anyway? Who do you think you are, Mom?"

Thad inhaled sharply, as if I'd slapped him. Pierce stopped midchew and frowned at me. It had only been six months since our mother passed away, and we were all dealing with it the best way we could. Thad had taken her death the hardest. They'd been super close and had done everything together. When he'd lost her, he'd lost his best friend.

Before I could apologize, Thad's hazel eyes turned copper in anger. "Fine. I'll stop. If you're satisfied with being the first worthless warlock in the Blackmoor family, then keep doing what you're doing. Nothing."

He stomped up the stairs.

I glanced at Pierce, who silently shook his head before following Thad.

This day just got better and better.

I SAT in the kitchen, drinking root beer. The sweet, slightly licorice taste of my favorite beverage helped take the sting out of what I'd done. I hadn't meant to be such an ass, but dammit, Thad seemed to bring it out of me more than anyone else. He'd always taken a more parental role with me than a brotherly one. It was like he saw me as a screwup he had to fix.

And since Mom had died, well, it had only gotten worse. As had the distance between all of us.

I didn't need another mother. I needed a brother. When was Thad going to realize that?

Still, I had to apologize, which wasn't something the Blackmoors did easily. It left a bad taste in our mouths, as if it somehow weakened us, and warlocks shunned things that did that above all else.

Of the three orders, our black magic was the wildest, much more so than white or gray. It was far more unpredictable and derived directly from the chaotic energies that emanated from the Gate.

That was partly why I found it so difficult to control. I had a harder time dealing with chaos than the rest of my family. I gained a certain amount of pleasure from order, like the wizards of the gray. Sure, they were boring as all get-out and about as much fun as a wet blanket and an army of ants at a Sunday picnic, but their lives weren't affected by the sometimes-nagging pull of the chaotic black magic or the extremely pure white. They had balance, and I sometimes envied them that.

"Who's got you crying in your root beer?"

My father stood at the entrance to the kitchen. He was dressed in his favorite black suit, which brought out his dark hair and the deep blue of his eyes. He scratched at the facial hair he'd grown in the past few months. Pierce believed he'd done that to sex himself up in preparation for bagging some hotties. Thad didn't agree. According to him, Dad had grown the beard and mustache in an attempt to separate the man he saw in the mirror in the morning from the one who stood next to our mother in the family pictures scattered throughout the house. It was his coping mechanism or some shit.

Whatever the reason, he looked great.

"Who else?" I asked.

He nodded and walked over to the fridge. He took out a root beer, which was his favorite too, and sat opposite me at the breakfast bar. He popped open the can and took a hearty swig. "So Thad's home, huh?"

"Yup. Pierce too."

"I know," he said. "His motorcycle is parked in my spot in the garage."

"Why does he always do that?"

He snuffed. "To piss me off."

Dad only pretended to be annoyed. He actually enjoyed these little power plays of Pierce's. After all, when dad was no longer with us, Pierce would assume his mantle as high priest of the Blackmoor coven, and it was important that our leader be the strongest warlock in the family.

"What happened between you and Thad this time?"

I swallowed down the bitter taste in my mouth. "I don't wanna talk about it."

"What do you want to talk about, then?"

Holy shit! I'd almost forgotten. "I need to tell you what happened at school today." When I'd finished filling Dad in on the dead body and what Miranda, Elliot, Edith, and I had learned, the worry crease in his brow deepened. "That is bizarre. Miranda sensed nothing at all out there?"

"Not a thing."

"What about you?" he asked. "Witches are sensitive to a life's passing, yes. It disturbs their more life-affirming ways, but warlocks are far more attuned to death. It represents chaos at its strongest, especially if it was a murder, which your description clearly indicates to be the case. What did you sense when you cast your spell?"

His raised eyebrow told me he already knew the answer. I hadn't cast one. Truthfully, the thought never even crossed my mind. Thad was right. I was worthless as a warlock. "I didn't cast a spell," I finally admitted. "But I didn't sense any magic whatsoever, and I don't need my abilities for that. It's just something we can all do."

My father stared at me in silence.

"I guess, since Miranda didn't sense anything, I didn't see any reason to cast my own spell."

He nodded and finished off the root beer. "And that is yet another mistake," he said. His volume had dropped to barely a whisper. When he was really mad, he didn't yell. He got deadly quiet. "I understand that you don't feel comfortable with your powers, but not using them isn't really going to solve that, is it?"

I shook my head.

"We are a proud warlock family, Mason. Our ancestors were chosen generations ago as a protector coven. You do realize the honor in that, right?"

Why did my family have to remind me of things I already knew every time they were disappointed in me? But saying that right now wouldn't be smart, so I nodded instead.

"You need to start using your magic and that brain your mother and I gave you. Out of all of you on that field, you had the best chance of revealing what we need to know. You could have called upon the dark energy of death and manipulated its lines for information. Miranda can't do that."

His nostrils flared, and his hands clenched. Warlocks had hair-trigger tempers, and when they were set off, you had to either duck or hope you were wearing a bulletproof vest. I'd been on the receiving end of so many of my father's angry outbursts that I'd grown almost immune to them. That was a perk of being the sole member of the family whose incompetence constantly pissed everyone else off.

"You need to think about what you could have done," he said before standing. He evidently realized he needed to put some space between us before a stray gesture sent me flying through the kitchen wall. "I need to go wash up for tonight, and so do you."

By the time Dad's footsteps reached the top of the staircase, I'd swallowed the rest of my warm root beer and tossed the can at the trash basket. I missed, and it skidded across the marble-tiled floor.

It looked like this day was going to suck all the way around.

AFTER QUICKLY putting on dress slacks and a blue button-down shirt in my room, I ran down the steps to the main floor. I had to get downstairs before everyone else. I wasn't ready to deal with their disappointment. Through the wall I shared with Dad's upstairs study, I'd overheard him talking to Pierce and Thad about what I'd told him. They'd taken the news about as well as expected.

Pierce had snorted in derision while Thad went on and on about how lax I'd been in my magical studies, so I didn't want to be up there when they all came out of Dad's room, shaking their heads in judgment.

I was frustrated enough with myself that I didn't need to add their further displeasure to the dark tidal wave of failure under which I drowned.

But how was I supposed to fix things? Thad didn't think I pored over the books we had or studied the family incantations in our Grimoire. But I'd been doing that. I had read through a lot of our books, and whenever Thad didn't have our family's book of spells by his side, I'd tried to cast the spells it contained.

It never worked right, and I'd been on the verge of giving up.

After what Dad had said, though, I couldn't toss in the towel. I had to find a way to connect to the magic that was my birthright and manipulate it the way our species had learned.

I closed my human senses and tried to clear my mind, opening myself up to the constantly flowing energy. I reached out to it with my thoughts, but it jerked away from me, as if I were something it didn't recognize. The patterns suddenly went crazy, surging left and right, trying to get away. Was it running from me or from something else?

But then a faint whisper drifted on the breeze. I strained to hear what it said, but the voice was too low. I could tell it wanted me to go outside, though.

I stood at the top of the stone steps leading down to the sprawling, manicured rear lawn of Blackmoor Manor. A stifling, hot breeze shifted the air around me, buffeting my lightly bronzed flesh with scorching waves of heat more suitable for south Texas than northeastern Massachusetts. A heat wave had settled into our little town about a week ago, and it seemed in no hurry to slink back to the southern border of the country.

I drew the searing air into my lungs, and I detected the light, breezy aroma of the asters growing along the perimeter of the estate. The heat had not only scorched the flowers but singed their scent as well. A burning, almost pine-like odor drifted with the typically sweet bouquet.

It made my nose twitch.

But on the air drifted another smell, something foreign yet familiar, subtle but still unmistakable. It hid underneath the hundreds of other scents that floated around me. My sense of smell had always been better than my family's. I sometimes wondered if I was part shifter or something, the way I could detect the slightest changes that traveled on the wind. But that was foolish. Both my parents were full-blooded warlocks, and no shifter blood intermingled with our magical lineage. We were pure members of the Order of the Black.

I sensed something, though. Why did it remind me of pancakes doused in bleach? It was an odd combination, but the unpleasant odor intrigued me. It called to me and to my magic, which lay dormant inside, crackling within my soul.

I took several deep breaths, centering myself as my father had instructed. To access my power, I had to become one with myself. I had yet to learn how to truly accomplish that particular task, but the strange scent tugged at me, daring me to follow its trail back to its source.

It was a challenge I wasn't about to let go unanswered.

That wasn't what a warlock did. If I'd been a holier-than-thou white-magic witch, I'd have been burning sage and anointing myself with patchouli oil in order to establish a connection with whatever crept around the outskirts of ordinary perception. I'd have been conjuring up a spell to create a bond and connect my spiritual force with whatever was out there.

That wasn't lame at all, right?

Thankfully, black magic was more about manipulating the energies instead of trying to create some kind of magical kumbaya. I just had to find the right words that would lead me to the source.

As I was about to speak the incantation that would spirit me away to whatever lurked in the forest beyond the house, a jolt of electricity sizzled into my left shoulder and sent me tumbling down the steps to the warm carpet of grass below.

I shook the haze from my vision and rubbed my aching shoulder before snapping my attention to my attacker. From the top of the steps, Pierce snickered. His eyes were mostly dark blue except for the small brown spot I knew to be at the top of his left eye. They narrowed as he waited to see how I would respond. He'd obviously done that partially as payment for screwing up at school earlier today. Being my pain-in-the-ass big brother, however, was the main reason.

"Dammit, Pierce. I was just about to do something."

"Like what?" he asked, nonchalantly crossing the distance between us. As the most powerful of my brothers, Pierce feared nothing except our father's disapproval. "Were you trying to hex someone from school again? You know how well that worked the last time."

As if I needed to be reminded. Accidentally turn yourself into a roach one time, and no one ever lets you fucking forget it.

I rose and charged forward, but before I took two steps, ice formed around my feet and held me fast. Just my luck, Thad was getting in his hits too.

"What the fuck do you think you're doing?" I asked Thad, who approached from the side of the house.

"Keeping you from getting hurt," he replied coolly as he brushed a strand of his strawberry blond hair off his forehead. He was still annoyed with me.

I'd had just about enough. "*Dimitte me,*" I said with a wave of my hand. The ice Thad had used to stop me broke away and crumbled in response to my release spell. I had to admit, I was pretty damned impressed. "I'll take the both of you on right now."

"And you'd lose," Thad said matter-of-factly.

My pretend anger suddenly turned real, and I couldn't stop the snarl that curled my lip. Thad's cold fish routine always pissed me off.

I uttered the Latin word *propellit*, and Thad flew off his feet and skidded on his ass across the lawn.

Another point for me.

Pierce broke into hysterics at my side. He slapped my shoulder with his big oafish hand. At six foot four, he was six inches taller than me and at least double my muscle mass. While he might be the strongest, both physically and magically, it had always been tough for him to get the drop on Thad, who was the cleverest of us all.

"I wouldn't be laughing if I were you." I was feeling a bit cocky now that I'd managed two successful spells in a row. Why not try for a third?

Pierce studied me while I recited a spell that should have caused Pierce's pants to drop around his ankles.

Wouldn't you know it? My streak came to an embarrassing end.

Pierce doubled over in laughter as I stood there completely naked from the waist down. My dress slacks and boxers suddenly appeared in the branches of a tree about ten yards away.

Thad, who'd sprung to his feet to retaliate for being knocked down, joined Pierce in laughing at me while I covered up my junk.

"It's not funny!" I yelled, trying to keep a straight face. I hated being the butt of jokes, but even I had to admit this was pretty damned hilarious.

Pierce tried to say something that would likely be shitty, but he was laughing so hard he had trouble breathing. Tears poured down his cheeks, and Thad couldn't stop snickering long enough to be his usual smartass self.

I wanted to be pissed off, but I couldn't.

We only got together these days for special occasions like Sabbat celebrations, which was why we were all together today.

It was the autumnal equinox known as Mabon, and we had a celebration to attend.

"Is there a reason you're standing out here butt-ass naked?" Our father stood at the back patio door. He cleared his throat and struggled to speak. He was clearly a few seconds away from joining the make-fun-of-Mason bandwagon. The warlock temper I'd stirred up had finally started to fade. "You do remember what today is, right?" he asked, his voice broken by hiccups of laughter.

Although Mabon wasn't Yule or Ostara, on this day all orders of magic—white, gray, and black—gave thanks for what the earth provided.

"It's their fault," I said, pointing at my brothers. Unfortunately, I gestured with the hand that had been covering my cock and balls. My complete nakedness caused Pierce and Thad to die in place.

"I see you're definitely still our little brother," Pierce teased as he held out his pinkie finger and wiggled it.

"Bite me." I walked over to retrieve my clothes. I yanked my pants from the insistent tree limbs, but my boxers were out of reach. I entertained the thought of using magic to bring them down, but with my luck the branch would fall on my head. I'd never gone commando to a Sabbat celebration before, but there was a first time for everything.

"We need to leave in fifteen minutes, Mason," my dad said as he escorted Pierce and Thad inside. "We don't want to keep everyone waiting."

Nope. We sure didn't. The warlocks, wizards, and witches that would be at the ritual didn't appreciate tardiness.

I nodded and slipped my pants up my thighs. My father paused at the threshold of the house. He peered at the farthest reaches of the property, into the army of trees that stood sentry along the perimeter. Had he sensed what I had smelled earlier and what had whispered to me on the wind?

But after a few seconds, he switched his gaze from the forest to me. He nodded for me to hurry and then went inside.

Maybe there wasn't anything out there after all, but I didn't believe that. I took one final look over my shoulder at the house and darted toward the woods.

I WALKED under the canopy of white pine, red maple, and northern red oak for about five minutes, trying to home in on what I had sensed, but whatever had smelled like pancakes and bleach seemed to have left. Maybe it had sensed my father's magic. He wasn't someone to be messed with, especially since he was close to being inducted into the Council of Black.

Even without that endorsement, he still kicked major ass. He scared the shit out of me, and I was his son. We weren't super close or anything. That was his and Pierce's deal. Pierce was the firstborn, the golden child, the one who mastered magic and every-fucking-thing else with little effort. Thad came next. He was the bookworm, poring over the dusty family books in the library and keeping our Grimoire at his side.

It was obvious he studied hard so he could hand both Dad and Pierce their asses in a magical showdown.

I wanted that too. I first had to master my magic and finally tap into my active power the way Pierce and Thad had.

A rustling of leaves about thirty feet to my left caught my attention.

I spun around, trying to sense movement among the overgrown bushes and vines that tangled the saplings, which stretched for the treetops. I saw nothing, but I heard more rustling and the unmistakable sound of heavy breathing and grunting.

Could kids from my high school be back here getting it on? It sure as hell wouldn't be the first time. If it was some kids from school, my magic might scare the shit out of them and make them think twice about coming back.

I was drawing closer when a figure exploded out of the bushes. It was that damn new kid from lunch. He leaped over a bush, placed his hands on the side of an oak, and somersaulted over a collection of rocks. I stood in amazement as the blur continued running over, around, and off obstacles in his path.

What the fuck was he doing?

Without missing a beat, he reached up to a tree limb on the other side of a rock and swung himself to the left. Before him was a crumbling brick wall, the remnants of a cistern. He pulled himself up in a single bound and then leaped like a cat down the other side. When he landed, he sprinted forward a few feet, kicked off the trunk of a tree, and went straight for the small stream only a few yards from where I stood.

He picked up speed as he rushed toward the water, which was lined with rocks on either side. What was he going to do? Jump? It was about ten feet across. There was no way he could do it.

But as he reached the water's edge, he launched himself off one of the rocks jutting out of the water, propelling himself forward while flipping in the air and landing with a small splash on the other side.

He hadn't made it, but he'd come pretty damned close. I was impressed.

He smiled and looked back at the path he'd taken. He was pretty pleased with himself, and I couldn't blame him. He'd run in a straight line and nothing, not the trees, rocks, or stream, had stopped him.

"Enjoyin' the view?" he asked through ragged breaths, his Southern accent still as pronounced as earlier this afternoon.

He turned to me. He combed his fingers through his shaggy, dark blond locks, brushing the sweat-matted strands to the side. He moved his hands to his hips and regarded me with suspicion.

He was even hotter in his tank top and running shorts. His shoulders weren't broad. They were as lean and strong as the rest of his tight body. Nice muscles defined his thighs and calves, probably because he bounced around like a cartoon kangaroo, and the tight-fitting shorts really showed off his ass. It made me hungry.

Even though his body got me going, his attitude still sucked. He snorted at me, and a crooked smile hitched up his lips. He evidently was used to both girls and guys fawning over him.

It made me hate him even more.

"Not really," I replied with a shake of my head. "Just watching a crazy fool running like mad in my forest."

He arched one dark, bushy eyebrow at me. "Your forest? I didn't realize a forest could belong to someone." His drawl was so thick he just had to be from Texas.

"Well, it does." I opened my arms wide. "And it's all mine."

Still on the other side of the stream, he took a few steps closer until he was directly across from me. "You know, I kinda hoped you might be different from your dumbass friends, but I can see you're just as much a fucktard as they are."

I bristled. I was two seconds away from doing something he'd regret. He might not have said retard, but he'd come pretty damned close. "You know I don't like that word."

He replied with a half smile and a nod. "So how can someone my age own a forest?"

Fuck! I was going to need a translator to talk to this guy if his accent got any thicker. "It belongs to my family. We've owned this land for five generations." He seemed more annoyed than impressed. "You're not from around here."

"How'd you guess?" he asked while a smirk tugged the right corner of his lips.

"Well, besides the fact that you talk like a refugee from a rodeo, most people in Havenbridge know this area belongs to the Blackmoors, and we're not too fond of unexpected visitors."

He nodded. He might not be from around here, but he'd evidently heard of us. "Right. My aunt Millie told me about your family."

Millie? Did he mean Millicent Carpenter, the grumpy old hag who'd used to run a local grocery store until my family's supermarket chain ran her out of business? She didn't speak like some hick. "And what did your aunt Millie tell you about us?"

"That you were a bunch of rich bastards who acted as if y'all owned the earth." He gazed around at the woods and let fly a single chuckle. "I'm guessin' she was right."

"We don't own the earth. We're working on it, though."

"Why am I not surprised?" he asked with a snort.

If I could guarantee a hex wouldn't backfire, I'd have turned this smug son of a bitch into a tapeworm. But I couldn't risk it. I was already tempting my dad's fury by not being at the house and ready to leave. Having to undo one of my misfired hexes wouldn't endear me to him or our family to the other covens.

"Well, I wish I could say it's been nice talkin' to you, but my momma always told me not to lie right to people's faces." He turned around, searching the woods for where he'd run off to next.

I don't know what made me do it, but before I could stop them, the words flew right out of my mouth. "What's your name?"

He glanced over his shoulder, a wicked grin sliding across his perfect pink lips. "Name's Drake," he said. "And you're Mason."

I tilted my head to one side. "How the hell did you know that?"

Drake responded with a laugh before taking off at full speed. He cut through the bushes, leaped over more rocks, and then bounded off a tree trunk before the overgrowth stole him from my sight.

I was suddenly overcome with the desire to find out everything I could about the latest addition to our town.

CHAPTER 3

AFTER I got back from the woods, my father led me to the car. For almost the entire ride, he proceeded to scold me for almost making us late. I sighed quietly as he reprimanded me. Didn't I realize how arriving late would make him look to the others? Did I not care that my family's reputation could be tarnished?

I nodded in strained contrition while Pierce smirked at me and Thad gazed out the window, most likely imagining he was back in the library reading his books.

Dad's words eventually turned into a low hum. My thoughts returned to Drake. Since I knew who his aunt was, finding out more information on him would be relatively easy. Havenbridge wasn't that big, and I just had to figure out what that guy's deal was. Why did it seem like he knew more than he let on?

There was a secret there, and I had to figure out what it was.

He wasn't one of us, that was for sure. Magical beings emanated an aura that other magic users could sense. Drake gave off no such energy.

But there was something there. I could tell because it made the back of my brain itch.

"Are you listening to me?"

I nodded at my father through the rearview mirror. His eyes narrowed in disbelief, but instead of calling me on it, he continued his tirade while I went back to my thoughts.

I could cast a spell. That might get me the information I needed. Of course, I could also fry my brain if I didn't get it right. Knowledge spells were tricky and precise. One incorrect word, and all the information that existed in the world could overload my brain, causing it to virtually explode. That wasn't something I wanted to experience, no matter how badly I wanted to learn as much as I could about Drake.

But why was that exactly? I typically didn't give a flying fuck about most people, magical or otherwise. What was it about this jackrabbit douche bag that intrigued me so much? It wasn't just his lean body, gorgeous eyes, or fantastic hair. If this were purely physical, I could understand that. He was a hot guy.

And I was more than particularly hard up. I hadn't had a good make-out session since last Samhain.

But with Drake, it seemed to be much more than that, and I had no clue why.

"We're here," my father said as he parked. He turned around in his seat and glared at me. "And do your best to behave yourself, okay?"

I nodded. Dad was right. I had to stay focused on our duties. Drake was going to have to wait.

We exited the Jaguar and strolled down the sidewalk, which ended at a two-story Victorian-style home. Dad had told us many years ago that it was Folk Victorian. I didn't really care. The house was pretty but simple, certainly nothing like the sprawling elegance of our place.

A covered porch with a beige-painted wood railing stood at the center of the house, tucked between two bay windows on either side. Gray shingles decorated the second story of the house all the way to the cornice that eventually formed two gables, one each to the left and right of the porch. They were as sharp in design as a stereotypical witch's hat. No doubt the white-magic Debbie Downers like Miranda Proctor hated that part of the architecture.

But this house wasn't where witches or their white magic lived. It belonged to the Stonewalls, wizards of the Order of the Gray. They sought balance above all else, and their magic and their lives were ruled by devotion to stability and order. It was even reflected in their style of house.

"I hate coming to these things," I said as we drew nearer to the front door. The drone of dozens of voices merged into a constant buzz as a strange brew of magical beings mixed inside. "They're so dull. I'd rather french-kiss Miranda."

Pierce snorted while Thad remained distant. He had yet to forgive me for sending him flying across the lawn. "Yes, well, as much as I'm sure you'd enjoy kissing a girl, this is what we do," my father said as he ascended the four wooden steps to the porch. "Mabon is an equinox and ruled by gray magic."

Like I didn't know that already. Mabon was a time to give thanks for what we had and honor the darker aspects of life, calling upon that which was devoid of light. Through meditation, communing, and giving, we celebrated the balance by which the world survived. "But the Stonewalls are so boring."

My father spun around on his heels.

"You've done it again," Pierce whispered after an impatient sigh. Thad simply chuffed in contempt.

"Mason, why do you feel the need to provoke me and question every part of our culture? Of our species' tradition? You may not embrace your magic the way the rest of us do, but we have been blessed, and part of that blessing is being thankful for that gift, whether it's for gray magic and Mabon, the white magic of Ostara, or the black magic of Samhain."

I twisted my lips in regret. Apologizing never came easy for a Blackmoor. Thankfully, father understood the gesture.

He leaned in closer to the three of us, an impish grin lighting on his lips before he sighed. "I agree with you about the Stonewalls, though," he whispered. "They're bland and tiresome, but they are a protector coven, as we are, and we have to work within the laws to which we are all bound, right?" When we all nodded in unison, he smiled and straightened. "Besides, no one can be as badass or awesome as us."

I grinned in reply while Pierce pumped his right fist in the air and hooted. Thad, who always looked as if he felt like he was wasting his time when his nose wasn't buried in books, crossed his arms and tapped his foot.

Suddenly the door opened. Miranda stood at the threshold, wearing a white button-down blouse and floral skirt. She nodded respectfully at my father and thinned her lips at my brothers. When her gaze settled on me, she frowned. "You're almost late," she mumbled under her breath, then waved a finger at the door. It opened all the way, causing the droning voices to spill out onto the porch.

"Almost late isn't late," my father replied. He walked past her without another word and my brothers trailed him inside.

When I attempted to follow suit, she stepped in front of the door.

"Move it or lose it," I grumbled as she flipped her chestnut-colored hair off her shoulder.

"Or what? You're going to turn yourself into a roach again?"

I rolled my eyes. "That news is about as tired as I am of looking at you."

"Ooh. Burn," she said, mocking my attempt to insult her.

"If it's you on the stake, then I'm there."

"Will you two stop it?" someone behind Miranda asked.

It was her older sister, Charlotte, who was home from school for the weekend festivities. She wore the same white blouse as her sister. It was the standard Proctor uniform, it seemed. But unlike Miranda, who had a sultry appearance with her perfect, rosy lips and long, straight hair, Charlotte had a more understated beauty. She didn't care about her appearance like Miranda did. Her clothes swallowed her petite frame, and her short dark brown bangs made her look fifteen instead of eighteen. Since she wasn't as annoying as Miranda, I could tolerate her in small doses.

"I'd love to," I said to Charlotte, who moved her sister aside. "But Miranda gets her jollies by making my life miserable."

"Everyone needs a hobby," Miranda said as she walked away.

Charlotte closed the door behind me, and together we cut through the crowd of magical families, who were chatting only with other members of their order. Sticking with our own kind was the standard operating procedure ever since we first evolved as a species. Only the protector covens could mix when necessary, but we usually kept to our own too. But on this Sabbat, covens of all orders across the northeastern part of the state traveled to Havenbridge for the festivities and a chance to be in our presence.

We were celebrities in the magical world.

"Greetings, Mason Blackmoor." It was Leopold Edwell, a fellow warlock who lived across the river in Salem. He was short and squat and reminded me of the Penguin from the Batman comics. His wife, Agnes, stood at his side, her contempt hidden behind a thin smile. The Edwell family was richer than we were, but they envied our status. They were among the few families considered by the Council of Black back in the seventeenth century to become the chosen protector coven for our order, and to this day, every single member of the Edwell coven resented the Blackmoors for our blessing.

"Greetings, Mr. and Mrs. Edwell," I replied with a bow of respect. He returned the gesture, though he silently seethed.

"Does your family take crap from other white-magic covens?" I asked Charlotte after we left the Edwells and their group of friends.

She frowned. "You should know better than that. Our order doesn't engage in such pettiness."

Charlotte was right. I *should* have known better. Witches prided themselves on being practically perfect in every way. Fucking Mary Poppins wannabes! "Then explain your sister to me. She seems to get off on it."

She shook her head. "If I could explain Miranda, I would. But I've given up trying to understand her. Every family has a black sheep."

I couldn't argue with that. In my family, that was me.

"Heya, Mason." Adam Proctor cut through the crowd to stand along the back wall with his sister and me. Like Charlotte, Adam wore a white button-down shirt and went out of his way to say hello. I believed he did that to piss off Pierce. The two of them loathed each other to excess. It went beyond even the usual white- and black-magic animosity that typically existed between our two orders. Unlike most of the others gathered here tonight, I didn't instantly dislike the other factions. I busted their chops because that was who I was. Take it or leave it.

In order for me to hate you, you had to earn it. Like Miranda. And now perhaps even Drake. He was well on his way to being at the top of my shit list.

Other than that, I didn't fall into the magical cliques everyone else stuck to. I did my own thing, and it upset my family to no end.

"Aren't you going to say hello?"

Adam's question pulled me out of my thoughts. "Of course," I said before holding out my hand. "How's your last year of grad school?"

The smile on his lips practically made him glow as he shook my hand. "Pretty wonderful," he said. "I've met lots of great people, but it's still tough being away from home. I'm sure Thad says the same thing."

I chuckled. "My bookworm brother talks to his dusty old books more than he does to me."

Adam laughed. "Yeah. He's always in the library, and he's usually alone."

They went to the same school. "Doesn't surprise me at all."

He gazed out of the corner of his eye at Charlotte, who smiled knowingly at him. "Um, I wanted to, uh, ask you something," he said between sputters.

"What's that?"

Why was Adam so nervous all of a sudden? An uncertain smile tugged at his lips as he raked his fingers through his light brown hair, which was cut short and tight at the sides but longer and looser on top. When he couldn't get the words out, I looked back and forth between him and Charlotte. "What's going on here?"

She snickered. "What my speechless big brother is trying to ask you is—"

Adam cut his gaze to her, and she stopped. "Charlotte, I can do this."

"Well, then do it," she said with a Cheshire grin.

Adam had let loose a long exhalation in preparation to speak when the clinking of a fork against crystal cut through the crowd.

Everyone turned to the front of the room where Lawrence and Rachel Stonewall stood. Like my family and the Proctors, the Stonewalls were one of the three protector covens. Even though they were boring as all get-out, they were a striking couple. Mr. Stonewall's bright smile gleamed against his mocha skin, which stood in contrast to Mrs. Stonewall's pale and delicate features. "Greetings and blessings to you all."

"Greetings and blessings to you," we all responded.

Mrs. Stonewall held her husband's hand. "Let's head outside and begin."

We filed into the backyard, and everyone immediately formed a huge circle in the middle of the lawn. After we were all in place, we turned to face the east.

"All hail the Watchtower of the East," we said, reciting the prayer that would evoke the elements, which gave us our powers. "The element of air, I do summon you forth to guard and protect this circle. Be here now."

When a warm breeze blew through the yard, the Stonewalls' eldest, Edith, walked to the center of the circle. She carried a candle with her. She blew across the wick, which suddenly danced with flame.

We continued calling the elements. After air came fire, after fire was water, and the last was earth. After each invocation, one of the four Stonewall children stepped into the circle and lit the candle in their hands.

When it was Mrs. Stonewall's turn, she proceeded toward her children and joined their circle, carrying a much larger candle. Their bodies formed the human pentagram that was needed to invoke the fifth and most powerful element of them all.

"Spirit, the quintessence," we said. "You are the bridge between the physical and the spiritual. Your touch binds us today as it did when you first gifted us with the essence of the Gate, creating the Spellbringer, the first of our kind. We summon you forth to guard and protect this circle. Be here now."

As on Sabbats past, I suddenly felt as if I were flying. The fifth element had arrived. We had the blessings and the protection of the Five.

We then joined hands. I held onto Charlotte's right while Adam held mine. He rubbed his index finger over the back of my hand and smiled. What the hell was going on with him?

Mr. Stonewall launched into prayer. As head and high priest of his family, the duty fell to him to lead us in thanks. "We celebrate the balance of Mabon, equal hours of light and darkness. For all that is bad, there is good. For despair, there is hope. For pain, there are moments of pleasure. For all that falls, there is the chance to rise again. May we find balance in our lives as we find it in our hearts."

"And so shall it be," we all answered.

The candles flickered out, and for a moment we stood under the starlit sky. In a few minutes, the candles would relight and the ritual would be over. We could then eat, commune, and go our separate ways for the evening.

But instead of flickering back to life, the candles erupted into columns of flame. Loud gasps and low murmurs followed. After the candles returned to their natural state, within the circle stood nine robed and hooded figures. Three were in black, three were in gray, and three were in white.

The Conclave, the ultimate authority of our species, was here. They never made personal appearances at celebrations. They instead watched all rituals from afar. What had brought them to Havenbridge?

SHORTLY AFTER the Conclave's arrival, the Mabon celebration abruptly ended, and all the guests left. Only the protector covens remained behind, and my father, Mr. and Mrs. Stonewall, and Mr. and Mrs. Proctor met with the Conclave inside.

I stood in the backyard with the rest of the kids, which is what we were basically considered. The only true children here were Keaton and Kate Stonewall. They were only twelve. It made perfect sense for them to be excluded. But the rest of us should have been in there. We ranged in age from eighteen to twenty-eight and were definitely *not* children.

Not that many of us seemed to mind. Keaton and Kate ran around their big brother and sister, Elliot and Edith, who sat cross-legged in the grass, meditating. Adam and Charlotte were carrying on what appeared to be a serious conversation that I couldn't help but feel involved me somehow. They occasionally glanced over to me while they talked. Not even my brothers seemed bothered by what was going on. Pierce chatted on his cell with someone he was most likely banging while Thad sat on one of the swings, reading something on his phone.

The only other person who seemed annoyed was Miranda. Like me, she was staring through the back window at our parents. They sat in the Stonewall living room, speaking with nine of the most powerful of us all.

"This blows," Miranda said as she crossed to stand next to me. "This is probably about that poor woman on the football field. We should be in there."

I nodded. "But that's not how we do things," I said, doing my best to mimic my father.

She chuckled. "Yeah. I hear that from my dad all the time." She cleared her throat and lowered her voice. "Miranda, why can't you be like your brother and sister and just do what's expected of you? Why do you have to be so difficult all the time?" She blew out a quick puff of air. "As if I want to be anyone else but me. I'm a witch with her own mind, and yeah, I'm grateful for what we can do and for our status, but that doesn't mean I don't ask questions or voice my opinions."

I couldn't help but gape at her. How could someone I despised so much be just like me?

"What?" Her usual grimace curled her lips. "Don't look at me as if I'm a freak, or I'll warp your sorry ass into the middle of Cape Cod Bay." Warping was what Miranda called her active teleportation power. It was both uncommon and powerful because it derived from spirit, the most potent element of them all. White magic drew its power straight from the five elements, and most witches tapped into fire, water, earth, or air. Not Miranda.

"No, thanks," I said. "I experienced your warping once before, and I was nauseous for days."

"Then don't look at me like that, and we won't have a problem."

Her father was right. She was difficult. "Look, I don't think you're a freak. I feel the same way you do." Even though I had her full attention, she grimaced at me. She clearly believed I was pulling her leg. "I'm constantly getting in trouble for not toeing the family line. For pushing the boundaries of what is acceptable for my order. I mean, I shouldn't even be talking to you, right? Unless we're on official business. You're white magic. I'm black. We're supposed to coexist because we have to. That's the way our world works, but that's bullshit. That's the way things used to be back when we first evolved, but that's not the way they have to stay. Sure, you're a pain in the ass." Miranda crossed her arms and raised one eyebrow at me. "I should dislike you for that, not because we're different species. But I think that's changing. Because of us."

I motioned to the others, who had stopped what they were doing and started listening to me. "Take Charlotte and me for example. She's always been kind to me. And so has Adam. Hell, I remember when Pierce and Adam were close, even though they aren't now." Pierce and Adam cast sideways glances at each other before returning their attention to me. "We're changing, and with it, magic is changing. It's becoming less black-and-white."

"More gray?" Kate Stonewall asked. She grinned, her dazzling white smile shining from skin darker than her father's.

Even though I shuddered at the thought of all of us becoming as boring as her parents, I shrugged. "I don't know. Maybe."

"What the fuck's the matter with you?" Pierce asked. He crossed the lawn and towered over me. "Black magic will always be black. I'm never going gray." He growled at Edith and Elliot, who had risen from where they sat and now stood in front of Kate.

I sighed. "I didn't mean it like that, Pierce. We're different. I get that. What I mean is that our attitudes about each other are changing. How else do you explain why I'm friendly with Charlotte or Adam or why they're friendly with me? If we were sticking to the ways of our parents, we'd all despise each other as much as our parents do. They're only cordial to each other during Sabbats because that's what we have to do. But that's not the way I want to be, and I don't think it's the way you all want to be either. When Elliot and Edith had the flu last year, I brought them their homework. And dammit, I like Elliot. I always have."

Elliot flashed me a big smile. He obviously felt the same.

"Sweet little Kate gives me a wildflower every time she sees me in the park, and how many of us have stopped to push Kate and Keaton on the swings in the playground?"

They looked at one another and nodded. My words rang true. Over the years, we'd developed more than just working relationships. We were a dysfunctional extended family, whether anyone wanted to admit it or not. "Acting the way our parents do doesn't make sense. There have been strict divisions among all three orders since our race evolved from the humans. But why? What's the purpose of keeping us separate? No one ever seems to question that. Why are the members of the Conclave allowed to work together as one when we can't? All of us have the same job, but we do it separately. Wouldn't uniting make us more powerful? Wouldn't it make more sense to protect the Gate together?"

"Makes sense to me," Kate replied from behind her older brother and sister.

"Kate, hush," Edith said.

Keaton joined hands with Kate. The Stonewall twins were closer to each other than anyone else. "Don't tell her to hush. You're not Mom or Dad."

Elliot was quick to defend his twin. He shook his finger at them in reprimand.

Keaton and Kate snorted in reply.

"See what you started?" Edith asked me.

"All I'm saying is we shouldn't blindly follow tradition. It's not who we are. Our race is a result of humans challenging the laws of the universe. Without them, we wouldn't be here. We shouldn't dishonor any of our ancestors."

"You mean the way you're doing right now?"

I spun around to my father's voice behind me. All the parents now stood on the back lawn with the still-hooded members of the Conclave behind them. None of them appeared pleased.

"It's time to go," my father said. He jerked his head to the left. Pierce and Thad immediately obeyed and crossed the lawn toward the back door. The other children responded similarly to their parents' gestures. Only

Miranda remained at my side, but after a few moments, even she departed, though not before casting one final, remorseful glance at me over her shoulder. It was perhaps the kindest look she'd ever given me.

When only my father and the Conclave remained, I opened my mouth to speak, but he held up his hand to quiet me. "Not. One. Word."

I nodded and walked past him and the robed figures. All nine members of our governing council turned their heads to watch me depart. I couldn't see their faces, which were shrouded beneath the dark folds of their hoods, but I sensed the contempt with which they silently regarded me.

But there was another emotion hanging in the air. Why did it smell like fear?

THE RIDE home was much different from the drive to the Stonewalls'. Instead of lecturing, my father remained quiet. He focused on the darkened road before him, and he gripped tightly onto the steering wheel. Why didn't he just yell at me? That was certainly better than the silent treatment.

It didn't help that neither of my brothers would look at me. Both of them stared out the windows, distancing themselves from me and the wrath I'd face at home. When we finally pulled up into the circular driveway of Blackmoor Manor, Pierce and Thad hopped out of the car. They opened the huge mahogany front door of the house and dashed for the protection of the interior.

I was left alone with my father, who, for the first time, stared back at me through the rearview mirror. "Meet me in the library," he said before shutting off the engine.

I nodded and exited the vehicle. I went inside and walked down the long, narrow foyer that was the hub of the house. Along the rear was the great hall that spanned all three levels of the structure. More than anything else, I'd rather be sitting at my spot on the third floor, sprawled on one of the bay window benches and taking in the view. I'd even settle for obsessing about the mystery that was Drake, as I had earlier that evening.

But instead of going up the stairs, I took a left into the library.

The room was quiet, and the sweet scent of cherry wafted in the air from the materials used to panel the room and construct the bookcases. I inhaled deeply, hoping the soothing aroma might help calm my nerves. It didn't. I crossed the hardwood floor over to the carpeted reading area, where two chocolate leather couches sat in a V shape that opened toward the huge fireplace and the massive mirror that adorned the wall above it. Thanks to the reflective surface, the room seemed to be even larger than it already was. The bookshelves along the first and second floor appeared to go on forever.

"Sit down," my father said as he strolled into the room.

I immediately complied, taking a seat on one of the leather couches. He sat in the red wingback chair diagonal to me.

"I'm sorry," I managed to choke out. I'd rather turn myself into a roach again than utter those two words.

He sat back with a sigh. "And what exactly are you sorry about?"

To be honest, I didn't have a clear understanding of that. I knew I was in trouble. Beyond that I wasn't really sure. I could only guess that our parents and our bosses had heard what I had said and viewed me as insubordinate.

"Just as I thought." He laced his fingers together and called my brothers. Within moments Pierce and Thad, ever-dutiful sons that they were, appeared at the library entrance. He gestured for them to take seats next to me, and they did as asked, but not before glancing at each other and then giving me the stink eye. They evidently believed I had somehow gotten them into trouble too. "We obviously need to have a discussion."

"About what?" Pierce asked. "What did Mason say we did? Because it's not true."

I chuffed. "Will you grow a pair already?"

"Fuck you, Mason! I'm not the one who screwed up again."

"I thought you were twenty-eight, not twelve."

Pierce clenched his fist in anger, sending sparks of electricity crackling through the air.

"Enough." Dad's voice immediately stopped our arguing and reined in Pierce's powers. Pierce sat back and faced forward, and I did the same. "You made a serious error tonight, Mason. And your lack of understanding gravely concerns me."

"Just what did I do?"

Father glanced at Thad, who nodded in reply. He stood and proceeded to the iron coffee table that squatted between our dad and us.

He turned to face me. Disappointment and exasperation were in the hazel eyes that reminded me too much of our mom. She too had often looked at me much the same way.

"You challenged the very premise upon which our community is founded," he said. "The different orders of magic exist for our safety. Separating our races wasn't some arbitrary decision made generations ago to complicate our lives. It safeguards us. If you'd studied our Grimoire, or any of the other books in this house, as much as I do, you'd know that already."

If I'd had an active power, Thad would be feeling the brunt of it right now. "I'm not an idiot. I know that. We *all* know that. All I was suggesting was that we don't need these divisions among our orders. We're charged with protecting the Gate. Wouldn't doing that together instead of separately be more effective?"

"No," Thad said without a moment's hesitation. "Our species has been hunted to near extinction from the moment we evolved as the *homo magus*. When we intermingled, we exposed ourselves to danger. It has only been withdrawing from human society, separating ourselves from them, that has allowed our species to thrive."

"It's also made us shortsighted bigots," I added.

"It has also kept us pure," Thad said. "Or don't you remember our history?"

"That was almost three thousand years ago, Thad. I think we've evolved a bit more since then, don't you?"

"You just don't get it." It was Dad's turn to speak. "How can gray magic remain neutral if it is constantly influenced by white or black? How could white magic promote spiritual connections if tainted by the selfish nature of our ways? For that matter, how would our black magic fare if we didn't focus on our individual wants or needs? In order for us to remain safe, for all magic to remain stable, and for this world to persist, we have to exist as we are and as the Gate meant for us to be. To abandon those rules and our roles would threaten everything there is. Whether anyone likes it or not, our traditions must be followed."

I still didn't buy it. There were huge holes in his logic, but everyone refused to see them. "If what you say is true, then why does the Conclave work together? They don't seem to be destroying our way of life."

"That's because their connection to the Gate is stronger than ours. The picture they see is bigger than what the rest of us see, and their combined power ensures stability is maintained and the rules that allow it are followed. When you question the rules, you question them." Dad paused, no doubt for effect. "And no one wants to do that, right?"

I swallowed hard. Considering how powerful each member of the Conclave was individually, I couldn't imagine the power they wielded together. But that only made me more curious about the need for the divisions. Did keeping us separate keep them in power? Would banding together somehow threaten that? But those were questions I wasn't going to voice. I was in enough hot water as it was.

My father cleared his throat, wanting an answer.

"No," I finally answered. "I don't."

He motioned for Thad to rejoin us on the couch. "Good. Because we have something far more important to deal with than you questioning our way of life."

"Is this about the murder at Mason's school?" Pierce asked, sitting forward on the couch. He was typically the first to goof off, but when it came to business, he was always ready to get started.

Thad sat down next to me, studying our father's expression. Trouble was obviously brewing, and the protector covens were needed.

"Perhaps. We told the Conclave about it, and they were not pleased."

"Wait a minute," Thad said. "They didn't already know?"

Dad shook his head. A curious expression played across Thad's face. He glanced over at me, as if contemplating something he didn't want to admit.

I had no doubt I'd find out what that was about later. "Then what brought them here?" I asked.

"A great enemy is coming, and we must be prepared."

"Enemy?" Thad asked. "Who?"

He sighed and shook his head. "We don't know. The Conclave senses a great disorder on the horizon, and not even their combined magic has been able to pierce the veil and reveal the identity of our foe."

That wasn't good. Anything that could hide from them was an opponent not to be taken lightly.

"Is it the witch hunters?" I asked. They had pursued us since the earliest of our race first cast a spell in front of nonmagical humans. Their sole purpose in life was to exterminate us as well as the threat we posed to their mundane lives.

"Doubtful," he responded. "They are thorns in our side, yes. But they don't have the power to shield themselves from the Conclave. They are just humans, after all."

"How can anyone or any*thing* hide from the Conclave?" Thad asked.

"They don't know, but it's being done. They sensed a riptide within the river of magic that flows from the Gate, and when they tracked it to its source, they realized Havenbridge had suddenly turned into a blind spot for their powers. They have been unable to sense anything that happens here for almost a month."

"And that's why they didn't know about the murder?"

Dad nodded.

"And they didn't tell us sooner?" Pierce's temper was ready to flare out of control. "That's information we should have known from the start."

"I can't argue with that," he agreed. "We asked them why they waited so long to inform us. Their answer was that they had their reasons."

"Of course they did," I said. Everyone obviously knew what was on my mind. I could see it in the way they stared at me. This was one more reason why we should question everything and accept nothing at face value. Thad's gaze lingered on me. Why did I get the feeling he might be agreeing with me now?

Dad snapped his fingers at us to regain our attention. "We've been charged with keeping our eyes open for anything or anyone suspicious."

"And the woman on the field?" Pierce asked. "What about her murder? We don't know if magic was involved or not."

"The Proctors have been assigned the task of determining if magic was used in connection with the woman's death. If they find out there was magic involved, they will inform the Council of White, who will notify the Conclave."

"That doesn't make sense," I said. "You told me warlocks have a stronger connection to death than witches. I may have screwed the pooch this afternoon, but that doesn't mean we can't figure it out now."

From the tense expression on my father's face, I could tell he agreed with me and was equally concerned by the Conclave's decision.

"The Conclave believes too much time has passed to manipulate any lingering death energy."

"But they don't know for sure," Thad said. "They told you they couldn't sense anything in Havenbridge anymore."

"Yet that is their decision. The Proctors are tasked with the murder, not us."

Pierce punched the couch. "That's bullshit! Finding out if magic was used in her death should be our task. Once we make that determination, the Stonewalls should be the ones putting all the pieces together. They're the logical ones. And the Proctors? They should have been given our assignment. Mr. Proctor works for HPD, and isn't defense their family specialty?"

Father gripped the arms of his chair tightly. Was he angry at our words or at the Conclave's ridiculous decisions? He blew out a lungful of air and said, "The Conclave suspects our enemy is already here in Havenbridge and the Gate is already in jeopardy. We don't have time to debate their orders. We have to find out who or what might be responsible for cloaking the events of this town from them."

"Holy shit!" I said, standing up. "I think I might have a lead."

Pierce and Thad peered up at me in amazement.

"Who?" Dad asked.

"I met a boy today in the woods."

Pierce groaned. "Your lack of a sex life has nothing to do with this."

"And neither does your big fat head, so shut up." Thad chuckled at my comment while Pierce silently fumed. I'd likely get zapped in the ass before bed tonight. "Can I continue?"

Dad motioned for Pierce to be silent and gestured for me to go on.

"Something drew me outside this afternoon before we left. I didn't know what it was, but it smelled weird. I was about to cast a spell, use my magic like you told me, to figure out what it was, but this big oaf," I said, smacking Pierce upside the head, "interrupted me. By the time I managed to get out there and check, the smell was gone."

"I didn't smell anything," Dad said. "But I did sense something earlier. I attempted an amplifying spell to heighten my senses, but I detected nothing unusual."

I briefly contemplated telling my family that it smelled like bleach and pancakes, but I didn't feel like being teased. Thad would find some way to make fun of me by telling me to think with my head and not my stomach, so I decided against it. "Like I said, it was gone before I got there. But that was when I ran into Drake. He was bounding all over the forest."

Thad looked at me askance. "What do you mean?"

After I relayed my encounter with Drake, the room grew quiet.

"I don't believe this Drake could be the enemy the Conclave has sensed, especially if he's human, as you say."

I nodded. "He is. I sensed no magic from him whatsoever."

"That doesn't mean someone hasn't bound his powers to avoid detection," Thad said.

Fuck. I hadn't even thought of that. If someone had bound his powers, it would also remove all traces of magic from our senses. Maybe I did need to read our books more.

"That's true," our father replied. "Mason, since he goes to your school, I want you to learn as much information as you can about this boy. While I'm certain it's just coincidence, no one is above suspicion."

I'd planned on doing that anyway. Something about him tugged at me in ways I'd never experienced before. Perhaps it was my magic's way of warning me of danger. If Drake was my enemy, I'd make him regret ever coming to Havenbridge.

CHAPTER 4

I SPENT the next few days following Drake around school, which was pretty fucking boring. The kid was about as exciting as a bowl of cold oatmeal.

He went to class, did his homework, chatted with friends he'd made—which aggravatingly included Miranda—and got to and from school by running and jumping over every fucking thing in his path.

I spent so much time thinking about him, I'd started dreaming about him too. And some of the dreams were wicked hot. My favorite was when Drake waited for me in the bathtub after school, his naked, smooth body dripping water as he played with the white towel that hid what I longed to see the most. He pulled me into the tub, but before I hit the water, I woke up.

That happened far too often. Right before I was about to touch him or feel his lips against mine, something interrupted us. When he walked down the empty hallways at school, performing a striptease, my alarm would go off as he was about to lose his underwear. When I got him into the backseat of my car after ripping off his clothes, the annoying beep would wake me for school before I could grab his dick.

It was fucking aggravating getting cockblocked in my dreams, but not as frustrating as the nightmares that played in between. In them, something chased us, and it wouldn't stop until it had us.

"You will be mine," the whispering voice that always followed us through the dreamscapes often repeated. It didn't matter where we were—in the woods, at school, in my car—the gravelly voice said the same thing over and over as we tried to escape. "You will be mine." But what made the dreams even stranger was that along with the voice drifted the ever-present smell of someone burning breakfast.

I sat up in bed after escaping the voice for the third time that week. Drake and I had been in the forest behind the house, getting ready to get it on, when the voice spoke and the tree limbs suddenly turned to long claws that had finally managed to grab us.

It was the first time whatever had been chasing us had made contact, and I didn't like it one bit.

My heart jackhammered in my chest and an uneasy drunken feeling set the world spinning like a top. What the fuck was going on?

My door was suddenly flung open, and I yelped in surprise. Pierce stomped into my room, dripping perspiration and wearing only his gym shorts and a fuck-you grin. "Dad says to get your ass out of bed. You've got shit to do today, remember?"

"Don't you ever knock?" I asked as I swung my legs out of bed. "Or shower?" The stench of moldy gym socks and stale sweat polluted my room.

"What?" he asked, raising his right arm and sniffing his ripe pit. "You don't like the smell of greatness?"

"Not when it smells like your ass," I replied as I shoved him out of the room and locked the door behind him.

"Stick with the plan," Pierce said from the other side of the door. "Don't screw it up."

"Don't worry about me. Worry about yourself." I hated that my reply made me sound like a little kid, but it pissed me off when my family naturally assumed I'd fuck things up.

Pierce replied with only a snort before his footsteps padded down the hall.

Since I didn't have time to start what would likely turn into a wrestling match, I flipped him off from my side of the door before I hopped in the shower, got dressed, and shoved some breakfast down my throat.

A few minutes later, I was driving into town in my black BMW 335i convertible. It was time for a more direct approach, and the best place to start was at Drake's aunt Millie's house. I pushed the button that lowered the top, anticipating that the breeze from the drive would calm my agitation. Usually the whipping of my dark locks and the gentle brush of the wind across my skin centered me. It lifted my spirits when I felt like a failure as a warlock and as a Blackmoor.

But it did nothing to ease my still-fluttering heart. It was taking longer for the aftereffects of my nightmares to dissipate. What did that mean? I contemplated telling Thad or my father about the dreams, but I didn't want a lecture.

I'd figure it out on my own.

Maybe some music would help. I turned on my XM radio, and "Fancy" blasted through my speakers. "Hell yeah." This was my fucking jam. I rapped along with Iggy Azalea, and when Charli XCX sang the chorus, I belted it out because dammit, I *was* fancy!

By the time I reached the stop sign at the intersection of Winston and Salem, I'd hit the second verse and was in full-out karaoke mode. Whether it was the song, the drive, or a combination of both, I'd started feeling better.

And then someone suddenly slid across the hood of my car.

It was Drake. He landed on the other side of my BMW, glanced over his shoulder, and gave me a devious smile before sprinting off down the street.

"I don't fucking think so," I said, more to myself than anyone else. Drake sure as hell couldn't have heard me since he was already about fifty yards away. I slammed on the accelerator and sped off in the direction he'd run.

He leaped over a mailbox before vaulting the fence on Mrs. Littlejohn's property. When he found traction, he continued on in a straight line that would take him to a picnic table and a brick wall. But instead of going around either, he leaped across the table, landed on the other side, and propelled himself onto the wall. He grabbed the top, climbed over, and flipped to the other side. Where the fuck was he going in such a damn hurry?

I did know where he was going to end up, though. If he continued on his current path, which nothing seemed capable of stopping him from doing, he'd have to jump over the fence on Goodwine Road, and that was where he'd find me.

I sped over there and threw my car into park. He'd have no choice but to stop now. Goodwine was the narrowest street in Havenbridge. It was really no bigger than an alley. With my car between the fence and the rear of the small convenience store to my right, there was no way Drake could keep going.

"Nice try," Drake said as he leaped onto the fence and jumped over my car. He caught the wall of the store with his right foot, and then he propelled himself to the left and in front of my car.

What the fuck was he? A cat?

I suddenly sat up in my seat as Drake bounded down Goodwine. Maybe that was exactly what he was—a goddamn shifter!

Unlike my magic, their shifting abilities came from some ancient spell cast during a dark part of our history. I couldn't remember the specifics and really didn't care, to be honest, but I did recall that shifters had developed a means of masking themselves from nonshifters as a self-defense mechanism. That explained why Drake could do what he did and why I couldn't detect anything magical about him. He was a motherfucking shifter!

I put my car back into drive and hauled ass after him.

This was amazing! Shifters were practically extinct. Most of what I knew about them could fit on an index card, but I did know one thing: shifters had departed our world for some magically shrouded island a long time ago.

And if they were back, they could very well be the enemy the Conclave had sensed.

When I turned onto Pleasant Street, Drake was nowhere to be found. I'd lost him. But as I drove by the Abbott Public Library, I saw an orange tabby cat lounging in the sun. It looked up at me with what looked like a shit-eating grin on its face and then proceeded to clean its fur.

The bastard! He'd shifted to avoid me catching up to him. There was nothing I could do right now. He'd won this round, but he couldn't evade me forever. He'd eventually have to shift back into his human form.

When he did, I'd be waiting.

I SAT at the Starbucks across from the library. I sipped my fizzy root beer, studying Drake the Cat, who was stretched out in the sun. Every now and then, he'd stop licking himself and stare suspiciously at whomever strolled by. When he was satisfied they weren't a threat, he went back to grooming, which included lifting his leg over his shoulder and swabbing his tongue across his more delicate parts.

Did he do that in human form too?

Suddenly an image filled my mind of Drake lying on his bed, naked, with his legs stretched behind his ears. I imagined settling between them, his hard cock only centimeters from my lips, and flicking my tongue across the engorged head.

Under the table where I sat, I squeezed the throbbing erection in my jeans as I mentally took Drake in my mouth, sucking on the head of his prick while jacking his hardness in eager anticipation of my warm reward.

"Are you followin' me?"

I glanced to my right to find Drake standing next to me. Both my cock and I jumped in surprise.

He blew his long blond locks out of his eyes and crossed his arms over his lean, muscular chest. In his stare brewed a surprising mixture of suspicion and smug satisfaction. Had he guessed what I'd been imagining from all the way across the street?

I glanced over at the library steps, where Drake the Cat had been a few moments before, and of course the tabby was gone. If I could have hexed myself, I would have. I'd been so preoccupied with that bizarre little sucking fantasy, I'd lost my chance to follow Drake and catch him in the act of shifting. Fuck my teenage hormones!

"Hey!" Drake snapped his fingers in front of my face.

I scowled in reply. Thad did that to me whenever I spaced out during one of his rambling lectures about needing to take my magical studies more seriously. "Don't do that," I warned.

"Yeah, well, don't follow me."

Even though that was precisely what I'd been doing, I scoffed. "Don't flatter yourself," I replied, taking a sip of my drink. I shifted in my seat and hoped the burning flush that had previously reddened my cheeks had subsided. The last thing I needed was for Drake to think I found him attractive.

"Then why do I get the feelin' I just caught you with your hand in the cookie jar?" He asked the question with a provocative arch to his eyebrow. I immediately withdrew my hand from my groin.

"So what?" I replied with a shrug. "I like cookies."

"I can tell," he said, pulling out the chair and joining me at the outside table.

"Is that your thing or something? Sitting down where you're not welcome? I don't recall asking you to join me."

"And I don't recall needin' your permission," he said with a grin.

Drake kicked his feet up onto the table and leaned his chair back as if he owned this place and everyone who inhabited the town. The light golden fur that spread across his toned legs made me want to lap at the skin and follow the trail up to the nice bulge in his shorts. An impish grin snaked across his lips as he gazed out at the warm sunny street. He either knew exactly what I was thinking and loved it or didn't give a fuck. It was difficult to tell.

What was the deal with him? Could this hick really be the threat the Conclave had sensed? I had my doubts.

Sure, he seemed to be a bit of a prick, but most people said the same thing about me. Being a shifter didn't necessarily mean he was some big bad enemy, especially not with that accent. From what I remembered from the books my father used to make me read, their species was only dangerous when provoked.

I sensed no impending threat from him, but there was something about him. It pulled at my stomach with the same intensity that made me rock hard when I imagined him naked in bed. It was very similar to the feeling I'd had in the woods before the Mabon celebration. It was like the universe was reaching out to me, trying to tell me something I was too blind to see.

Was that what was going on? Was I being somehow directed to Drake? It certainly made some sense, considering my dreams. Although I was able to bend magic to my will, it still had a mind of its own.

But if that was the case, what was the reason and why was he here?

"So do I have to get a restrainin' order or somethin'?"

"What the fuck are you talking about?"

Drake snorted. "I know you're followin' me, and I don't like it." He let his chair fall back to the ground and sat forward. His scent suddenly filled the space between us. It was an intoxicating mixture of cedar, herb, and fruit that reminded me of earth, wind, and water. It also sent the blood rushing back into my dick.

I willed the rising lump in my denim back to its normal, lazy state, but it wouldn't listen. It lengthened and snaked down my thigh.

"Why?" I asked. My voice was thick and heavy like my cock. "You hiding something?"

"Doesn't matter," he replied. His Southern drawl got stronger the more emotional he got. He clearly didn't like me, which was a pity. We could have had a sweaty good time. "Back off, or else."

It was my turn to lean forward. I wasn't about to let Drake think he could tell me what to do. I was a fucking warlock, and it was about time he learned a lesson or three. "No one tells me what to do."

"I'm not tellin' you to do nothin'. I'm just givin' you a bit of friendly advice."

"When I want your advice, I'll let you know." I angled in closer until we were practically nose to nose. "And I'll say this so even you'll understand. You and me, we ain't friends."

He chuckled and rose. "Honey, you ain't tellin' me nothin' I don't already know." He practically moseyed away. His slow, even pace was meant to tell me that he wasn't frightened of me, that he could take whatever I dished out.

And as I watched his ass sway back and forth, I had no doubt he could.

COULD I be any more of a fucking screwup?

I hammered my fist on the tabletop, drawing uneasy glances from a couple strolling by. A guy a few feet away who'd been washing down the sidewalk with a hose glanced at me from the corner of his eye. I sneered at them, and they turned around, going about their business.

I might not be as physically intimidating as Pierce or as cold as Thad, but I'd been told when I was seriously pissed off, I could look pretty menacing. I wouldn't be a warlock if I couldn't do that, but my physical appearance also played a part in people's reaction to me. Like everyone in my family, I had inherited the badass dark looks of a warlock, which often made people uncomfortable around me. That probably explained why my only friends at school were Brandon, Simon, and Eddie.

At times like this, though, I regretted not having my active power. Frying a nearby car engine or giving someone a severe case of frostbite would make me feel a lot better than repelling strangers with my appearance. Especially since I had to go home and explain to everyone how I'd fucked up my plan right off the bat.

I'd never hear the end of it.

Because I hadn't come up with anything during the first couple of days, Thad had wanted to take over. He believed casting a spell might help determine if Drake was the threat. But since the Conclave couldn't break through whatever veil hung over Havenbridge, our father doubted it would work. True to his battering ram personality, Pierce proposed a more direct approach: snagging Drake from his bed in the middle of the night and zapping his balls with electricity until he revealed all. Strategy had never been one of Pierce's strengths.

My suggestion was subtler. Instead of tailing him, why not try to be his friend? He was new to town and most likely pretty lonely. So was I for that matter. Brandon, Simon, and Eddie weren't exactly the pick of the litter. Sure, we hung out and got drunk, and I could always count on them to back me up if I needed them, but they were often too crass and unpleasant even for me. And I was a warlock.

I'd have liked to have more people in my life than my family, who thought I was a screwup, and the other covens, who didn't respect someone with my clear lack of skill. If I could be friends with Elliot, that would be great. We could have been best friends, but that was something our parents had quickly nipped in the bud years ago.

So even though Drake and I had gotten off to a rocky start in the woods, I was confident I could get him to see past that. There was something in the slump of his shoulders that told me he could use a friend too. Why else would he be sitting with complete strangers at lunch or running like a madman in the forest, if he wasn't searching for something?

My brothers hadn't agreed.

Pierce had snorted, and Thad had silently rebuked me. Dad had been the only one to truly hear me out. I'd convinced him we couldn't rely on our usual bag of tricks. Hexes, spells, and power plays might backfire on us, especially if Drake had the power to hide from the Conclave. Someone with those skills had to be handled in a way he wouldn't suspect.

But when I'd realized he was a shifter, I'd had to improvise. Drake's instincts would have told him I was a warlock. Maybe that was why I'd sensed Drake knew more than he let on back in the woods. Trust was one thing most people didn't give us. Warlocks had a reputation for using whatever or whomever we needed to get what we wanted.

"Did you mess up your assignment again?"

The question pulled me out of my thoughts. Behind me stood Miranda and Charlotte with some other witches who'd come to town last week for the Mabon celebration and had yet to hop on their brooms to fly back to their respective cities. Shouldn't they have gone back to school by now?

Fuck. It really sucked to be me right now.

"I'm not in the mood," I grumbled, hoping she'd take the hint and leave.

"Oh, but I am," she said. She crossed into my line of vision and grinned. She was only ever that pleased when she was hell-bent on making my life more miserable than it already was. "You always have the same look when you've screwed up. Shoulders slumped like a vulture and pouty lips like Angelina Jolie after her collagen injections." She leaned in close and whispered so the guy washing down the sidewalk behind us couldn't hear. "So what did the little warlock who couldn't do now?"

The girls behind me giggled while Charlotte shushed them all. It seemed that news of my sucking at magic had spread beyond the borders of Havenbridge. "Will you please give it a rest, Miranda?" Charlotte was suddenly at my side, looking down at me as if I was some pathetic mongrel who constantly peed on the floor because he couldn't help himself. Her pity pissed me off more than Miranda's bitchiness.

"Fuck you," I said to Miranda before standing and looking over my shoulder at the girls behind me. They all wore white somewhere in their outfit, on their purses, blouses, shorts, or hair bows. They looked like those carbon-copy young actresses you could see on any Nick Jr. show. "And fuck you too." They gasped in shock.

"Mason," Charlotte chided. She wasn't a fan of cursing.

"And you too, Charlotte." She jumped back as I turned the gun of my anger on her. "I'm sick and tired of all of you. I don't need Miranda's crap and I especially don't need your fucking pity."

Suddenly, Miranda stood between Charlotte and me. Her angry brown eyes had become slits. She was ready to throw down right here and right now. "Don't talk to my sister that way," she muttered. "She's only ever been nice to you, even though you don't deserve it."

"What's going on here?"

Adam stood behind me, his mouth slack. "Great! Just what I need. Another goddamn Proctor dressed in white."

"Whoa!" he said, walking toward me. "Where's all this coming from?"

He reached out to touch me, and I jerked away. What was up with this touchy-feely crap? It had started during the Mabon prayer and now it was happening here.

"Mason, what's wrong?" His voice trembled for some reason.

"We're not supposed to be friends, remember? Much less friendly." I'd tried to make them see differently last week, but they'd left when the going got tough. They obeyed their parents like the good little magical soldier-children they were. What pissed me off even more was that they had all evidently agreed with me. Our ways didn't make sense to them either. But instead of standing with me, they'd thrown me to the wolves. "We work together when we have to, and we get together for celebrations. That's it. You have your assignment, and we have ours. Our kind doesn't mix, remember?"

Charlotte winced. "You've always been sweet to me even though it upset our parents. You never cared what we were *supposed* to do. This isn't you."

I scoffed. "Yeah, well, it's the new me."

Charlotte turned away, gnawing on her thumbnail.

"Let's go somewhere," Adam said. The previous tremor had been replaced with a low, soothing tone. "So we can talk."

"No."

He took two steps toward me anyway. The man with the hose was practically standing behind us. Either he was working his way down the sidewalk or he wanted to eavesdrop on what we were arguing about. Either way, it didn't matter. Seeing him gave me an idea.

"*Madesco*," I whispered. I couldn't wait to see my little spell in action. My hex would upset the man and his hose, and he'd get the Proctors and their little friends wet.

When the man tripped over the hose, I eagerly waited for the water to spray them from head to toe. Instead, the hose turned on me.

My breath caught in surprise as the cold water shot in my face. Gasping for air, I held up my hands to deflect the spray, but the hose had developed a mind of its own. It wiggled like a snake in the worker's hand, drenching me to the bone.

Miranda and her friends laughed. The only other sound I heard was Adam. He mumbled, "*Aqua, averte*," and the water instantly shut off.

"Jesus Christ!" the man who'd been fighting the hose said. He gaped at the hose and then back at me. "I don't know what happened. Are you okay?"

"I'm fine," I replied, wiping the water from my face. I glared at Miranda, who was practically rolling on the pavement in laughter. Charlotte walked away to spare me the pity that no doubt hooded her eyes, and Adam opened his mouth to say something before thinking better of it.

When he closed his mouth and trailed after Charlotte, I walked in the other direction.

I WALKED the few blocks to the common nestled in the quadrangle that made up the downtown center. A construction crew busily worked on the courthouse remodel along the western side of the square. It had been going on for over a year and still wasn't finished. Scaffolding covered the entire front face of the building, and men in jeans and hard hats worked like ants across every level of the wood-and-steel structure.

A crane operator was preparing to lift a pallet filled with the new twenty-foot-tall windows the town fathers had insisted be a part of the new building's look.

While the men fastened the bundle to the crane, I made a beeline for the white gazebo in the middle of the open town square. There, I'd be out of the shade of the tree-lined perimeter, and the sun would have a chance to dry my sopping wet clothes. Once I no longer squished while I walked, I could head back to where my car was parked in front of Starbucks.

By that time, the Proctors would be long gone, and I could get in my car without getting the interior all wet.

I lifted my face to the warmth of the sun's rays and let its heat sap the anger that still boiled in my blood. If there was one bad thing about being a warlock, it was our tempers.

Wizards were our complete opposite. They were the calmest of all. Their gray magic demanded balance in all things, emotion included. They were the strategists, the thinkers, the ones who could see all sides of a problem and figure out a solution. Witches were superior at defense. Their charms and protection spells were a bitch to bypass because they added an important ingredient to their spells—their hearts.

Warlocks were the muscle. We made up the offense and were ruled by our emotions as well, but they were a different set than the witches used. We incited fear, we used intimidation, and we harnessed and directed our anger like a missile strike to obliterate our enemies.

That was why a protector coven from each order was chosen. Together, we had what it took to keep the Gate safe from those who wished to destroy it.

Well, at least everybody but me did. I couldn't even work a simple spell on a fucking hose!

That wasn't Charlotte's or Adam's fault. Not even Miranda's. They didn't deserve the fit I'd pitched. Well, maybe Miranda did. She deserved to have a house dropped on her head, especially since I'd thought we'd turned a corner. She'd stayed by my side longer than everyone else.

Who was I kidding? She was never going to change, and maybe neither was I.

I might never learn to master spells or tap into my active power. It had happened to others across all three orders. No matter how hard they tried, they never quite got the hang of it. They were what my father called magical lemons, because they were a defect in our species.

And I had the privilege of being the first lemon in the Blackmoor family. How lucky was I?

I blew out all the air in my lungs and sat up. I peeled my T-shirt off and wrung out the water before placing it on the rail inside the gazebo. If I wouldn't have been accused of being a perv, I'd have done the same thing with my jeans. I sure as hell didn't have a problem with my body. I wasn't muscled like Pierce, but I had a decent physique. I doubted the parents who walked around the square with their kids would approve of me in only my briefs, so I sat there with a swampy butt and crotch, wishing I could use my magic to get myself dry instead of what I'd likely do, which would be to set myself on fire.

A blur of motion caught my attention, and I turned to my left.

Who else could it be but Drake?

He leaped over trash cans, swung off lampposts, and bounded off walls, all the while avoiding the people who stood in his path or hurried out of his way. I laughed as one crotchety old man screamed after him when Drake nearly knocked him down.

Drake didn't let that stop him. He kept moving, staying focused as he always did on that imaginary straight line that no one else but him could see.

But there was one thing he probably wasn't taking into consideration—the construction going on in front of the courthouse. He'd have to find a clear path through and had completely missed the hundreds of pounds of thick glass that hung suspended from the crane overhead.

I saw something: a figure crouching at the top of the crane. Darkness draped it, as if it had somehow bent the light to keep itself hidden. The form crawled down the cable of the crane.

I got up, and before I knew what was happening, I was dashing through the square on an intercept path. I had to get to Drake fast. The back of my brain itched, and it only did that when something was about to go terribly wrong.

"Stop!" I yelled at Drake, who couldn't hear me over the noisy construction crew. Other people along the common heard my warning, and so did the hidden figure on the crane. It stopped its progress, and though I couldn't see its eyes, I felt its gaze on me.

Time was running out. In less than a minute, Drake would be dead.

How the hell did I know that?

I pumped my legs faster and wished for the first time in my life for Miranda. She could warp Drake out of harm's way, because no matter how fast I was, Drake was faster.

I wasn't going to make it.

Without thinking, I uttered, "*Ocius*," and energy I'd never experienced before rushed through my body until it hit my legs. I shot forward as if I'd been fired out of a cannon. Within seconds I appeared in Drake's path. He yelped at my sudden appearance and tried to stop, but momentum carried him forward.

He slammed into me, and we tumbled, head over feet, at least three times across the pavement. My bare back skidded across the cement, causing searing flames of pain to burn across my skin, and to make matters even worse, Drake's head slammed into my nose as we slid to a stop.

My eyes watered, and pain exploded across my face. Drake rested on top of me, a groan escaping his lips.

Even his moans had a slight Southern drawl to them. "Jeez, man. What the fuck?" he asked as he raised his head to gaze down at me.

Before I could answer, all hell broke loose.

"Move!" another voice screamed as a loud snap thundered around us.

We both looked up as the line holding the bundle of glass snapped. For a few moments, the package remained suspended in midair before plummeting toward us. I wrapped my arms around Drake and rolled us toward the building. The glass struck the scaffolding, which buckled and splintered before giving way to the weight, and the scaffolding collapsed.

I pressed Drake as tight into the wall as I could, shielding him with my body. I looked up at the debris headed our way. I held out my hand toward what was just seconds away from killing us and muttered, "*Protegat nos.*" While most of the wreckage fell around us, the wood, iron, and glass immediately above us stopped midfall before sliding sideways and missing us completely.

We lay safe underneath the rubble in a small bubble of protection.

"What the fuck?" Drake asked from beneath me.

I couldn't very well confess to being a warlock, even if Drake happened to be a shifter. Admitting what we really were, especially in a public place with so many humans around, went against the laws the Conclave enforced. "Lucky, I guess," I said with a shrug.

His lack of response told me he wasn't buying what I was selling. And why would he? He already knew what I was anyway. I just couldn't admit it here.

"Are you okay in there?" someone outside the rubble asked.

"We're fine," I called back. "Just want to get out of here."

"Sit tight," the man yelled back. "We'll have you out of there as soon as possible."

I nodded, even though the man couldn't see me. My thoughts had suddenly become preoccupied. Not by the fact that Drake had acted as if he didn't have a clue what was going on or the fact that we'd both almost died.

What I couldn't stop thinking about was that I had just used my magic. Twice. And both times it had worked.

AFTER WHAT seemed like an eternity but was most likely only half an hour, rescue crews managed to clear away enough debris for Drake and me to crawl out. Paramedics rushed at us, checking our vital signs, bandaging our wounds, and asking questions. I didn't respond. As they led us to the rear of the ambulance, I could only look back at the tangled heap of wood, iron, and glass where we had just been.

No one should have walked away from that alive, but we had. Because of me.

I gazed down at my hands. They didn't look any different from a few hours before, but with a gesture and two words in Latin, I'd managed to save our necks. How could my hands be exactly the same? Shouldn't there be some kind of visible sign that would let me know this wasn't a fluke? That I'd managed to finally get something right with my spells?

But there was nothing different about me. Had it really happened?

All I needed to answer that question was to look at Drake. He hadn't stopped staring at me since the moment I saved us.

"Besides the bloody nose and scrapes along his back, I don't see any serious wounds on this one," the paramedic who tended to me told his dark-skinned partner, who was checking on Drake.

"None on this one either." The man with the tanned face gazed at us in amazement. "It's a miracle."

"Yeah, a miracle," Drake replied. He swept his gaze up the crane, down to the wreckage, and then back to me.

"We're still gonna need to take you to County Memorial," my paramedic said. "Run some tests. Make sure everything is okay."

"I'm fine," I said, removing his hand from my forearm. I sure as hell wasn't going there. That place held nothing but bad memories for me. "I just want to go home."

"You can't," he replied. He looked at his partner before turning back to me. "You need to be checked out. You could have a concussion."

And if I did, home was the best place to be. Dad could cast any spell he wanted, and Thad could brew up a healing potion that would take care of everything that would hurt like a motherfucking bitch in the morning. "I'm good." I gave him one strong nod.

The paramedic sighed. "If you get dizzy or start vomiting, you need to come to the ER right away."

I nodded and waved his concern away. Right now, my focus was somewhere else. What had been on top of the crane and why had it tried to kill Drake? And speaking of Drake, why had he appeared so shocked I'd used magic? If he was a shifter, he should have sensed what I was. Either he wasn't what I thought he was, or a shifter's ability to detect us had been overexaggerated.

How was I going to find out which it was?

"Mason!" someone called. "Are you okay?"

Adam was standing outside the yellow tape the police had used to cordon off the area, studying me from head to toe. Next to him, Charlotte gnawed on her thumb. Her gaze shifted from me to Drake and then to her brother while Miranda and her friends stared at the mess and shook their heads. They most likely assumed one of my misfired spells had caused the destruction.

"I'm fine," I replied, walking past the emergency personnel over to where they stood. I glared right at Miranda. "I managed to save the day."

She stared blankly at me, clearly not buying a word.

"What happened?" Charlotte asked. "We heard this horrible crashing sound and came running only to see all this." She shivered as she scanned the mess. "And then when we saw you crawling out, well, I can't believe you're okay."

"Because I fuck up all the time?" There went that infamous warlock temper again. Charlotte was expressing concern, nothing else.

"That's not what she meant, and you know it," Adam replied. He was clearly growing tired of my foul mood. And so was I.

"You're right," I said, looking at Charlotte. That was as close to an apology as she was getting. She let out a long exhalation before nodding. My apology had been accepted.

"Are you sure you're okay?" she asked. "Because I could— you know."

I did. Charlotte drew her abilities from the element of water, and she'd mastered some pretty tough healing spells. I touched my nose, which throbbed in pain, but it wasn't broken, just severely bruised. "I'll live," I told her.

"You gonna tell us what happened or not?" Miranda asked. "I'd sure as hell like to know what you were trying to do when you"—she gestured to the scene behind me—"did this."

Maybe I should tell them what I'd seen; they might have some insight. But as I was about to start talking, Drake suddenly said, "Mason, can you and I have a word?"

I nodded. "I'll be right there."

Adam glared at Drake as if Drake were getting ready to steal candy from a baby. Miranda's friends had stolen her attention, so she had returned to her little witchy world, but Charlotte was another story. She studied him intently. Why was she looking at him that way?

"That's Drake. He's new to Havenbridge," I replied. Charlotte remained fixed on Drake. "What's wrong?"

Her attention lingered on him for a few moments longer before she focused on me. "Nothing." She was lying. I could tell by the thinly forced smile. It was the same one she gave Miranda whenever her sister either confused or worried her. She was battling the mother-hen role she assumed so often.

"Why don't I believe you?"

She shrugged and said no more.

"Mason," Drake called.

"I'm coming." To Adam and Charlotte, I said, "I'll see you two around."

Adam forced a smile. "Sure."

As I joined Drake, one of the construction workers who'd been surveying the damage cried out, "Holy shit! We've got a dead body here."

When they uncovered the mangled corpse of one of the construction crew guys, I gasped. The side of his neck had been torn open.

DRAKE AND I walked back through the town square. He'd called me away from Adam and Charlotte as if he were dying to talk, but since the discovery of the dead body, neither of us had said a word.

When the police arrived, we couldn't answer any of their questions. We had no clue how he'd wound up in the rubble or who he was. No one else had any answers either.

What I did know, I couldn't share, and if I had, they wouldn't have believed me anyway. Saying I'd seen a shadowy figure climbing the crane cable would have earned me a one-way trip to the psych ward.

Miranda suspected I knew more than I was letting on. Her twisted lips told me that much, but the witches didn't ask me any questions. They must have figured I wasn't going to share anyway.

"Does crap like this happen a lot in this town?"

The usual hostility in his tone had softened. I guessed saving his ass made me less of a jerk in his opinion. "Freak construction accidents and dead bodies?"

He nodded.

"All the time. We're the deadliest place to live in the entire country." It was a joke, but not too far from the truth these days.

He shoved his hands in his shorts, and we continued on in uncomfortable silence.

"Can I ask you somethin' else?"

"Why not? I've got nothing better to do."

He exhaled. "Are you always this difficult?"

"Is that really the question you wanted to ask?"

"Jesus H. Christ!" he exclaimed. "You're probably the most aggravatin' guy I've ever met."

I couldn't stop the smile that crossed my lips. "I take that as a compliment."

"Why am I not surprised?"

Drake drew his lips into a thin line. Whatever truce my saving him had earned me had just about expired. I playfully nudged his shoulder, causing him to stumble a few steps. "What was your question?"

He studied me, no doubt trying to determine if I was done being a dick. Even though it gave me great pleasure to yank his chain, it was time for some slack. "Where's your shirt?"

"My what?" I looked down and was surprised to find myself topless. I'd left my tee in the gazebo. "Fuck," I groaned. "I left it in the middle of the town square."

Drake swept his gaze down my bare flesh, taking in every dip of flesh and curve of muscle. When he unconsciously licked his lips, I had to force myself not to smile. He obviously liked what he saw. That made it harder not to grin like an idiot. I had to pretend-cough in my hand for a few moments before my goofy smile slunk away.

"You okay?" he asked, patting my back. When his warm hand made contact with my flesh, I inhaled sharply and started choking for real.

"I'm fine," I managed after I recovered. "Just swallowed wrong."

"Do you normally walk around without a shirt on?"

The unfortunate memory of my failed spell on the water hose came rushing back. I shook my head. "I got wet," I admitted with a frown. "And before you ask, I don't want to talk about how or why."

He nodded, and we continued on in silence. I contemplated running to the gazebo to snag my shirt. It was one of my favorites, but my closet was full of clothes I didn't wear, so I decided against it. Besides, I didn't want to chance running into Miranda or any of the rubberneckers from the accident again.

I just wanted to get home. I had a lot to sort out, starting with the fact that my spells had finally started working right and then trying to figure out what wrinkle the new dead body added to things.

"Those people you were talkin' to back there. Are they friends of yours?" Drake asked.

That was a good question. "I don't really know."

"You don't know if they're friends of yours or not?" If he were any more puzzled, he'd be scratching his head. "As my daddy used to say, 'That don't make a hill o' beans worth o' sense.'"

I chuckled. How could I argue with that? I really had no clue what type of relationship I had with them. No, that wasn't entirely true. Miranda and I hated each other. But Charlotte and Adam? I wasn't exactly sure where we stood. If the Conclave and our parents had their way, we'd hate each other to our cores.

"It's complicated," I finally answered.

He nodded. "And none of my business. I get it."

"That's not what I meant at all." Why was I going to explain myself? I never did that. "Our families don't really get along. Kind of like the Hatfields and the McCoys, you know?"

He cocked his head to the side and jutted out his chin. "You pokin' fun at me?"

"What? No."

He didn't seem convinced. "I know folks around here think I sound weird, but to me, it's all y'all that sound funny. Y'all have an accent too, in case you didn't know."

What the fuck was he talking about? "I don't have an accent."

"Are you shittin' me?" He cleared his throat and spoke in an exaggerated Boston accent. "Oh, look," he said pointing to my BMW. "There's where you pahked the cah."

I frowned. I did *not* sound like that.

"I might not be from around these parts, but I'm not just some hick. I'm actually pretty damn smart." He raised one blond, bushy eyebrow at me. "Like for instance, you were speakin' Latin back there."

I schooled my face as if I had no clue what he was talking about.

"Don't play dumb," he scolded. "It doesn't suit you. You said 'protegat nos,' which means 'protect us.'"

If my jaw dropped any lower, I would be able to swallow my own feet. "You know Latin?"

"I told you. I'm not as dumb as you might think I am."

"How do you know Latin?"

"How do *you* know Latin?" he asked.

"School, I guess."

"Not me," he replied with a smug look of superiority. "I've always been interested in other languages. It's one of my hobbies, I guess. I'm pretty good with 'em too. Taught myself Latin, Spanish, French, and German. *Wie viele Sprachen sprechen Sie?*"

"What the hell did you just say?"

"My point exactly," he said with a chuckle and a nod. "That was German, by the way."

I'd never heard German spoken in a southwestern twang before. "Okay, fine," I admitted. "Maybe in terms of language, you might be smarter than me."

Drake rolled his eyes. "It's more than just language, I'm sure."

It was my turn to roll my eyes at him.

"Why were you speakin' Latin back there?"

I shrugged. "Just a prayer my mother taught me."

He twisted his lips and regarded me carefully.

"Is there anything else?" I asked as I unlocked my car and opened the door.

There clearly was. He leaned against the door, but the weight of his eyes—no, his entire presence—rested on my soul. "Why'd you do it? Save me, I mean." A longing I hadn't really noticed before flickered within him, as if a spark of hope struck within the well of loneliness that existed within. "You and me haven't exactly gotten off on the right foot, you know?"

That was the understatement of the year. "Just a momentary lapse of judgment, I reckon." I was doing my best to mimic him because I somehow knew he'd appreciate it. It would make the distance between us seem more like misunderstanding than anything substantial.

He punched me lightly in the arm. "Stick to your Yankee speak. You couldn't pull off a Southern accent to save your life."

I got in my car. "I'll remember that," I said, starting the engine. "You want a ride home?"

He contemplated it for half a second before saying, "Nah, I prefer to walk. It's what we country bumpkins do." This time he smiled, and it was genuine. It didn't have that cocky or devilish edge to it like any of the others he'd flashed at me. "And thanks."

I smiled. "Let's just not make it a habit or anything."

"You've got my word on that," he replied.

As I drove away, I glanced in my rearview mirror. Drake stood in the middle of the street, watching me drive off. A smile crept onto my lips. Maybe I hadn't screwed things up after all.

CHAPTER 5

"WELL, SAY something already."

I'd just finished telling my father and brothers that I'd saved Drake's life by finally managing some pretty decent spells. I hadn't gotten to the weird shadow on top of the crane yet, because I wanted to revel in their appreciation of my magical skills. After I was done basking in their praise, I'd finish filling them in.

At least that was my plan had things gone my way. I should've known better.

Instead of cheers and rounds of applause, I got silence.

My father sat with his arm extended across the back of the couch. His distant gaze told me he'd retreated to his thoughts. Why the hell did he look so concerned? Wasn't this what he'd always wanted?

Pierce was lying on the couch, his hands covering his face, while Thad sat rigidly on the piano bench to my left.

"What the hell is wrong with you?" I asked. For the first time in my life, I'd actually gotten something right with magic, and they couldn't at least pretend to be happy for me. "Did you not hear what I said?"

"We heard you," Thad replied. If his words had been daggers, I'd be bleeding. "Did you hear yourself?"

"What the hell does that mean?"

"Are you fucking serious?" Pierce asked. He bolted upright. "You can't be that much of a fucking dipshit, can you?"

I'd had about all I could take. I leaped onto the couch and landed on top of Pierce. My right fist connected with his jaw before he had a chance to blink. By the time my left fist struck, he'd managed to shove me backward. I landed with a thud on the mahogany wood flooring, and a few seconds later, Pierce had me pinned. He raised his massive fist, ready to deliver one powerful haymaker, when he suddenly flew off me and slammed into the ceiling, his arms and legs splayed.

My father stood in front of the couch, his right hand upturned and his arm at a forty-five degree angle in front of him. With just a gesture, he'd managed to not only lift my brother off me but keep him confined to the ceiling until his temper tantrum subsided. Dad's stern expression told us he'd been pushed beyond the limits of his patience.

"Dad," Pierce gasped from above. "Stop."

But our father didn't listen. He growled at me sprawled on the floor. There was that damned warlock temper again, and when my father lost it, the ramifications could be deadly. I half closed my eyes, waiting for him to turn his powers on me. Unlike the rest of us, he didn't have to speak Latin to call forth his abilities. He'd long since evolved beyond spoken magic; a gesture got the job done. I was thankful he wasn't like the members of the Conclave. Their thoughts triggered their powers, and right now, my father's thoughts would have likely ripped me in two.

Thad stepped between him and me. His typically clipped tone had softened. "Dad, stop." His whisper of a voice broke through our father's anger. "You're crushing Pierce."

He glanced at the ceiling, where the force of his magic continued to push against his oldest son. He shook off the red haze that had momentarily blinded him and turned his hand palm down, lowering it about ten inches.

The force applied against Pierce eased, and he slowly descended from the ceiling until he was gently placed on the couch.

"I shouldn't have done that," Dad said to Pierce. Apologizing, even when it was necessary, didn't come easily for him either. "I let my temper get the best of me."

Pierce nodded. He clearly feared reigniting the anger that had almost flattened him into a pancake. Either I wasn't as scared of our father as he was, or I was dumber than Pierce said I looked, because once Pierce was safe, I jumped up and let Dad have it. "What the hell's the matter with you?"

"Mason," Thad whispered. He placed a firm hand on my shoulder. "Not now."

I shrugged off his touch and snarled at him over my shoulder. He stepped back in surprise. Once I was satisfied Thad was going to keep his mouth shut, I faced our father. "You could've killed Pierce. Do you know that?"

He nodded. Regret had been replaced by dread.

"It's okay," Pierce coughed. The big badass he pretended to be slunk away. He'd been reduced to the little boy he really was,

especially when it came to our father. All it took was one look of
disappointment, and Pierce was devastated for days. To have been on
the receiving end of such a powerful spell would likely haunt my older
brother for months.

"No, it's not." I took another step forward. "Dad is always telling
us how we need to control our tempers in order to better manage our
powers. Hell, he's been hounding me about that for years. What just
happened isn't exactly the picture of control, is it?"

My father's eyes drew into slits. His anger fought again for
control, but he knew I was right. I could see it in the slight grin that
hitched up the right corner of his mouth. "Mason is correct," he finally
said. "Would apologizing make it better?"

I snorted. I was pushing my luck, but I couldn't help it. "It would
be a start."

He turned to Pierce and said, "I'm sorry, son. I shouldn't have
lost control like that."

Pierce forced a smile. "No worries."

"Better?" he asked.

I nodded.

"But now we need to deal with the mess you've made."

Oh, for crying out loud. "What did I do now?"

"Is he serious?" Thad asked. The gentle tone had departed in
favor of his usual condescension.

"What?" I asked.

"Mason, you broke the laws of the Conclave."

I glanced nervously from my father to my brothers, who shook
their heads at me. "What? How?"

"You cast a spell in front of a human," my father answered.

I opened my mouth to defend myself, but words wouldn't form.
He was right. I'd been so caught up with protecting Drake, I hadn't
even considered the fact that I was breaking our cardinal rule—magic
must remain hidden at all costs.

I PACED in the living room, trying to figure out exactly how screwed I
was. Casting spells in front of humans wasn't only forbidden, it was
grounds for the binding of the offender's powers. I could spend the rest of
my life forever cut off from my magic, even banished from my coven.

I had to find a way out of this new mess I'd gotten myself into.

"Drake doesn't know it was a spell," I told my brothers, who sat in the living room with me. Our father had left the room to answer a phone call. "I told him it was a prayer Mom had taught me. So even though I cast a spell, he doesn't realize that's what it was. That's got to mean something, right?"

I could hear the desperation in my voice as I grasped at straws, but I didn't care. I loved being a warlock. I didn't want to lose my birthright for one mistake, especially not since I had finally managed to do something right with the abilities I had.

Maybe I should also tell them my suspicions about Drake being a shifter. I had no proof except how he bounded all over the fucking place, but if he was a magical being, technically I hadn't broken the law.

But I couldn't bring myself to say the words. If I was wrong and Drake wasn't a were, I'd be needlessly placing him in danger. I couldn't do that, not even to save my own skin. What the hell was that about?

"Don't know," Pierce finally answered with a shrug. He glanced at Thad, who still sat at the piano. "What do you think?"

Thad didn't immediately answer. He clasped his hands together with only his index fingers pointing up. He brought them to his face and tapped them against his lips. It was Thad's standard thinking pose. He had a lot of information rattling around in that egg head of his. It sometimes took him a few moments to find exactly what he needed to answer a question. "Maybe," he finally responded.

"Maybe?" I asked. "That's it? With as much shit as you read, that's the best answer you can come up with?"

He straightened the creases in his perfectly pressed shirt and sighed. He only did that when he was about to get really bitchy. "Yes, well, I'm not the idiot who broke the law."

"Fuck you, Thad."

"You can be furious with me all you want," he replied. "Your inability to control yourself is what keeps getting you in trouble."

"And being a cold, distant asshole is what you'd recommend?"

He nodded. "If it prevents you from having your powers bound by the Conclave, perhaps. What this family needs to learn is how to rein in the emotions that swirl like a tempest inside us. You may find me indifferent, and perhaps in a way I am. But that's because I've learned how to check the warlock tendency of losing our cool. Acting rashly typically gets warlocks nowhere but dead." He surveyed Pierce and me with one sweep of his gaze. "Or do we need a warlock history refresher course?"

"You know what, Thad?" Pierce asked as he rose from the couch. "I may let my emotions get the better of me from time to time, but I sure as hell don't need lessons on what it means to be a warlock." He clenched his hands into fists. A blue aura crackled around them, and the low hum of electricity filled the room. "Because I know exactly what and who I am."

"You only prove my point," Thad replied. "You fall back on picking up the hammer when a screwdriver would suffice."

Pierce's expression twisted. "What fucking hammer?"

"He's talking about your powers," I answered, to which Thad nodded.

"We're more than just the immense power we wield," Thad added. "It's time we all realized that. Even father. We rely so much on our magic that we ignore the baser sides of who we are. We evolved from humans, and we retain human characteristics. Yet we shun them when we should be embracing them. Because, as loath as I am to admit it, Mason might be right, and it will be our humanity that will ultimately make the difference, not our supernatural gifts."

I had to do a double take. Where was Thad Blackmoor, and what had this man done with my brother? He'd never, in all the years I'd been alive, ever said I was right about anything. "What are you talking about?"

Thad glided over to the living room door and poked his head into the hallway. After seeing nothing, he turned and answered, "What you said at Mabon raised questions I'd never once considered, and frankly the fact that you thought of it before I did was quite a blow to my ego."

"Gee, thanks."

"Something is wrong," Thad continued. He rubbed his arms as if he'd gotten as cold as his frigid abilities. "The Conclave doesn't just appear in the middle of rituals, and they don't suddenly have blind spots in their powers. But they did and they do. The questions we should be asking are why, and why is this happening now?"

"But what about everything you said last week?" He'd been the one to remind me of the reasons the magical orders had been separated. It was for the good of all magic. Where was that speech now?

Before he could answer, the clicking of our father's footsteps echoed down the hall.

"Not now," Thad said. "We can't do this in front of Dad."

"What?" Pierce asked. "Why?"

"It's for the best," Thad replied. He clutched at my and Pierce's forearms. "Just promise me you'll keep what we've talked about to yourselves and that you'll only discuss this again when it's just the three of us. No one else."

Pierce gaped at Thad as if he'd gone crazy. Pierce didn't keep anything from Dad. In fact, he was the first one to tell our father everything. But I couldn't dismiss Thad's panicked expression. He rarely asked us for anything. If he was concerned enough to seek us out, that was reason enough to give him my word. "I promise."

"Fine. Me too," Pierce said with a loud sigh. "But if I get in trouble because of the two of you, you'll both find out exactly what it feels like to be a lightning rod."

Thad nodded in acceptance of Pierce's conditions, and when our father came back into the room, he arched his eyebrow. It wasn't often he found the three of us huddled together.

His lips parted slightly as he scrutinized us. "What's going on?"

"Nothing," we answered in unison. That wasn't suspicious at all.

He shrugged and let it drop. There was obviously something else on his mind. "That was Charles Proctor on the phone," he said. "When were you planning on telling us about the new dead body?"

Everyone was suddenly glaring at me once again. Man, I just couldn't catch a break.

AFTER I filled them in on the body and what I'd seen at the top of the crane, the room grew silent except for the turning of pages. Thad was flipping through our Grimoire, searching for answers. "I'm not familiar with any active power involving the bending of light," he finally said.

"Neither am I," my father added.

"So what does this mean?"

My father turned toward the bookcases and eyed each and every book, as if he could somehow snatch the answer from within the collective knowledge contained in the room. "I'm uncertain. Perhaps we're dealing with a new species, one that has evolved from us as we did from humans."

That was a frightening thought I didn't even want to consider. We were a pretty powerful bunch. To suddenly come upon a race even more powerful than we were set my nerves on edge.

"I don't think so." A familiar smugness clung to Thad's tone. Mr. Know-It-All had found something. "We might be dealing with a shadow weaver."

My father crossed over to Thad. "I'd forgotten all about them," he said. "What Mason described definitely could be a part of their power set."

I glanced at Pierce, who gaped at me, then shrugged. "And what exactly is a shadow weaver?"

"An extremely powerful warlock with mastery over darkness."

"Darkness?" Pierce asked. "How the hell is darkness more powerful than directing a couple thousand volts of electricity down someone's throat?"

Thad motioned to the shadows that filled the room and the land outside. "Because darkness is everywhere."

I studied the shadows that enveloped the corners of the room. They crawled across the floor, up the walls, and even trailed behind us. If manipulating darkness was the active power of a shadow weaver, the kindling for its ability was always on hand.

"But what does that mean exactly?" I asked as I drew closer to where Thad and our father read from the book. "I get that darkness is everywhere, but so is air. The same can be said for earth or water. What makes darkness so special?"

"For one, it's extremely rare," Thad said as he ran his fingers over the text. "Only a handful of shadow weavers have ever existed. The last was one of the most powerful members of the Conclave, Bartram Kane."

I exchanged glances with Pierce. We remembered that name. The last time we'd heard it had been when we were trying to save our mother.

"For another," Thad continued, as if he hadn't evoked a painful memory, "it's also the only active power that has contributed to a truly corrupt warlock."

"What? How?" Pierce asked.

"It's the nature of the power itself," our father answered. He had finished reading over Thad's shoulder. "Typical warlock powers, while strong, have limitations. Take mine for example. I can change my body to stone, and while I assume the stone's strength and durability, it's still stone, an element bound by the physical world as much as water, earth, or air. But darkness is far more malleable." He stared at the shadow his hand cast onto the wall. He extended his fingers and its projection grew into talons. He curled his hand, and a spider danced across the wall. "Its uses are only limited by the imagination of the individual because shadows have no true form. They're an absence of light, and within that void, a powerful shadow weaver can do almost anything."

"Which has turned past shadow weavers bad," I said, to which my father nodded. It certainly made sense. Any power had the potential to corrupt whoever wielded it, and with limitless power at his disposal, a shadow weaver might be tempted to do things that shouldn't be done.

Like Bartram Kane.

"I'll inform the Conclave we might have a potential shadow weaver in Havenbridge," Dad said just as the doorbell rang. "But first I'll get the door." As he walked away, he said, "You can continue your plotting now."

As soon as he left the room, Pierce smacked both of us upside the head. "He knows we were up to something."

I rubbed the pain away while a fire flickered in Thad's amber eyes. It seemed to be taking everything he had to contain his anger.

"Remember," he said after a few seconds. "You promised."

Pierce nodded and said no more. While warlocks typically broke promises made to others if the ends justified the means, promises made to each other were considered sacred.

"Mason," my father called. "It's for you."

Who the fuck was here at this hour? I glanced at my brothers as if they had the answer. When I turned back to the doorway, my father stood with Drake at his side. He carried a gift bag in his right hand. Where was he going, to a late-night birthday party?

"What are you doing here?"

"Well, howdy and hello to you too," he replied with the same wicked grin he'd first flashed me in the woods. I evidently didn't annoy him as much as I had before saving his life. That was a step in the right direction.

"Aren't you going to introduce us?" Dad asked.

"I wasn't planning on it," I replied. It wasn't safe having Drake here, not after I'd cast that spell in front of him. And with a potential shadow weaver on the loose, there was no sense in tempting fate.

Drake turned to my father and extended his hand. "Name's Drake Carpenter, sir. It's a real pleasure to meet you."

"Oliver Blackmoor," my father answered, shaking Drake's hand. He nodded to me with a frown. "The aghast father to such a rude son."

Drake smiled broadly at my father's jab at me and then laughed. His face lit up like a little boy's. Did it have to make him so damn charming? My father certainly seemed taken by him. He usually greeted newcomers with a reserved distance, but there he was shaking hands with Drake and laughing beside him as if there might not be a powerful warlock out there murdering people for some reason.

"These are my other sons," my father said, motioning to my brothers. "Pierce and Thad."

Drake turned the charm on them. "Pleasure to make your acquaintance," he said to Pierce. He held out his fist for a bump, and I almost fell over when my older brother knocked his fist against Drake's.

"I'd say any friend of Mason's is a friend of mine, but Mason doesn't really have friends."

Drake laughed again, as if he was incapable of anything else. Where had this cheerful attitude come from? He hadn't been like this when I'd met him. Was he just trying to be a well-mannered guest? Maybe it was a Southern thing.

When he turned to Thad, Drake didn't make a move to shake his hand or bump his fist. It was as if he could read each one of us like a book. He simply nodded at Thad and smiled. "I can tell you're the brains of the family."

Thad couldn't have been more stunned if Drake had Tasered him. "Excuse me?" Thad asked, clearly taken aback.

"Vos yeux sont remplis de la connaissance au-delà de vos années."

A grin stretched across Thad's lips. "C'est très poétique et très correct. Merci."

"Speak zee English," I said in a mock French accent. "We are in America, you know?"

Drake and Thad looked at me and sighed before turning to each other and cracking smiles.

"My brother's love of language knows no bounds," Thad said, patting Drake on the shoulder.

"I can tell." He turned to me and said, "And in case you were wonderin', I told your brother that his eyes were filled with knowledge beyond his years, and he said I was both poetic and correct."

I groaned. "Don't encourage him. His head is big enough as it is."

"And yours could stand to be a bit bigger," Thad replied. He locked eyes with me before shifting his attention to my groin. "And by that I mean *both* of them."

Everyone burst into laughter, and once again I was the butt of the joke. I was used to it from my brothers but not from Drake. I had half a mind to cast the last spell he would ever hear in his soon-to-be short life.

Thad motioned for Drake to sit on the couch. What the hell was going on? We had other things to do than entertain visitors.

When Drake complied with my brother's request, Thad sat next to him while my dad and Pierce sat down on the love seat. The only place left for me to sit was on the other side of Drake.

"I detect a Southern accent," Thad asked. "Am I correct?"

"Right on the money," Drake replied. "I was born and raised in the great state of Texas. Dallas to be exact."

It was my father's turn to get all social. "What brought you to northern Mass?"

The sadness I'd briefly detected in Drake's eyes while he ran and jumped around town, the look that told me he was running *from* something, returned. It shoved aside the carefree, charismatic boy who had seemed to cast a spell over my typically leery family. In his place sat a lost little boy. Why did I suddenly want to put my arms around his shoulders and tell him he'd be okay?

"My parents died a few months ago," he replied. His gaze focused on the wood flooring, and he sniffled. I looked at my father and my brothers, and the same expression of grief had seized their features. My family knew a thing or two about losing a loved one. It was a fucking bitch. "But I don't like to talk about it."

I could understand that. My mother's death wasn't exactly a favorite topic of discussion.

"So why Havenbridge?" my father asked.

The question brought Drake's focus from the floor back to us. His eyes had turned wet, and the tip of his nose was red. "My aunt Millie lives here. She's the only family I have left."

I suddenly developed a new appreciation for my family. Pierce and Thad were the biggest pains in my ass, but they were my brothers. What would I ever do without them?

"Wait a minute," Pierce said. "Millie? As in Millicent Carpenter? That old bi—" I snapped my gaze at him when he realized what he'd almost said. "Um, you're related to her?"

Drake nodded.

"Well, even though you aren't here under the greatest of circumstances, I'd like to welcome you to our little town. It's not much, but we love it. Perhaps you'll come to feel the same way about it too one day."

The thin smile on his lips revealed Drake doubted it would happen.

"Well, I have a call to make, so we'll leave you two boys to your visit," my father said upon standing. Thad and Pierce did the same without even being asked to leave. "It was nice meeting you, Drake."

"Same here, Mr. Blackmoor," Drake replied as my father and brothers exited the room.

For a few moments after they departed, Drake and I sat in uncomfortable silence. What could I say after what he'd revealed? I couldn't tell him I understood, that I'd been there too. That would be super lame and likely sound as superficial as it often did.

How many times after my mother's death had people offered condolences that made me want to hurt them very badly? Perhaps it was because I could tell they weren't sorry for me. They were happy the tragedy we'd suffered hadn't happened to them. Their grief was actually joy that they had escaped the suffering that had found my family.

"I bet you're wonderin' why I'm here, huh?" Drake asked.

"The thought did pop into my head once or twice."

He picked up the gift bag he'd been carrying and held it out to me. "I brought you somethin'."

The only people who'd ever given me gifts had been my family. How was I supposed to react to a random act of kindness? "Why the fuck for?"

Drake sighed in exasperation and shook his head. Evidently cursing in response to a gift wasn't the path to take. How the hell was I supposed to know that? Our family only exchanged gifts on Samhain and Yule. We didn't celebrate every damn holiday with presents and celebrations the way witches or humans did.

"How about you just say thank you?" Since I hadn't reached for the gift, he scooted closer to me on the couch and placed the blue bag with white tissue paper on my lap. The sweet, woody scent that lingered around him filled the air once again. I took a deep whiff.

My breath caught in my throat, my heart fluttered in my chest, and my damn cock turned to steel. Drake's gorgeous blue eyes, the ones that had somehow entranced me the moment I saw them in the woods, made me almost take him in my arms.

What the fuck was the matter with me?

Drake's lips parted in a semigrin as he shook the fluttery blond locks that had fallen in front of his eyes out of his vision. "Well, aren't you goin' to open it?"

"I still don't understand why."

"Oh for Christ's sake!" he complained. He nudged me with his shoulder, and the slight physical contact sent pulses of electricity coursing through me. It was like getting zapped by Pierce, except this was far more pleasant. My dick agreed and throbbed in response. I was grateful the gift bag hid my erection. "Will you open it already?"

"Fine," I replied, pulling the white tissue paper out of the bag. "I just wish I knew why you—" And then I saw what was at the bottom of the bag. "My shirt!" I took it out and held it up against myself.

"See, it isn't all that special." Even though he was attempting to be humble, he was failing miserably. The pleased expression that pulled his mouth into a wide grin told me that much. "I figured you'd like to have your shirt back. It was the least I could do after you saved my life and all."

"The very least," I replied.

Drake's Cheshire grin retreated to a thin line. "Don't make me regret being nice to you."

"Don't make me regret saving your life."

His smile sprang right back. "Fair 'nough."

He sat back, the outside of his right thigh touching my left. The heat from his body spilled over to me. His warmth traveled across my lap and ignited a fire in my already smoldering groin. A long, cold shower before bed was in my immediate future.

"You've got a nice place here," Drake said as he inspected his surroundings. "It's not quite as cold an' stuffy as I thought it might be when you first accosted me for trespassin'. It's formal, but a warm heart beats underneath it." His gaze lingered on mine a few moments longer than necessary before he once again surveyed the living room. "How about you give me a tour?"

I'd show him around all right. Straight to my bedroom, where he could get a long look at the ceiling from his back. "If you insist," I said after standing up. I held out my hand.

He hesitated, eyeing my offered assistance. After a few moments, he took my hand, and the comforting warmth of our touch spread across me like an old blanket. I helped him to his feet and when we stood almost nose-to-nose, his sweet breath pluming across my cheeks, I had to take two steps back before I leaned in for a kiss.

Drake flushed, and he avoided eye contact. "Shall we?" he asked, withdrawing his hand from mine.

Desire I'd never experienced before stole the words from my throat, so I nodded and started the tour.

AFTER SHOWING him around the house, I took Drake out to the back patio. The sun had long since waved good-bye, and the moon had begun its steady ascent across the heavens, which were clearly visible in the cloudless sky.

The pale silver light reflected off the stone wall along the east side of the property and the tiny garden that was surrounded by a white picket fence. The shadows and the uncertain light transformed each rock of the wall into a shimmering, opaque pearl. The grass had become a richer, deeper green, as if emeralds had been tilled into the soil, and a perfumed scent wafted on the breeze.

It was like I was experiencing the world for the very first time.

"It's beautiful out here."

"I think so too." I walked down the steps to the yard and turned to face the house. I pointed to the third-floor window of the great hall. "I often sit up there and gaze out to the horizon."

"What are you lookin' for?" he asked as he joined me and looked up to where I pointed.

"Huh?"

"Well, it's always been my experience that when someone's starin' out as far as they can see, they're missin' somethin'. They don't always realize that." He paused for a few moments before repeating his question. "So what are you lookin' for?"

"I wasn't aware I was," I replied with a shrug.

"Well, you are," he said with confidence. "When you find it, you'll know."

Was he right? Was that why I spent so much time up there?

Drake left my side and turned from the house. He looked out onto the back property that stretched about a hundred feet back before merging into the forested area where we'd run into each other. I couldn't help but stare at him as the moon bathed him in its embrace. His radiant white skin practically glowed, and the long sandy strands of blond hair turned almost silver.

He was the most beautiful boy I'd ever seen. It certainly explained my reaction to him. He revved up my hormones and kicked them into overdrive more than anyone else had ever done before. There had been other boys I'd been attracted to, like Walter Howard, a teenage warlock who'd traveled through the state with his family during Samhain.

We'd hung out together all weekend, made out on my bed, and even got to third base, but once he left, I never really gave him another thought. The same went for any other boy who'd managed to snag my attention. They were useful for satisfying the urges that built inside me like a category-five hurricane.

But something was different here. I didn't want to chase and then discard Drake like I had the others. I wanted to hold him close and keep him safe. But why was that? Why had I put myself in danger to save his life and broken our laws without a second thought? I hadn't known him long enough to feel that way.

What was it about Drake Carpenter that intrigued me so much?

"I see you're enjoyin' the view again?" he asked. He hadn't even turned his head to look at me. He just somehow knew I'd been staring at him this whole time.

"You sure are full of yourself, aren't you?"

He chuckled. "Not at all. Just statin' the obvious."

"Yeah, well, you're wrong."

Drake turned to face me. A thin, troublemaking smile lingered on his lips. "You really are bad at this, aren't you?"

"What are you talking about?"

"I know your secret," he said, closing the distance between us.

I couldn't respond. All I could do was stare into his sapphire-blue eyes, which seemed to see only me.

"Did you hear what I said?"

I nodded. What further confirmation did I need? Drake was a shifter. He knew I was a warlock because his animal senses probably smelled the black magic in my blood as easily I detected the cologne he wore. "And I know yours," I replied. "So what do we do now?"

"Really?" he asked. "I'd reckon it was pretty obvious, wouldn't you?" His voice had gotten thicker, and the distance between us smaller. Even though we weren't touching, I could feel the pressure of his body against mine. It was like some wonderful spell had been cast that linked us.

"Not to me," I said, swallowing the huge lump in my throat. "You're the first one I ever met."

A knowing smile danced across his lips. "That explains a lot."

I guessed it did. How exactly? I wasn't quite sure, but I wasn't really thinking clearly. My hard cock pressed painfully against my jeans in a vain attempt to reach Drake. "What do you think we should do?" Only a few inches separated us, but it seemed more like miles. "Tell my family?"

He laughed. "I'd say that's puttin' the cart before the horse, wouldn't you?"

I wasn't entirely sure what he meant, but I got the general idea. "You think?"

"Well, yeah," he said. He wrapped his arms around my neck and pressed against me. The contact was warm and comfortable, like a fire in the middle of a dreary New England winter. I couldn't tear my gaze from the sight of his creamy skin against my tanned flesh. It was mesmerizing. "We take things much slower where I'm from. Give folks a chance to get to know each other before lettin' the horses outta the barn. Once those suckers run free, there's not much chance of corrallin' them back up, if you know what I mean?"

I thought I did. If I told my family Drake was a shifter, the Council and the Conclave would immediately intervene. They'd descend and take him to be interrogated so they could learn why he was here instead of on shifter land, or whatever their damned island was called.

I wouldn't like that one bit. We were looking for a shadow weaver anyway, not a shifter. And if I revealed Drake's secret, I wouldn't be holding him in my arms like I was doing right now.

"You still with me?"

I tore myself from my thoughts and focused on Drake. "Yeah, and you're right. I won't say anything to them."

He smiled. "Good."

I leaned in to sample his tasty lips, but Drake stepped out of our embrace. I tried to pull him back into my arms, but he grabbed my hand and grinned. "I said slow, remember?"

Fuck. Did that mean for us too? I hadn't agreed to that. "What about if I promise to kiss you real slow?"

Drake patted my shoulder and walked back up the steps. "I'll show myself out," he said. "But I look forward to seein' you at school on Monday. Maybe next time you won't be such a dick."

"I make no promises."

"How did I know you were fixin' to say that?"

I shrugged and Drake laughed before he left the backyard, passed through the foyer, and went out the front door.

For a few minutes, I stood there. My thoughts raced through my mind as quickly as my blood filled my cock. A shifter. I had the hots for a fucking shifter.

No. That wasn't quite right. Whatever existed between us went deeper than just wanting to jump each other's bones. It was almost magical, as if from the moment we met, Drake and I had been spell bound.

But that couldn't be possible. We were too young for a magical bonding, weren't we?

CHAPTER 6

THE NEXT morning I was wide awake by the time the first rays of the new day streaked through my windows. Not because I was ready to get the day started, but because I'd spent most of the night tossing and turning. I couldn't shut my mind off long enough to drift to sleep. Ever since Drake left, every single thought had been about him, and it made my head spin.

Everything had happened so fast. One moment we hated each other, and the next I was saving his life and holding him in my arms in the backyard.

Could it really be the magical binding of two spirits we called being spell bound? As Drake would say, that was "puttin' the cart before the horse," right?

Being spell bound only happened on extremely rare occasions, and it was the Gate's way of recognizing love, like that shared by my parents, reborn through the ages. It allowed soul mates to find each other again after each reincarnation.

There was just no way that was what was going on. There had to be another reason, and that was why we had to take things slow and figure out exactly what we felt. Maybe it was pure sexual attraction. Maybe Drake's shifter pheromones were to blame. Perhaps we'd make out, maybe even have sex, and then find out it was physical, nothing more. That happened to Pierce all the time. He fell in and out of lust so quickly, it gave me whiplash.

Someone lightly rapped on my bedroom door. It sure as hell wasn't Pierce. He'd just barge in. "Come in."

The door opened, and Thad poked his head inside. "Can we talk?"

I nodded, and he closed the door behind him. "What's up?"

"Drake."

Like I hadn't seen this one coming. As the rule follower in the family, Thad was most likely going to lecture me on blurring the lines. Drake was my assignment, not my love interest. "What about him?"

"You like him." It wasn't a question.

"I don't know what I feel for him, but, yeah, there's something there. So what?"

He sat at the foot of my bed and sighed. "This could complicate things, don't you think?"

I couldn't argue with that. It moved things so far beyond complicated, it was a calculus problem. "Yeah, it does." He opened his mouth to speak, but I had to say something before the lecture started. "Look, I know I screwed up when I cast that spell in front of him. I wasn't thinking. I just reacted. And I know that doesn't make it any better, and the Conclave might bind my powers, but I couldn't let him die. I had to do something to save him."

"And yourself?"

"Well, yeah," I said. "But I wasn't thinking about myself when I did it." Thad regarded me carefully. I hated when he did that. It was like I was on a glass slide under a microscope. "What? Why are you looking at me like that?"

"I don't think I've ever heard you think about someone before yourself. You've always been very much a warlock in that regard. Focused only on your wants and needs, and to hell with everyone else, including this family."

Was Thad trying to start a fight? "That's a damn lie. This family means a lot to me."

"I have no doubt." There was no sharp edge to his words, which wasn't Thad. Maybe he didn't want to start a fight after all. "But to you being a warlock has always been about a show of strength, a projection of power, an image of some badass motherfucker." I had to suppress my laughter. Thad rarely cursed, and when he did, it sounded strange. Like hearing a five-year-old accidentally scream *shit*.

"What?" he asked. "Why are you smirking like that?"

"No reason," I replied with a wave of my hand. "Go on."

He glared at me for a few more seconds before he continued. "I find it interesting that your spells seem to work now that you have apparently cast that false image aside."

"False? Are you saying we aren't badass motherfuckers?" Coming from my lips, cursing worked.

He shook his head. "We are, but that's not all we are. Yes, we're powerful, and yes, our kind is far more selfish than any of the other orders. But we aren't evil, and we aren't some stereotype. I think that's how you saw us. All of us."

Maybe he was right. I always felt I had to live up to the family name, to honor the reputation we carried. In order to do that, I had to be perfect. Had I been putting too much stress on myself? Was that why I hadn't been able to master my magic, because I was standing in my own way? "You could be right."

"I know I am, but I don't think you see it that way anymore. I think you now realize that being a warlock isn't a reputation, it just is. Our magic doesn't define us. We define it, and when you look at it that way, it makes it easier to manipulate."

This was the best talk Thad and I had ever had. He was actually talking to me like my brother and not my parent. "You're right. It does."

"So on those grounds, I think whatever is going on between you and Drake might be good for you and your powers. But you need to be careful."

"I know. And I also know I have to face the consequences of my actions. If the Conclave binds my powers, I'll accept the decision and won't embarrass the family."

"That's not going to happen," Thad said as he rose from my bed.

"What? Why not?"

"The Conclave can't see into Havenbridge right now, right?"

Shit. I hadn't even thought about that. "They have no idea I broke the law."

He nodded. "The only ones who know are your family."

"But you're required under law to report me. If you don't, the entire family could have its powers bound."

"Correct," Thad replied as he opened my bedroom door. "But you're family, and the Blackmoors take care of their own first. That's how we badass motherfuckers roll," he said with a wink.

I burst into laughter as he left and shut the door.

With my family behind me, how could anything go wrong?

ABOUT AN hour after my talk with Thad, I sat in front of Millicent Carpenter's house. Going up and knocking on the front door wasn't going to be easy. Millicent hated the Blackmoors. We'd ruined her business, and she thought we were rich lowlifes. At least that was what Drake had told me.

And maybe from her perspective, we were. My family had tons of money and influence, and we weren't shy about using them when we needed to further our own interests. That was how her grocery store went from being the most popular in town to going bankrupt.

Finding me on her doorstep, calling on her nephew, wouldn't exactly be a welcome event. But that wasn't going to stop me. I got out of the car, strolled down the sidewalk, and knocked on the front door.

"Coming," a kind, elderly voice sang from the other side. She was evidently in a good mood. I had to hope it would last after she realized who I was. When the door opened, a gray-haired woman with wrinkled brown eyes peered at me from behind the screen door. Her brows stitched together. She recognized me from somewhere, but she obviously couldn't tell from where. "Can I help you?" she asked as she dried her hands on a kitchen towel.

"I'm here to see Drake. Is he home?"

She nodded. "He's out back doing the gardening he refused to let me do." After opening the door, she motioned me inside. Deep wrinkle lines crossed her face, but they couldn't hide the strong woman who'd weathered the storms of life. Strength and wisdom reflected in her bright eyes and in the proud carriage of her jutting jawline. She obviously appreciated Drake's helpfulness, but she didn't like it. "I've been taking care of this place since my good-for-nothing husband ran off some thirty years ago, and I'll continue to do just that till my dying day." She punctuated her statement with a firm nod.

"I have no doubt you will, Mrs. Carpenter."

She snorted. "It's *Ms.* Carpenter. I went back to my maiden name a *long* time ago."

"Of course. My apologies."

She waved my apology away and gestured for me to follow her through the house, which was a simple half-Cape. The outside had a broad, strong frame just like Drake's aunt, but the inside was anything but traditional. Vibrant blue and green paint covered the walls instead of the customary neutral colors associated with a Pilgrim-styled house. The furniture wasn't Quaker or thrifty. A light green couch with white cushions rested along the far right wall opposite a custom white entertainment center that resembled a giant jigsaw puzzle.

This décor was stylish and chic. There was nothing old lady about it. "You have a beautiful home."

"That's very sweet," she said as we entered the kitchen, which included polished stainless steel appliances. She nodded at the back door. "Drake's out there. Why don't you wait a minute, and I'll give you some cold lemonade to take outside for the two of you?"

"That would be great."

"I'm guessing you're the young man I have to thank for saving my Drake from that awful construction accident."

"That would be me."

She clasped her hands together before rushing over to give me a hug that almost squeezed all the breath out of my body. "I could never thank you enough for risking your own life that way." When she backed up, her smiling eyes had filled with playful teasing. "You're either very brave or very stupid."

I laughed. This woman was awesome. "I'd have to go with stupid."

She clicked her tongue. "As I suspected. I said the same thing to Drake after he told me what happened. When that boy runs, he doesn't notice anything but where he's going."

That was most likely the shifter in him. They could be pretty narrow-minded at times. "So I've noticed." But if Drake was a were, did that mean Millicent was one too? That would certainly explain the strength in her arms and the spring in her step.

"Let me get you those drinks," she said after staring at me for a few seconds. She grabbed glasses from the kitchen cabinet. The wheels of her memory were obviously turning, and she was trying to figure out where she'd seen me before. It wasn't me that she was recalling, though. She and I had never officially met. It was my father she knew, and we closely resembled each other.

"What's your name?" she asked as she poured. "You look extremely familiar, but I can't place you."

"I'm Mason."

She hesitated for a minute before resuming her task. "I don't think I've ever met anyone by that name."

It was now or never. "You may have met my father."

She crossed to me with both glasses in her hands and a smile on her withered lips. "And who's your father, Mason?"

"Oliver Blackmoor."

At the mention of my father's name, she stopped cold. She looked me up and down as if she could assess my worth solely on my appearance. "Well, damn," she said with a sly grin. "I never thought I'd ever have a member of the Blackmoor family in my house."

She handed me the drinks and motioned to the back door. Had I somehow passed muster? "Would you like to join us?"

She shook her head and smiled. "The last thing two young boys need hanging around is an old lady like me."

"It would be an honor if you joined us." And I wasn't lying. I liked her, and I regretted what my family had done to her.

"You've got a silver tongue like your father," she said as she shooed me out the door. "Just make sure that tongue doesn't develop a fork in the middle, and you and I will do just fine. The poor boy has been through enough."

"Yes, ma'am," I said before heading out the back door.

DRAKE WORKED in the garden, pulling up weeds. His back was to me, and he was listening to music through the earbuds that connected to his iPhone. I was grateful he couldn't hear me approach because it gave me time to take in the sight of his shirtless body as he dug in the ground. His lean muscles flexed as he pulled out weeds. Sweat glistened across his back, and beads of perspiration snaked lazy trails down his spine before disappearing beneath the waistband of his blue denim cutoffs.

The cleft of his butt crack peeked out at me. I had to restrain myself from rushing over to him and lapping the sweat that dotted his pale skin before following the trail to his musky center.

But I had to gain control of myself. I couldn't stand here with lemonade and a boner. At least not with Drake's aunt more than likely watching from somewhere within the house.

I took several deep breaths and then crossed the lawn to where Drake worked. I kicked at his feet. When he looked up, a smile stretched across his hot, flushed face. "Aww," he said as he pulled the earbuds free. "You brought me somethin' to drink."

I handed him his beverage. "Yup. Made it myself."

After gulping down half the contents, he shot me an even stare. "I thought your name was Mason, not Millicent."

I crouched beside him. "That's my middle name."

"What? Millicent?"

"That's correct." Drake playfully shoved his shoulder into me, which upset my balance. I fell backward on my butt and landed in the grass, spilling lemonade all over my shirt.

"Now look at what you've done." I glared at him and raised one eyebrow in mock anger.

"That's what you get for fibbin'," he said, tossing a weed at me. Naturally, it hit my chest and showered dirt on me and into the remaining liquid in the glass.

"Aw, man. Now you've ruined my lemonade. Plus you got my shirt wet *and* dirty." I leered at him and then pulled my tee up and over my head.

Drake's breath caught in his throat as he swept his gaze over my chest and down my smooth, tanned abdominals. A thin smile stretched across his lips before it retreated. Was he playing hard-to-get? "Any excuse to take off your shirt, huh?"

I gestured toward his half-nakedness. "What's that, Pot?"

"Oh please. I'm workin' out here in the heat."

"And I got wet and dirty. What's your point?"

Drake shook his head and then placed his glass beside him. "So what brings you by?"

I lay on my side in the grass, propping my head up on one elbow. "I came to see you."

"Why?"

"What do you mean 'why'?"

He glanced at me, his blue eyes twinkling with the sun's light. "I really don't know how else to ask that question. It's pretty simple."

Now I was confused. After last night, I figured Drake would be expecting to see me today. Or was that not taking it slow? Was I supposed to wait a day or two? I had no clue. Instead of answering, I stammered.

Drake chuckled. "You really *are* bad at this."

I still couldn't speak. Instead I let my arched eyebrows express my continued confusion.

He stopped working and covered my hand with his. His touch was cool and refreshing from the mud he'd been working in. "What's the reason you came over here today?"

I stared down at our overlapping flesh. He ran his finger along the back of my palm, urging me to answer his question.

"To spend some time with you, I guess." My response made my cheeks burn.

He patted my hand and sat back with a smile. "See? That wasn't so hard, was it?"

I snorted. "Says you."

He shook his head before saying, "My daddy always said it's best to just speak your mind. It keeps people from havin' to guess what you're up to." The mention of his father caused the sadness that occasionally overcame Drake to descend upon him. It was a shadow that followed him and wrapped around him like a bad nightmare.

"You must miss them a lot."

"Somethin' awful."

I could tell he wanted to say more, but his throat had clenched up. Tears had probably lodged in his throat. It happened to me all the time when something reminded me of my mother. Like when I looked at Thad's reddish hair and hazel eyes. He resembled her so much it was uncanny, and it sometimes made me sad. He was a reminder of what I no longer had. If it was tough on me, I couldn't imagine how difficult it was for my brother to look at himself in the mirror every day. "I miss my mom too."

Drake stopped working and shifted his gaze to mine. "Did your momma recently pass?"

I cleared my throat. "Six months ago."

He gathered his legs to his chest, wrapped his sweaty, mud-streaked arms around them, and gave me his full attention. He evidently wanted me to continue, but I didn't talk about her death with anyone, not even my family. We grieved in silence and by ourselves. It was the Blackmoor way. "What happened?"

Was he really going to make me do this? He wasn't sharing any information about his parents. He'd made it quite clear he didn't like talking about it, so why did he want me to open up, and why did I want to do just that? "Cancer."

He winced and scooted to me across the grass. He unconsciously rubbed his fingers against my chin in a show of support and comfort. I leaned into the gesture and continued. "She got sick about a year ago. Breast cancer. The doctors thought they removed it all with the mastectomy a few months before that, but it had metastasized in her bones and lungs. We tried to fight it."

"Radiation?"

I nodded. That and whatever healing spells we could find. Thad had cross-checked our Grimoire with every medical book he could find, mixing potions that would cause the cancer to go into remission. Nothing he tried worked. Dad wove spell after spell to cast out the malignancy, but nothing he did proved successful.

"I can't even imagine how tough that was," he said.

It had been hard on all of us. While father and Thad had searched for a magical answer, Pierce and I researched new treatments. Some were quite aggressive and weren't legal in the United States, but we didn't care. We had to save our mother.

But she didn't want to leave home. She was getting weak and wanted to remain with her family.

So Dad contemplated casting the spell most forbidden by the Conclave, the *immortalitus* spell. It was the trickiest and most complex spell in existence and had only ever been cast once in all of magical history. The results had been disastrous for humans and for us.

The Conclave at the time ordered the spell stricken from every warlock's Grimoire, every wizard's Magus, and every witch's Book of Shadows. Contemplating casting the spell, like my father did, was grounds for immediate binding of powers. Actually casting it resulted in death.

We were prepared to do it if we found any traces of the spell, but Mother didn't want that. Instead of fighting like we asked, she let go. She surrendered to the force that consumed her from within in order to prevent her family from doing what we were never supposed to do.

"It was the toughest thing I've ever lived through," I replied.

Drake drew closer, wrapping his arms around my neck like he had outside my house last night. He gently massaged the tension that had bunched up in my shoulders and rested his forehead against mine. His sandy-colored hair had fallen in front of his eyes, and I brushed it away.

"I know that words don't mean a hill o' beans at times like this. They can come off corny, clichéd, and without a whole heck of a lot of genuine emotion behind 'em, but I'm truly sorry for your loss." He nuzzled into the crook of my neck and held me tight. "No boy should be without his momma."

The words brought tears to my eyes, and from the sniffling I heard coming from Drake, they'd brought tears to his too. I patted his back, and he rubbed mine.

But more importantly, we held on to each other, and that seemed to take some of the pain away. Not a lot, not most, but some. And that was a start.

I HELPED Drake finish up in the garden, and about an hour later, Millicent stuck her head out of the back door. "You boys get in here for some lunch," she said, and from the tone of her voice, there would be no arguing.

"Yes, ma'am," Drake said as we finished watering the freshly planted winter flowers that would add color in the weeks ahead.

I turned off the water at the faucet and was headed toward the back door when I noticed Drake gazing at the earth and then at the sky. "What are you looking for?" I asked, remembering what he'd told me last night.

He flashed me a cheeky grin over his shoulder. "Someone pays attention. I like that."

My only response was to place my hands on my hips and glare at him. I wanted an answer.

"I'm just gonna miss the green, is all. The sun and nature always make me feel better. It's kinda my thing." As if that was news to me. Shifters loved the outdoors. "It's gonna get dark and dreary before we know it, so I guess if I'm lookin', it's for a butterfly." He bared his teeth at me as his cheeks grew rosy with embarrassment. "Pretty dopey, huh?"

Yes, it was, but it made me smile anyway. There was a refreshing honesty about Drake that eased my soul. I hadn't liked his candor when we first met at school. He'd come off too cocky. But it wasn't overconfidence, just confidence. He stood his ground, and he spoke his mind. We weren't really all that different from each other.

Well, besides being from two different magical species.

But seeing him standing there, searching each flower and tree along the fence for a butterfly, I decided to test the magic I'd managed to master yesterday. I closed my eyes and found the energy that connected me to everything around me. The entire backyard turned into one invisible latticework of colorful energy. I was surprised by how quickly I'd been able to lower my human senses and heighten my magical ones. It was like Thad said. I wasn't trying to be a warlock. I was one.

I reached out to the energy, plucking several strings and watching them resonate outward in gentle rolling ripples, and as the waves of energy flowed outward, I whispered, "*Papiliones, veni.*"

When I opened my eyes, a yellow- and black-striped butterfly flitted into the garden.

"Mason, look," Drake cooed. He pointed to the fluttering insect as it danced between us. "It's beautiful."

I nodded, and another butterfly flew into view. Drake covered his mouth with his hands, trying to hold back what would no doubt be a childlike, gleeful squeal. Then a blue butterfly joined the others. The silvery finish on its indigo wings made it sparkle. As it fluttered and flitted, it dazzled in the sun's light.

"Oh my God," Drake said.

I looked at him, but he wasn't staring at the butterflies in the yard. His wide-eyed gaze had shifted to the fence behind me. When I turned to see what had him so awestruck, I couldn't believe my eyes either.

A cloud of butterflies, both yellow and black and blue and silver, swarmed into the backyard. They performed a silent aerial ballet around us, dipping left before rising high, or swirling in circles before darting to the left or right. Some landed on Drake's head and clung to his clothes. He giggled like a school kid.

"Auntie, you've gotta come out here," Drake called.

"What is it?" she said, but when she opened the back door, all she managed was "Oh my."

The prancing performers responded to Millicent's arrival and fluttered around her, kissing her cheeks with their wings.

I held out my arms, silently calling them to me, and some answered. They lighted on my arms, waving their paper-thin wings in greeting. I smiled at them, sending a mental note of thanks for responding. No doubt they were perplexed. Warlocks didn't usually cast spells such as these, as there was nothing to be gained by it. This was more of a witch's spell, but even though an unfamiliar voice had called, they'd come.

The Gate's energy hummed within all living creatures.

But it was time for them to go. I could sense it in their movements. Staying in one place, gathered in such a large number, was dangerous for them, so I said one final thanks, and the swirl of color lifted from the backyard.

It hung over us for a second before, one by one, the butterflies continued the journeys they were on prior to receiving my call.

"I've never seen anything like that before," Millicent said. One persistent butterfly still fluttered at the edge of her nose. "I don't know what else to say. It was…."

"Magical," Drake said as he crossed over to me. His gaze never left mine, and when he reached my side, he grabbed my hand and pulled me toward the back door. "That was like the most awesome thing that's ever happened to me. And whenever I'm this pumped up, I get ravenous. What about you?"

"I'm so hungry I could eat a horse."

He groaned as he held open the door. "What did I tell you about stickin' to your Yankee speak?"

"I guess I'm just like you, then," I said. "I don't really do what people tell me to do."

Aunt Millicent chuckled behind us. "You boys are two peas in a pod."

She was right. I could feel it, and I think Drake could too.

WE STUFFED ourselves full of hearty sandwiches made with homemade bread, some sliced apples, and another tall glass of lemonade. I was about ready to pop. "Ms. Carpenter, that was perhaps the best sandwich I've ever eaten."

"Call me Millie or Aunt Millie. Everyone else does," she said as she collected our plates. "And I'm glad you like it. I pride myself on my sandwiches, as Drake will tell you. They used to be the highlight of the delicatessen at my old grocery store."

That was right. I remembered going in there with my mom and brothers when I was a kid. I used to push my face against the glass container, overwhelmed by my choices. It had been too difficult for me to decide what I wanted, and Pierce and Thad complained I took forever. My mother always shushed them, though, and told them to let me have my time to choose. According to her, it wasn't my fault they ate the same thing every time while I tended to try something new each visit. "I have some good memories of your store," I said, helping her with the dirty dishes. "My mother used to take my brothers and me to your store every week. I think I tried all the sandwiches you ever made, but my favorite was the fried egg."

Her eyes sparkled. "The Perfectly Fried Egg Sandwich," she corrected.

"That was it." I turned on the water and started washing. "It had cheese, avocado, bacon, and was just all around yummy. I really miss it…." I trailed off. It was my mother I missed most right now.

Aunt Millie wrapped one arm around me and gave me an affectionate squeeze. "I was very sad to hear about your mother. Priscilla was a beautiful woman, and the way she doted on you kids, well, I could tell you three were her most prized possessions in the world."

I wiped a stray tear from my cheek and nodded. My mother had loved me. I never doubted that, but there had always been this occasional distance between us, as if there was some secret I was unaware of. It didn't prevent her from loving me, but it kept her guard up.

As I continued washing, I stared over my shoulder to see where Drake was. He hadn't said a word since we finished lunch. When I saw him sitting at the table staring at me, I arched an eyebrow at him, wondering why he had gone mute when he usually couldn't stop talking.

He responded with a big smile that made my stomach flutter.

"How is your family doing with everything?" Aunt Millie asked.

"In the usual Blackmoor way, we don't really talk about it."

She nodded. "That's the trouble with men," she snorted. "Bottling up their emotions instead of dealing with them. It's not good to keep it all inside. Sometimes you just have to let it out. Cry. Scream. Hit things. Whatever it takes. Just get that venom out of your soul before it tears you apart."

"Auntie!" Drake scolded.

"Oh, hush!" she said. "You're no better, mister, and you know it!"

He had no comeback for that one.

"Don't get me wrong," she continued. "I'm not a sexist. Certain men can be open about their feelings, but they are few and far between. I dated this man once. You might have known him, Mason. Gerald Wa."

I nodded. Gerald arrived in Havenbridge about five years ago. He was a solitary wizard of advanced age without a coven. While most of our kind stayed with our families, a lone wizard, witch, or warlock wasn't uncommon. Either they were the last of their coven, like Gerald, or they'd ventured off on their own, preferring a life of solitude to the often-complicated life of communal magical living.

Gerald had come to Havenbridge to be close to the Gate before he passed.

"He was a wonderful man," she said, "and a great companion for a few years." She pulled a gold chain out of her blouse. "He was the one who gave me this." She showed off what was obviously a very prized possession. Hanging from the chain was an emerald stone mounted in gold. A lily with its petals open had been carved in onyx across the gem face.

It was an exquisite piece of jewelry. I was shocked that such a gift had come from a wizard. They weren't known for their good taste in baubles. "It's beautiful," I said.

"Thank you." On her face was a smile of pride.

She flipped the charm over in her tiny fingers, and I glimpsed what looked like a triangle on the other side. It vaguely reminded me of something I'd seen before, but I couldn't place it. I wanted to ask Aunt Millie if I could have a closer look, but her careful handling of the trinket told me such a request would likely make her uncomfortable.

"He was an exceptional gift giver."

She nodded before chuffing. "But talk about closed off. He was so quiet and logical. I could barely get a rise out of him even when I tried." That was because Gerald was a typical gray wizard, free with logic but closed with his emotions. "But he was a breath of fresh air after my husband. Now Vincent, he wasn't shy about expressing his emotions, even though he didn't have a lick of common sense. He didn't like that I was smarter than he was, and that's probably why he left," she added with a shrug.

"He was a fool," I said, turning off the faucet.

"Maybe," she said with a laugh. "But he gave me the greatest gift of our marriage when he walked out on it. I send him a thank you card every year on the anniversary of our divorce."

Drake snickered. "Aunt Millie, you do not!"

"I sure do," she said with a satisfied nod, and Drake and I burst into laughter at the sheer pleasure Aunt Millie got from socking it to her ex-husband every year.

"You're my kind of woman, Aunt Millie," I told her, at which she smiled and nudged me. "And that's why I need to apologize."

Confusion clouded her typically clear eyes. "For what?"

"For what my family did to you and your business," I said. "It was an institution in this town, and we should've found a way to work together instead of forcing you out. No one deserves that, especially not you."

Tears welled in her eyes as a smile inched its way across her lips. Unable to speak, she swallowed hard and nodded. "Thank you, Mason," she managed after getting her emotions under control. "You might be the first Blackmoor I actually like."

I chuckled and leaned into her. She pressed back and smiled. "I'm honored."

"You should be," she said. Evidently it was time to bring the sappiness to an end. "I don't like many people. I am a crotchety old woman, you know?"

"So I've heard," I replied with a fake grimace.

She tossed the towel on the sink and then yawned. "I think it's time for my nap." She looked from me to Drake. "What are you boys going to do?"

Drake shrugged.

"If you don't mind, I was thinking about taking Drake out for the afternoon. Show him around town some and maybe go to a movie."

"That sounds nice. But behave yourselves," she warned. She gave both of us stern glances.

"I promise to be a gentleman," I replied.

"Can I promise just to have fun?" Drake asked, sticking his tongue out.

She glared at her nephew before turning to me. "You're a good boy, Mason, and I know you'll take good care of my Drake."

My eyes met Drake's before I replied, "Yes, ma'am. I will."

"Good," she said before tucking her necklace and its charm back into the safety of her blouse. "Now you boys have fun." She gave us a wink as she shooed us out the front door, and as I turned around to wave good-bye, she returned the gesture and rubbed her hand lovingly along the hidden necklace.

AFTER A short drive around town, we arrived at the movies and bought our tickets for *Guardians of the Galaxy*. It was a movie we both wanted to see. Since Drake had paid for the tickets, even though I'd been the one to invite him, I insisted on springing for the snacks. Of course, he argued with me over that too.

"You saved my life," he said. "The movies are on me."

I shook my head. "You already paid me back with my shirt."

"I said I'm buyin'."

I'd been about to argue some more, but his blank expression told me I was going to lose. "Are you always this difficult?"

He snorted. "If you think this is difficult, you're in for a world of hurt later."

I grinned and wiggled my eyebrows at his comment.

"Get your mind out of the gutter," he said with a playful swat at my chest. "Is that all you ever think about?"

"Maybe," I said with a shrug. "I'm a growing boy."

He crossed his arms and let out a long exaggerated sigh. "And you promised Aunt Millie you'd be a gentleman."

"And you promised you were going to have fun," I reminded him before slyly drumming my fingers across his lower back.

Drake's pretend annoyance melted away at my touch. He leaned back into the contact and smiled. "Well, I am havin' fun. It's been a long time since I have."

The smile in his eyes faltered as memories of his parents most likely floated to the surface. That happened to me all too often. One moment life was going along just fine and then *bam*, my thoughts turned to my mother. "I'm glad," I said, rubbing his back in comfort. "It's been a while for me too."

He wiped away the tears he refused to allow to fall. "I'll be right back," he said, stepping out of the line. "I'm gonna visit the men's room."

"Take your time."

He dug into his pocket and took out some money. "Can you get me a large buttered popcorn and a root beer?"

"Root beer? Really?"

His brows stitched together. "Yeah, so?"

"I love root beer. It's like my favorite drink in the world."

"Only because it's the best," he replied before putting the crumpled bills in my hands. He walked away, but before taking five steps, he turned and said, "Oh, and don't forget the extra butter."

I snorted. "As if I would."

When Drake finally disappeared into the restroom, I tucked the money he'd given me in my pocket and took out my wallet. I was going to pay whether he liked it or not.

"Well, doesn't someone look like he's on top of the world?"

I grimaced. Miranda stood behind me in white capris and a light blue shirt. She had curled her typically straight hair, and it bounced off her shoulders with every step she took toward me. She was actually quite stunning, not that I would have told her that in a million years. "I'm in a good mood today, Miranda. Don't ruin it."

"But ruining your day is the best part of mine," she answered when she'd joined me in line.

"You need get yourself to the end of the line," I said, pointing. "You're cutting. And while you're at it, get yourself a new hobby."

"You mean like the one you got?" she asked, completely ignoring the fact that she now stood in front of me.

"What are you talking about?" I stepped ahead of her and snarled.

She snorted and nodded toward the men's room. "It's obvious Drake turns your crank. You'd have to be blind not to see it."

I grabbed her by the elbow and pulled her away from where other kids from our school had gathered. Sunday was evidently a big movie night in Havenbridge.

She glanced at my hand on her arm before staring me down. "Remove your hand before I warp it back to your house."

I released my grip and backed away. The thin smile that stretched her cherry red lips showed she approved. "We're not going public with that."

She grinned. "Mason, you do realize the power you've just handed over to me, right?"

I nodded. What choice did I have? I had to appeal to the good witch she was instead of the bitch she liked to pretend to be. I wasn't the only one in the school who acted a part. I had mine. Miranda had hers. "We want to take things slow. See where it goes. If people know, it'll only make things harder."

She stared blankly at me. "You do realize most people already assume you play for the other team, right? The only one who's still holding out hope is that skank Laura. She seems to think her *V* will cure you of your taste for *P*."

I had *not* known that. "Really?"

If she sighed any longer, she'd have passed out from lack of oxygen. "It's not going to be any big surprise that you're gay. Believe me. We've been talking about it since middle school, I think."

"Are you serious?"

"Are *you* serious? Do you think your tough-guy routine fools anyone into believing you're straight? Every time Laura hits on you, you scamper off like a scared rabbit. You haven't shown any interest in one girl the whole time I've known you. And I've known you far longer than I'd care to admit. You're here. You're queer. We've all gotten used to it."

Wow. I'd had no idea. "I don't know what to say."

She snorted. "That's no surprise."

"Will you do it?" I asked. This time when I touched her arm, I did so gently, the way a friend might ask another friend for help. "Will you keep quiet? I'm not ashamed of who I am or anything. I kinda want Drake and me to be able to figure this out on our own without all the high school busybodies shoving their noses into our business."

"Fine," she said. "Since you're being uncharacteristically nice and everything."

"Thank you." I couldn't stop the huge smile that practically cracked my head in two.

"Jeez," she said. "Dial down the happy, or I'll announce it over the school's intercom."

I wiped the smile from my face and nodded.

"Much better. But how about I give you some advice?"

"Okay."

"You're not going to keep it from people for long. I picked it out the moment I first saw you two together in the cafeteria, and we all noticed it when you climbed out of the rubble yesterday. The way you two acted around each other, pretending to be pissed off, wasn't ringing true. What was real was you saving him and the two of you walking off together like you've always known each other. You're not going to be able to hide that."

"Thanks for the heads up."

"One more thing."

"What's that?" She averted her eyes and chewed on her lower lip. When had Miranda ever held her tongue before this? "Spit it out already."

She rested her brown eyes on me, and there was great sadness there. As if her heart was breaking. "Try not to be so happy around my brother, okay?"

Adam? What did he have to do with this? "I don't understand."

"I know you don't. Just think about it," she said before getting back in line with the friends who'd suddenly arrived.

THE ENTIRE drive home from the movie, Drake and I laughed and talked about the film. We'd enjoyed it, and Rocket Raccoon was our favorite character. By the time we pulled up in front of his aunt Millie's house, my face hurt from laughing so hard. When was the last time that had happened?

But what really blew my mind was when Drake sat sideways in his seat and laced his fingers with mine. All night I'd done my best to be respectful of his wish to go slowly even though what I most wanted to do was jump his bones.

"I had a great time," he said, leaning against the headrest. His lingering gaze made me tremble. "Are you cold?"

"Maybe a little," I lied. I couldn't admit he drove me crazy and made me want to strip him naked. He wasn't like the other boys I'd been interested in. He was different. Special.

"Then let's go in," he said.

I held his hand, refusing to let him go. "Not yet."

A slight blush reddened his cheeks. He clearly liked my answer. "Okay."

We sat in silence, relishing the weight of each other's hand. Drake skimmed his fingers across my palm. The light, feathery strokes made me gasp, and when he scratched his fingernail across my flesh, I held my breath.

"What's going on?" I hadn't meant to voice the question, but it leaped from my lips before I had a chance to stop it. "Between us, I mean."

He smiled, shrugging. "I don't really know, to be honest. It's been downright strange. But a good strange, if that makes any sense."

It did, and I told him as much with my smile.

"I've never met someone like you."

"Well, I am a truly unique individual," I said with a grin.

He squeezed my hand and gave me the stink eye. "I'm tryin' to have a serious conversation here."

"What makes you think I'm not serious?" I asked, pretending to be offended. "I really am one of a kind." Drake's blank stare informed me he was about two seconds away from letting go of my hand. I gripped onto him even tighter and grinned. "And you're pretty unique too."

"Really?" he asked. Why did he sound so surprised? "You're not just sayin' that?"

"Not at all," I replied with a firm shake of my head. "Why do you ask?"

He twisted his lips in thought before responding. "I guess I'm just used to the boys back home. In Dallas there seem to only be two types of gay teens. The oversexed party boy or the undersexed closet case. Neither of which is all that attractive." Even though he still held my hand, he switched his gaze from me to the night beyond the windshield, as if the past he had left behind stretched out before us. "I didn't quite fit in with other kids at my school."

"Did they bully you because you're gay?" The thought of anyone pushing Drake around riled my warlock temper. I had half a mind to put a hex on his last high school.

"Not at all," he answered. Why did he seem so surprised by my question? "As difficult as it might be for you to believe, Texas isn't as backward as you Yanks like to make it out to be. Well, not Dallas at least. I didn't fit in because I didn't screw around like everyone else. Most of my friends were doin' each other every which way from Sunday. The fact that I wasn't kinda made me stand apart from them, I guess. They treated me as if I was a picky queen who thought I was too good for them. But that wasn't it at all. My parents raised me to respect myself, and the way they hopped in and out of each other's beds didn't seem all that respectful, you know?"

Even though I didn't know, I nodded. I had yet to have sex with anyone but myself.

"So you've never had a boyfriend?"

My question drew Drake's eyes back to me. They beamed with hope. "Nope."

"Would you like to have one?"

A smile cracked his lips and spread to his sparkling blue eyes. "I thought we agreed to go slow."

I snorted. "I wasn't asking you to be my boyfriend. I was asking if you'd like to have a boyfriend. There is a difference."

"Yeah, right," he said, staring at me askance.

I poked his side, pretending to be annoyed. "Will you just answer my question?"

"Yes," he said. "I would like to have a boyfriend one day."

"Then maybe you will. And maybe he'll even be a truly unique individual with dark, brooding good looks, a kickass car, and a charming personality."

Drake sighed. "He sounds yummy. I'd love to meet him." I glowered, and he snickered. "Come on," he said after letting my hand go. "Let's get inside. Aunt Millie is no doubt waitin' up for me."

But before he could open the door, I leaned across the console that separated us. He drew in a breath, his eyes locked on my lips, which hovered inches away from his own. I cupped his cheek before trailing my fingertips around pink lips that puckered in response to my touch. He was special, and he had to know that. I wasn't into him because of what I might get in return. "Just so you know," I whispered, my breath fanning across his flushed skin. "I'm not like *any* of the boys back in Texas, okay?"

He bit his lip and leaned in for a kiss.

And even though I craved nothing more than to taste his lips, I pulled away and shook my finger at him. "Slow, remember? I only kiss boyfriends."

He cracked a smile and nodded before resting his head against the window in a loud sigh. "I'll do my best to remember that."

"Please do," I said before exiting my car and escorting Drake up the walk. When he unlocked the door, he glanced at me over his shoulder and grinned. "What's that smile for?"

"For being you," he said, brushing his lips across my cheek. "Thank you."

He walked inside and closed the door behind him. I stood on the porch. The memory of his lips pressed against my skin made me lightheaded, and the feeling didn't go away during my drive home or when I slipped beneath the covers of my bed.

And when I closed my eyes, I dreamed of Drake, except this time no one chased us. All we did was kiss.

CHAPTER 7

THE NEXT morning, I woke up with the biggest smile and the hardest boner ever. It was like I'd erected a tent in the middle of the night. And even though I was dying to get to school to see Drake, there was no way I was going to be able to focus if I didn't take matters into my own hands immediately.

I flipped back my covers and shoved my shorts to my ankles. My cock flopped onto my smooth stomach, already slick with precum. I closed my eyes and danced my fingers across my aching shaft as my thoughts returned to Drake.

His big, beautiful eyes gazed at me as I stroked my cock, and the earthy scent that clung to the air around him filled my nostrils. Everything about him, from his looks to his confidence, excited me.

It made me want to be with him, protect him. Show him he wasn't alone, and he didn't have to run anymore.

And his smile seemed to acknowledge that he knew that.

As I ran my fingers around the head of my dick, I imagined it was Drake who touched me, and the contact signified his acceptance of me. Of us.

His caresses on my palm the night before fluttered now across my hardness. His lips pressed against my cheek, kissing a trail to my mouth before his hand engulfed my prick and pumped it in a slow, measured rhythm.

I bucked my hips into his touch as his tongue wormed inside my parted lips. His hot breaths filled my lungs, and he fondled my balls before trailing over my cock and swabbing the precum that wept from the slit.

He rubbed the clear liquid around the head, lubing his fingers before bringing them to our lips for a shared kiss. Our tongues dueled through the sweetness of our kiss, and my cum solidified there was more between us than just the physical. Whatever we felt, whether it was being spell bound or not, was real, and it was something both of us had waited all these years to find.

My breathing turned ragged, and my hips bucked harder and faster against his expert hand. He pulled and tugged my cock, working his grip in circles around the head before jacking up and down the shaft.

My balls drew up to my body, the cum churning inside.

I was getting close, so I drew Drake to me, wrapping my arms around his neck, forcing my tongue deeper into his mouth. The hand that had so furiously pumped my dick slowed to an agonizing rub. He gripped the base before pulling all the way to the head, and the change in rhythm drove me wild.

I moaned as he continued the brutally slow hand job, but once I'd grown accustomed to the change in pace, he picked up speed again. This time, he wasn't stopping.

He pumped my cock and pulled on my balls, forcing the roiling cum out of my nuts. I grunted as my spunk arced through the air and splattered my stomach and chest.

I lay there, panting. There was no way I could move. My legs had turned to jelly, and my vision swam. Had I ever had such a mind-blowing orgasm?

I sure as hell couldn't recall ever coming like that before. What was going to happen if Drake and I got naked together in real life?

No. It wasn't a question of if but when. But that wasn't going to happen as long as I stayed here, so I grabbed my sheets, wiped off the sticky mess, and entered the bathroom.

I COULDN'T get to school fast enough. I broke every speed limit there was and made it in record time. I still made time to rub out another load in the shower before I left. Fuck! That was how wild Drake made me.

How I still had any cum left in my balls was beyond me.

When I got to school, I couldn't find Drake anywhere. We didn't have any classes together, but I'd thought for sure we'd run into each other at least once during the passing periods between classes. We had for the past week, but today I caught no glimpse of his shaggy hair or beautiful smile.

By the time the lunch bell rang, my cheery disposition from that morning had turned into a foul mood. If I didn't see him at lunch, heads were going to roll.

When I walked into the cafeteria, the silence that followed my entrance quickly descended. I didn't have time to relish it. I needed to find Drake. But a quick scan of the room revealed he was nowhere to be seen.

Where the fuck was he?

I passed Laura McBride's table. She said something, but I didn't hear her daily come-on. I blew past her to where Brandon was waving me down to our usual spot.

"I got you a corn dog today," he said as he held aloft a drink. "With some root beer."

Normally that would have made me happy, but it only pissed me off. I didn't want root beer. "Have you seen Drake?"

Brandon glanced at Simon and Eddie, who shrugged. "Who?"

"Drake Carpenter. The new kid."

"The one who sat at our table a week or so ago?" Eddie asked.

"That's him."

Simon frowned. "The guy who pissed us off and called us retar—" He stopped when I froze my gaze on his. "The one who was making fun of us? That guy?"

"Yes," I replied, rubbing my temples. I had to calm down. They had no clue that Drake and I had been spending time together, mostly because they'd been in and out of trouble the past few days. "Have you seen him?"

"No," Brandon answered. He unwrapped my corn dog and placed it before me. "Why? What did he do? Do we need to take him out back and kick the shit out of him?"

"Do that, and I'll snap you in two." I clenched my fists at my sides and glared at Brandon.

Eddie cleared his throat, and Simon leaned back on his bench. Brandon just stared at me. I'd never threatened him that way before. Well, never that seriously. Everyone could tell that this time I meant it.

"Do you three understand?"

"We get it," Simon said. "You like this guy."

Well, shit. I'd gone and done what Miranda had warned me not to. "What do you mean?"

"No worries, Mase. We know you're gay. That's cool," Brandon said. He smiled and pushed my drink in front of me. "If you like him, there's no need to threaten us. We're your buds. We'll watch out for him like we watch out for each other."

Was I hearing this right? Simon and Eddie nodded in agreement.

"Just tell him not to make fun of us," Eddie said. "That's not cool."

I smiled. "No. It's not." I didn't know what else to say. I'd thought these guys were no deeper than the shallow shits they always pretended to be, but maybe they were more like me than I thought. Maybe they were putting on an act too. "Thanks."

Brandon patted my back. "Now eat up. Then, if you want, we can see if we can find Drake for you."

"I'd like that." I took a bite of my corn dog, and they all snickered. "What?"

"Nothing," Simon giggled.

But when I looked around the table, my friends could barely contain themselves. Eddie was laughing so hard, he banged his head on the table to get himself to stop, and Simon had tears in his eyes. Brandon's mouth was open so wide in laughter I could've driven my car through it.

"*What?*"

"It's just that—" Brandon said between howls of laughter that were drawing the attention of everyone around us. "That—" He broke into more hysterics that made speech impossible.

Even though I had no clue what was going on, their laughter turned infectious. I couldn't stop giggling. "What the fuck is going on?" I picked up the corn dog and waved it at them. "Tell me."

When I did that, they lost it completely. Brandon fell off the bench, and Simon and Eddie collapsed on top of each other in fits of crazy laughter. I eyed the corn dog and tossed all three of them a fake sneer before dropping it on the table. "You guys suck."

That made things worse. Brandon rolled on the floor, Simon had snot and tears streaming down his face, and Eddie seemed to no longer be breathing. His face had almost turned purple.

"I hate you. I hope you know that." But I didn't. For the first time since we'd become friends, I actually appreciated these guys. I'd taken them for granted, and they'd had my back in more ways than I even realized. Even though I was the butt of their joke, it was the first time in my life it didn't bother me. "Are you guys done now?" I asked as their hysterics finally started to taper off.

Brandon struggled to his feet. "I think so," he twittered.

Eddie, who'd finally managed to breathe normally again, nodded, while Simon gave me the thumbs-up sign.

"About fucking time."

"Sorry, Mase," Brandon said. This time I rubbed his back in true friendship instead of the condescending taps I'd always doled out. His smile told me he noticed the difference. "Are you gonna finish that?" he asked as a chuckle escaped.

Simon and Eddie snickered. They were on the verge of losing it again.

"No. Thanks to you three, I'm gonna go hungry."

"Then let's go find Drake," Simon said as he stood up.

"Right," Eddie added. "I'm sure he's got a corn dog that'll satisfy you."

All three of them burst out into laughter, and I rolled my eyes at them. "Come on. Let's go."

As we made our way through the cafeteria, I couldn't help but notice the perplexed expressions on everyone's faces. They'd always been afraid of us. Of me. But that fear seemed to have lessened after seeing the four of us act like fools. Maybe the intimidating walls we put up around ourselves had come tumbling down when we acted more like regular obnoxious teenagers than cold pricks.

I didn't know what that meant. All I knew was that I didn't care.

THE BOYS and I searched the patio around the cafeteria. Even though it was hot outside, the area was packed with students who'd already finished lunch and were waiting for the bell that would send us back to our classes.

"I don't see him anywhere," Simon said after surveying the crowd.

Yeah, neither did I. Where was he?

"Maybe he didn't come to school today," Brandon said. "Could be sick or something."

That was a possibility. I supposed even shifters caught colds. Warlocks certainly weren't immune to human diseases. We'd learned that the hard way.

"Have you called him?" Eddie asked.

"Not yet," I said, taking out my phone. But something wasn't right. The back of my brain itched, and I needed to find out why. I couldn't do it out here, though. I needed privacy if I was going to cast a spell, especially if it backfired on me. "I'm gonna give him a call and take a leak. You boys see if you can find him, and I'll be back."

I turned around, dialed Drake's number, and walked toward the boys' restroom.

"I was wonderin' if you were gonna call," Drake's voice said on the other end. Just hearing his drawl made me smile.

"Skipping school, huh?" I asked, pretending to be casual instead of immensely relieved. "You should have told me. We could've made a day of it."

He laughed. "I wish that's what I was doin'."

"Then what's going on?"

"Aunt Millie's not feelin' up to snuff," he said. "She had some heart palpitations last night, so we had to go to the emergency room. She's fine, but I'm not about to leave her alone for a while."

"Don't blame you. How about I come by after school? I could bring you both dinner or something."

"That's very sweet," he said. I could almost hear the smile in his voice. "I'd love to see you."

I liked the way that sounded, especially since I'd been driving myself crazy with worry. My mind had been going to all sorts of awful places. Unsolved murders in town could do that to you. "Well, good. Because I'd be okay with seeing you too."

Drake chuffed into the phone. "You're such an ass sometimes."

"You should consider yourself lucky," I said, grinning. "Because I'm usually *always* an ass."

"Can't argue with that. Just get here before seven, okay?"

"Why? What's happening at seven?"

"Ms. Wilkens is comin' over to sit with Aunt Millie while I go for my daily run."

Of course he was. When wasn't he bouncing around like a jackrabbit? "I'll head over right after school."

"See you then."

I hung up the phone, and the world didn't seem as dark or as heavy as it had before, but all wasn't quite right yet. Something was definitely in the air, and it was time to find out exactly what that was.

ONCE I walked into the boys' restroom, I checked the stalls for feet. I wasn't alone. A pair of Nikes was clearly visible under the last stall on the right.

Fuck. I had to get this guy out of here so I could work my magic. But how was I going to do that?

That was when I heard sniffling. Whoever was in there was crying.

"Um, dude, are you okay?"

The sobbing abruptly shut off.

Mason, is that you? The words in my head caused my brain to ache.

"Elliot, what's going on? You okay?"

It hurts, Mason. It hurts so bad.

Okay, that was more information than I needed. "Maybe you need to go see the nurse or something."

The nurse can't do anything about the voice. Why would I go see her about that?

What the hell was he talking about? "What voice?"

The one I told you about, remember? The toiled flushed, and he exited the stall. Tears stained his cheeks, and his eyes were red. He was the picture of misery.

I still had no clue what he was talking about, and it must have been evident in my expression.

Remember? I told you about the voice I heard the day the first body was discovered.

Oh yeah. I'd forgotten about that. "Some guy is still pissed off at me? And that's hurting your head?"

A lot. It scares me. He glanced around as if searching for some unseen threat.

"Do you know who it is?" Because if Elliot did, I'd go have a talk with this guy and set him straight. I wasn't about to let Elliot suffer for whatever hate-on this guy had for me.

No, I don't. His eyes darted everywhere. *But he's here.*

I followed his gaze as he scoured every tile and crevice in the room. The one flickering light over the far sink revealed there was no one here. It was just the two of us and our shadows. "Where?"

I don't know.

That was when I noticed a third shadow. It stood flat against the far wall. It didn't connect to anyone or anything. It existed on its own. "Elliot, I think you need to get out of here."

He searched the room. *Why? What's wrong?*

Before I could answer, the shadow shot off the wall and flew directly at me. It slammed into me as if it was solid, and I skidded across the sticky bathroom floor. Elliot yelled in my head before the shadow turned on him. It extended over Elliot's face, and his eyes went wide in horror.

He flailed about as if he were drowning, and his panicked eyes sought mine. It was trying to kill Elliot.

"Propellit," I muttered, and the shadow left Elliot and cast itself along the walls of a stall. Elliot fell to the floor, gasping for breath, and I rushed to stand over him. There was no way I was letting that thing get to Elliot again. As a mute, he couldn't access his magic through spoken spells the way I could. That meant it was up to me to deal with our enemy.

"Come on, you bastard," I said. "What the hell are you waiting for?"

Shadowy limbs suddenly shot off the wall to my left and right. They grabbed my arms and bound them together as they tugged me toward an open stall. I pulled back, trying to gain some ground, and Elliot suddenly sprang to his feet. He tried to strike the arms, but his blows went right through the shadowy projections.

Somehow, the silhouette was solid enough to confine me but immaterial at the same time. How the fuck was it doing that?

"Get out of here," I told Elliot as the inky arms pulled me toward the shadows. "Find your sister or Miranda. Quick!"

Only someone with an active power might be able to free me before I was pulled into the black void. I had no desire to find out what lived on the other side.

Elliot turned to leave, but two more black arms sprouted from the void and pinned him against the opposite wall.

Fuck. So much for the cavalry being called.

I placed my feet on of the walls of the stall, halting my progress as the limbs tried to force me in. I uttered as many spells as I could think of, but none of them had any effect. I was clearly out of my league, and Elliot was going to pay the price for my inexperience.

"Come out and fight me like a warlock, you chickenshit motherfucker."

In response, a huge oversized pumpkin head popped out of the wall. Its black mouth cracked into a snarl, and its big, hollow eyes examined me carefully. *"Enoménos mazí mas eísai."*

What the hell did that mean? It sure as hell wasn't Latin. "Speak English, you fucking freak!"

The shadow laughed and tightened its grip around my arms.

I'm sorry, Mason. But I have to do this. It's the only way.

Before I could ask Elliot what he was talking about, he screamed in my head. My vision immediately swam, and my head pounded in agony. I was on the verge of passing out, but I wasn't the only one affected.

The big black pumpkin-headed shadow reared back onto the wall and released me. I fell to the floor as Elliot's voice echoed in my head. The shadow form shook in evident pain from Elliot's ear-piercing, mind-numbing wail.

I covered my ears with my hands, trying to force the sound out of my mind, but nothing worked. Elliot continued to scream until the shadow retreated across the wall and folded itself under the crack of the door.

When it was gone, Elliot stopped. He knelt at my side and patted my shoulder. *I'm sorry, but I didn't have any other choice.*

"I know," I mumbled. Too bad I was going to have a migraine for the rest of the month.

What was that thing, Mason? And what did it say?

I had no fucking clue what it said, but I had some idea it was a shadow weaver. "I'm not really sure." I stood on unsteady legs. "But I think we need to tell our parents."

I CALLED my father and gave him all the details about the attack, including the fact the shadow weaver spoke some weird language. He planned on informing the Conclave, and hopefully by the end of the day we'd have some answers. While he worked on that, I had to finish the rest of the school day and then get over to Drake.

Being with him would settle my nerves. I'd been jumpy the entire afternoon. Every time I saw a shadow, I tensed and prepared for an attack.

When the dismissal bell rang at three thirty, I gathered my books and headed out the front doors. The heat of another blistering day immediately fried my skin. Sweat beaded across my forehead, and drops of perspiration slid down my back. A quick glance at the high school marquee, which displayed the time and temperature along with the weekly HHS events, told me it was ninety-seven degrees.

What the hell was up with our weather?

A sudden, hot breeze whipped up around the school. The trees surrounding the building swayed, sending leaves fluttering through the air. A familiar odor of bleach and pancakes filled me with dread.

I froze. Whatever I'd sensed in the woods behind my house was here somewhere. Was it the shadow weaver in corporeal form? It had to be, and I couldn't let it get away this time.

No matter how badly I wanted to be with Drake, my duty as a warlock had to come first.

I rushed over to my car and got in. I needed the relative privacy it offered from the swarming students around me in order to call upon my magic.

I rolled down all the windows and closed my eyes, withdrawing my senses from the external to the internal. The laughter of my classmates and the roaring engines of their cars slowly faded away until the only sound was my own breath. My flesh grew numb to the wind that caressed my skin. My blood sped through my body. In the darkness behind my closed eyelids, sparks of red shot across my vision like meteors falling from outer space.

Everything around me disappeared except for the smell of bleach and the taste of pancakes. Those two sensations became my entire world. Nothing else mattered but finding what was responsible for the return of that strange combination.

I focused all my energy on the scent until the smell of bleach transformed into a long red streak and the taste of pancakes became a yellow strand. The two threads of energy wove around each other like a magical rope and shot out into the forested area beyond the football field.

That was where I would find what I was looking for.

When I opened my eyes, the sun no longer shone overhead. Night had snuck up on me, and the first stars twinkled overhead. The digital clock on my car's dashboard told me it was almost seven. How the hell had I been out here for three and a half hours? It seemed like only minutes had passed since I'd left school.

The parking lot was empty. Everyone had gone home except for Mr. Matula, the janitor who cleaned the school after hours. His green van sat in the parking lot, four rows over.

Was it normal to lose so much time on such a spell or was it my inability to master my magic that had caused this? I'd have to figure that out later. I put my car in drive and sped out of the parking lot toward where the lasso of energy disappeared into the wooded area.

I took my phone out of my pocket and noticed I had several missed calls from Pierce and Drake, and a text from my father. Fuck! I'd promised Drake I'd head over after school. He no doubt believed I'd bailed on him. I'd make up a good explanation when I saw him. Right now, I had to call my brother.

"Well, well. Look who finally decided to answer his phone."

"Pierce, listen."

"Save it," he said. "When we couldn't contact you, Dad got worried and made Thad scry for your location." Scrying was a simple spell that involved a crystal and a map. It was so easy even I had no problem with it. "So what have you and Drake been doing in your car for the past few hours, huh?"

"I haven't been with Drake."

Pierce whistled. "Damn, bro. Already stepping out on him, huh?"

My brother had a one-track mind. "Will you shut the fuck up and listen to me? Tell Dad that whatever attacked me is here in the woods behind the school."

"Are you serious? How do you know?"

"What the hell do you think I've been doing all afternoon?"

"A spell?" Did he have to sound so impressed? "But it took you three hours?"

I didn't have time for this. I pulled up to where the lines of energy shot through the forest. "I'm gonna see where it leads."

"No." Pierce's voice grew stern. "Wait for us. You shouldn't go in there by yourself."

I got out of my car and scanned the trail that blazed before me. "Would you wait?"

He didn't reply, but we both knew the answer. The only reason he was telling me not to go in was because he didn't think I could protect myself. I had no active power, and my spells usually went wrong.

But I'd been making progress. I'd saved Drake's life, as well as my own, and managed to manipulate the energies around me to lead me to what I desired to find. I couldn't let whatever was out here get away again.

"You should be able to see the lines of energy I've created," I told Pierce. "You can use it to follow me in when you get here."

"Dammit, Mason!" he yelled before I ended the call.

I tucked the phone in the pocket of my jeans, let out a long breath, and then ran into the woods.

I FOLLOWED the magical trail for about five minutes before it ended about twenty feet away from where I stood. Whatever I was searching for was right up ahead. I hid behind a tree and closed my eyes, trying to sense anything that might tell me what this fucker was.

But no matter how hard I tried, I sensed nothing at all. It reminded me of the spell Miranda had cast on the football field. Like then, I should have sensed *something*, but I didn't, and something *was* here. Yet it somehow evaded detection. It had to be one powerful son of a bitch.

Waiting for my family would probably be the best course of action, but by the time they got here, it could be gone. I could get a glimpse of whatever it was and be able to identify it. At the very least, I could confirm it was a shadow weaver.

That would go a long way toward stopping it. Once we knew what it was, we could cast the necessary spells to either trap or defeat it.

There was no turning back now.

I slid out from behind the tree and kept low to the ground. I took extra precaution not to step on anything that would give my presence away. As far as I could tell, it didn't know I was here, and right now the element of surprise was all I had working in my favor.

A low grunt filled the air around me, and I froze. Had it heard or smelled me? I couldn't tell. Hell, I couldn't even see it yet, and it wasn't that dark out. The moon shone big overhead and illuminated much of the area, but the shifting shadows somehow kept it concealed from sight.

The smell of bleach and pancakes was even more overwhelming now.

Another noise drifted on the breeze. A low moan filled with pain. Shit. Someone else was out here with that thing. Maybe another victim getting its throat torn out, but whatever was out there, grunting and sniffing, sounded like some wild animal instead of something human.

I had to make my move. If I didn't, whoever was in pain might soon be dead.

But as I stood up, something shot through the woods about sixty feet to my right. A familiar grunt caught my attention, and so did the measured rhythm of footfalls.

It ran straight for where my woven energy rope ended, and if I heard it, then whatever was out there had heard it too.

When I spotted a familiar flash of blond hair, I held my breath. It couldn't be. Not here. Not now.

A few seconds later, Drake sprinted into view. He was on a direct path to the clearing where my enemy was. I tore out of my hiding spot and ran straight for him. "Drake!" I yelled at the top of my lungs.

He slid to a stop a few feet from the brush where he would run straight into danger. When he saw me, he panted and smiled. "There you are," he said. "I thought you were gonna come by Aunt Millie's."

"Get away from there!" I screamed as I barreled toward him.

"What?" he asked, looking around. "Why?"

That was when the bushes parted. A pair of pale hands grabbed him and pulled him into the thicket. "*Drake!*"

He yelled and whatever was in the thicket with him growled and hissed. A brief scuffle shook the dense thatch of leaves before all went silent. I crashed through the wall of branches, which slapped hard against my skin.

Drake lay unconscious at the edge of a clearing, which was no more than ten feet in diameter. I knelt beside him and checked for a pulse. It was strong and steady. Aside from being knocked out, he was apparently okay. I scanned the area for whatever had grabbed Drake. Instead of finding my foe, I spotted a man sprawled in the center of the clearing. He wore a gray uniform I saw every day at school. It was Mr. Matula, the janitor.

Even though I didn't want to leave Drake, I sprinted toward Mr. Matula. His brown eyes widened in terror. He clasped my arm and tried to talk, but all he managed to bring up was a gurgle of blood. Like the woman on the football field and the construction worker, he had his neck ripped open. But unlike them, he had blood freely spilling from the wound.

"I'm here, Mr. Matula," I said, tearing my shirt off and pressing it firmly to his wound. "We'll get you help."

His eyes locked onto mine before rolling back in his head.

"Mr. Matula! Don't give up on me."

I hadn't mastered healing spells, but I couldn't just let him die. I had to do something. "*Sana*," I whispered as I hovered my hands over the torn flesh. Golden light emanated from my palms as his skin stitched itself back together. As the gash slowly closed, something crashed into me from behind.

"No!" it railed before an arm wrapped around my neck. It lifted me in the air and away from Mr. Matula. Breaking contact with him before the spell was complete caused his wound to reopen and the blood to pour out of him once again.

Mr. Matula would die if I didn't get free, and then it would most likely go back for Drake. I couldn't allow that, but the viselike grip with which it held me grew as tight as a boa constrictor squeezing the life out of its prey. I wasn't some helpless animal. I was a warlock, and I had to get out of this.

As I gasped for breath, I clawed at its ashen flesh, but no matter how hard I dug my nails into its skin, I couldn't break the surface. Its flesh proved just as strong as the steely muscles that held me in their grip. I kicked against its legs and thrashed about like a fish flopping on a pier, but nothing worked.

If I could only speak, I'd be able to recite a spell that might give me the leverage I needed. But my foe knew that.

"I won't let you ruin the plan," it whispered.

How could killing the kindhearted Mr. Matula be a part of any plan? And why did its voice sound different than just a few hours ago in the bathroom?

I had to catch a glimpse of it, but I couldn't turn my head. Its hot breath plumed across the back of my neck, and every time it exhaled, the stench of pancakes and bleach filled my lungs.

What the hell did it pour over its short stacks, Clorox?

It inhaled deeply at my neck. "I can smell it on you. You were close to it. In the same room with it." It took another big whiff. "But that was yesterday, not today."

What the fuck was it talking about?

"Mason!" Pierce screamed from the wooded area around us. My family had arrived, and this fucker was going to have its ass handed to it.

It tensed against me. It apparently feared the combined might of the Blackmoor warlocks, as it should.

"Now's not the time for us to meet," it muttered before its tongue darted along the edges of my ear. I winced, but I couldn't do much more. I struggled for oxygen, and the world swam around me. In a few moments, I was going to black out. "But soon I'll thank you for leading me to what I seek. I promise."

It tightened its hold one final time before lightning arced through the air around us. Pierce was almost here. His powers always seemed to precede his arrival whenever he was truly pumped up.

In response, my unseen foe shoved me face-first into the ground and let go. I immediately sat up and gasped, drawing in oxygen by the lungsful. I wheezed and hacked as the life-giving air once again returned to my body just as Pierce and then Thad and my father burst through the thicket.

"Where is it?" Pierce asked. Lightning sizzled from his clenched fist and arced through the air around him, searching for a foe to fry.

I attempted an answer, but my itchy, raw throat couldn't form words, only rasping noises.

"Are you okay?" my father asked. I nodded as the coughing subsided.

"Where did it go?" Thad asked. He placed his arms on my shoulders and gently rubbed them. Who was this man who seemed to really care about my well-being? Was this a new thing, or had I always been blind to it?

I pointed toward where it had disappeared, and my father and Pierce disappeared after it. Thad stayed behind to help me.

"I'm fine," I finally managed before nodding to the two forms in the clearing. "Help Dad and Pierce. I'll see to Drake and Mr. Matula."

Thad inspected the fiftysomething, balding man with gray whiskers on his chin and cheeks. "I'm afraid it's too late for him," Thad said. "He's gone."

No. It couldn't be true.

But it was hard to deny the truth. His blood had turned the green grass red, and his skin had grown pale. Whatever purpose that thing had in murdering Mr. Matula, it had succeeded.

"Fuck!" I cursed before heading over to Drake. I sat on the ground and pulled him to me. If anything attacked again, I would be ready.

My father and Pierce emerged from the bushes. I glanced at them, hoping they'd caught the motherfucker so we could make it pay. But their hands were empty, and a fire burned in their eyes.

"He got away," Pierce mumbled before discharging lightning straight into the ground. A huge thunderclap exploded into the night.

"Did you see it?" my father asked.

I shook my head at the question but remained focused on Drake. A huge knot had formed at the base of his skull. It made me angry. It made me want to rip that bastard in two, but when I glanced over at Mr. Matula's dead body, the burning need for answers slowly calmed my boiling blood. What had that thing been looking for, and what purpose could there possibly be in killing a janitor?

It was time for answers.

I PACED in the waiting room of County Memorial Hospital. Being here brought up unpleasant memories of my mother, sick and emaciated from the cancer that had eaten her away from the inside. I'd done my best to avoid this place ever since, but here I was, along with the rest of my family, waiting for news on Drake and for Charles Proctor to come up from the morgue. But right now, all I really wanted was to be by Drake's side.

Along with being the high priest of the white-witch coven and father to the insufferable Miranda, Mr. Proctor also served as a detective for the Havenbridge PD. Having him on the force came in handy at times like this. He could make evidence that might reveal the existence of our species disappear without affecting the case.

"We'll hear something soon," my father said. He rested a hand on my shoulder to offer comfort, but it was my dad who needed reassurance. Painful memories welled in his blue eyes as well. Being here affected all of us, even Thad. He had propped himself in the far corner and was chewing on his fingernails. He'd only done that as a kid.

"Not soon enough," I mumbled, adjusting the paper-thin hospital shirt one of the nurses had given me. The police had collected my shirt, which I'd used on Mr. Matula's wound, as evidence.

The hospital doors swung open, and Charles Proctor entered the room. He had short silvery hair and dark green eyes that told the room he was definitely the man in charge. His long strides quickly brought him to us. He was obviously ready to get down to business.

"This makes number three," he said, taking out his pad and pen. "And this needs to be the last."

"I agree," my father said.

When he glimpsed at me, Detective Proctor's legendary compassion became evident. His stare reflected sadness, both for the loss of Mr. Matula and for the fact that I'd had to witness death once again. "Tell me everything that happened out there."

And I did. There was no reason to leave anything out. As I spoke, he scribbled in his pad, and my brothers gathered around us. He stopped every few minutes to ask follow-up questions, but when we were done, he sighed and motioned for all of us to sit down. "So you think it's a shadow weaver?"

"Yes," Thad said. "Everything Mason experienced seems to indicate that's what we are dealing with."

Detective Proctor shook his head and exhaled. "There hasn't been a shadow weaver in so long, I figured they had become extinct, a byproduct of Bartram Kane's foolishness. But if another warlock has tapped into the power of darkness and become as corrupt as he was, we could be heading toward some pretty rough times."

That was an understatement. Bartram Kane had almost destroyed the humans and us by casting the immortality spell. That dark time in our history had become the stuff of legends and popular fodder for fantastical stories that most didn't know were based in reality.

"But why kill Mr. Matula?" I asked. "Or any of the others? What plan was it referring to?"

"And what is it searching for? Those are the million-dollar questions," Detective Proctor said. "What is the motive here? What links these three deaths?"

"Isn't that your job, Detective?" my father asked. He and Charles Proctor got along about as well as a lion and a hyena.

"It is," he answered with a nod. "And I'll figure it out. I always do."

"In the meantime," I interrupted. We didn't have time for a verbal sparring match. "How do we stop him?" The only image that filled my mind was of Drake being pulled away from me by those hands. I'd never felt so powerless in my life, and it was something I didn't want to experience ever again.

"It took the combined magic of the Conclave to stop Bartram," my father finally replied.

"Then they need to get their asses here." Pierce scowled. Being in the hospital had set his nerves on edge. "What the hell are they waiting for?"

"Confirmation," my father revealed.

"They're just going to sit on their asses until we find indisputable proof of what we are dealing with?" I asked. "People are being attacked and killed here!"

My father was clearly concerned too. He didn't like their decision any more than I did. So why were they taking the wait-and-see approach?

"This doesn't make sense." My comment drew both Mr. Proctor's and my father's disapproval. Even though they didn't like each other, neither of them took kindly to the Conclave being so openly criticized. Doing that only led to trouble. "And before you tell me to shut up and do my job, at least hear me out. The fact that they aren't willing to step in right now and deal with this tells me something else is going on. We aren't getting the full story. They're keeping something from us, and I don't like it."

Thad nodded. "I have to agree."

If my brother had had a feather, he could have knocked me over with it. The amazement on everyone else's faces clearly revealed they were as shocked as I was. "You do?"

"Yes," Thad said with a nod. "The Conclave is not acting as they normally do. Where before they took action, now they wait. Why? It's almost as if they are afraid."

"Yes," I said. "I could sense it at the Mabon celebration."

"That's absurd," Detective Proctor said. He crossed his arms over his muscled chest and grunted. "What could make the most powerful among us feel fear?"

"That's precisely what we need to find out," I said. "They sure as hell aren't going to tell us, and I'll be damned if I let Drake be exposed to danger again."

"Mason?"

I whipped around to see Aunt Millie standing in the middle of the emergency room. She wrung her hands, and tears coursed down her cheeks. I ran to her and held her close.

"Thank you, dear," she said with a sniffle. "He's awake now if you'd like to see him."

That was the biggest understatement of the year. I nodded, and she led me through the hospital doors and down the corridor toward the boy I'd been waiting all day to see.

WHEN I entered the curtained area where Drake lay on the hospital bed, I couldn't help but smile. The sight of his perfect blue eyes staring at me set my heart fluttering, and I had to stop myself from crawling on the bed with him.

"It's about time you woke up," I said. "You'll do just about anything to get attention, won't you?"

His pink lips parted into a grin. "This from the guy wearin' a see-through hospital shirt. Did you lose yours again?"

I laughed and took his hand in mine. Even though our words were playful, we squeezed each other's hand tight. More than anything else, physical contact was what we needed.

"Thank you, Mason," Aunt Millie said from behind me. She placed her hands on my right shoulder and kissed my cheek. "You saved my Drake. Again."

I put my arm around her shoulders and hugged her to me. She needed to be consoled as much as we did. "I'd say 'anytime,' but I thought Drake and I had agreed we weren't going to make this a habit."

"And that's your fault," he said. "Not mine."

I glowered at him. "How do you figure that?"

"Well, you were supposed to drop by after school. With food if I remember correctly."

"I got sidetracked."

Drake raised one eyebrow at me. "By who? Laura McBride?"

"Oh, stop the teasing," Aunt Millie told Drake. She stepped out of my embrace and walked to the other side of the hospital bed. She took her nephew's other hand in hers. "I'm glad Mason didn't come by. If he had, he might not have been in the woods to save you."

"Listen to your aunt Millie." I tapped my finger on the tip of his nose. "She's one smart cookie."

"And just what were you doin' in the woods anyway?" he asked.

"I heard a scream." I couldn't very well tell him I was following my magic, but what I did share was only a partial lie. "And I'm glad I did. I don't want to even think about the alternative."

"Me either," Aunt Millie said with a nod. She shivered at the thought.

"Are you doin' okay?" Drake asked. "All this excitement can't be good for you right now."

I'd forgotten all about her irregular heartbeat from this morning. "If you're not, I'll go get a doctor."

She waved away our concerns. "My ticker might be old, and it might stumble every now and then, but I'll be just fine." She glanced between Drake and me. "But right now, I could use a cup of coffee, and you boys could use some time alone together. I'll be back in a bit," she said before parting the curtain and closing it behind her.

"Well, that wasn't very subtle," Drake muttered.

"Nope. Not at all," I said with a laugh. "But since we're alone and all." I wiggled my eyebrows at him.

Drake hitched up the right corner of his mouth. "I was attacked and conked unconscious, and you're hittin' on me?" If he had been any more exasperated, he'd have been climbing up the wall.

"Well, you do look darn cute in that hospital gown."

"I look darn cute in just about anythin'," he said.

I leaned in and rested my forehead against his. Even in the sterile environment of the hospital room, Drake's earthy scent filled the space between us. "I won't argue with you on that."

Drake swallowed hard. He focused on my lips as he held his breath. When he finally exhaled, he said, "Thanks for savin' me."

"I would say 'anytime,' but let's not do that again, okay?"

He nodded and bit his lip. "Okay."

As I pulled away, he wrapped his arms around my neck and brought me close. He held me tight, unwilling to let me move farther away, my forehead once again upon his. The fire in his eyes told me what he really wanted was to be as close to me as possible.

"Mason?" he asked. His voice was low and throaty.

"Yeah," I replied. A husk deepened my tone.

"Will you kiss me?"

I smiled and ran my fingers along his lips, which pursed against my touch. "I only kiss boyfriends, remember?"

He nodded. "Then kiss me." His lips quivered as he drew me to him.

"I thought you'd never ask."

I hooked Drake's chin with my thumb and tilted his head.

When our lips brushed, my body exploded to life. I'd kissed other boys before, but none of them had been like this. Drake's smooth skin on mine caused the magic within me to rise and fall like he was the moon and I was the tide. Whatever power resided within me had doubled—no, quadrupled—by kissing the boy who'd come to mean so much to me in a relatively short time.

Every part of me surged toward the magical pull he'd had on me since the day we met.

My toes tingled and my legs quivered. I pushed harder into the kiss, opening my mouth and slowly pushing my tongue into his hot, wet warmth. Our tongues wrapped around each other, sliding and dancing from his mouth to mine. I rustled my hands through his blond hair as his clutched at my bicep and chest.

His breath plumed across my flesh, and I moaned every time our lips parted for the briefest of seconds. I couldn't get enough. I dove back on his lips as he touched me from my chest to my face, which he cupped and caressed. Each flutter of his fingertips sent jolts of electricity more powerful than any Pierce could summon rippling through my body.

Drake pulled away, panting heavily. "We've gotta stop."

What was this crazy talk? "No, thank you," I said as I molded my lips to his once again. He moaned into the kiss and lay back in bed. My body followed, and I pressed my chest against his.

"We have to," he mumbled while his tongue darted once again past my lips. His body and his brain were not in agreement. I kissed my way from his lips to his neck, where I nibbled. He gasped and clutched at my shoulders as I inhaled his heady scent. "Please," he whimpered. "Not here."

Reluctantly, I pulled away. Drake was right. This wasn't the time or the place.

"I'm sorry," I said as I forced the air from my lungs. My rock-hard cock throbbed in my jeans and bent at an uncomfortable angle.

Drake blew out a lungful of air as well. "Don't be," he said. "It was nice."

I frowned at him. "Nice? Playing with a new puppy is nice. And that was definitely *not* what we were doing."

He laughed and laced his fingers with mine. "You're right. It was hot. Is that better?"

"Much."

"Good," he said, pressing his forehead against mine. "I really like you, Mason Blackmoor. I don't know how that happened, but I do."

"I'm glad. Because I really like you too, even though you're constantly getting yourself in trouble."

"Well, then, it's a good thing you're always there."

"And I will be there for you. That's a promise."

And it was a promise I intended to keep.

CHAPTER 8

TWO DAYS had passed since the attack in the woods, and we weren't any closer to finding the shadow weaver. The Conclave's lack of directions increasingly frustrated my father. They had promised to get back to us when they had a decision on what our next move should be. Until then, the protector covens were not supposed to act.

When we heard that bit of news, Pierce fried our television.

"It doesn't make sense," I practically screamed. My brothers and I sat in the great hall after my father left the house to meet with Mr. Proctor and Mr. Stonewall. What they were meeting about, he would not reveal. "What the hell is the Conclave thinking?"

"They aren't," Pierce growled. "And it's pissing me off."

Thad nodded. "This doesn't make sense."

No, it didn't. People were dying, and a corrupt warlock was on the loose. We had no clue what its endgame was. It could be after anything, including the Gate, which was the source of all magic in this world. If it was destroyed, not only would we be powerless, but the balance by which this world thrived would end. The result would be chaos and destruction.

"We're obviously missing a vital piece of this puzzle," Thad said. He sat on the overstuffed chair and placed his index fingers to his lips. He was in thinking mode. "Whatever is really going on must have the Conclave in disagreement. That is the only thing that makes sense. They usually act swiftly, but to not act at all means that perhaps they can't agree on what to do."

"So we're supposed to sit here with our thumbs up our asses while they figure it out?" Pierce asked. "That's bullshit!"

"I agree."

"You're the smart one, Thad," I said. "What do you think has caused this?"

Thad rose from where he sat and paced. "I'm not sure, but my gut is telling me one thing."

"What's that?"

"Whatever rhyme or reason is behind this, I have a feeling you are the key."

Pierce's open mouth communicated exactly how I felt. "Why do you think that?" I asked.

"I don't know. It's just the way the Conclave reacted to you at the Mabon celebration. It was like they were studying you, waiting for something they expected to happen. And you're right, Mason. They are afraid. I couldn't believe it before because of the power they wield collectively, but now, with the way they are acting, something has them scared so shitless, they don't know which way to turn."

"Is that why you don't want us to tell Dad anything about our suspicions?"

He nodded. "Dad can't be objective about the Conclave. As our high priest, he's honor-bound to follow their wishes."

"Yeah, well, so are we," Pierce added with a sniff.

"Yes, but we aren't scrutinized to the extent our father is," Thad added. "He has direct access to both the Council of Black and the Conclave. He travels in circles far more powerful than we do. We operate on the periphery, away from their prying eyes. Their magic could detect his apprehension or doubts. That's why we can't share what we think with him. It has to be our burden to bear. At least until we stumble upon the truth."

That made sense. It was difficult to keep thoughts and emotions from magical beings who could read people as easily as I read a book. If they caught even a hint of dissent from a high priest, the entire coven would suffer. "So how do we find out what's going on?"

"I don't know," Thad admitted. "I need to think about this. For now, we have to go about our business as usual."

I didn't like that answer and neither did Pierce. The low hum of his electrical powers filled the room.

But what else could we do?

AFTER MY talk with Pierce and Thad, I had to get out of the house. I called Drake and told him I was taking him out for the afternoon. Not that my invitation was any big surprise. Ever since our first kiss in the hospital, we'd been virtually inseparable.

I drove him to and from school, partly because I didn't want him being attacked again, but mostly because I enjoyed holding his hand while we drove. And, of course, there were the kisses.

Before I started the car and after I turned it off, I'd draw Drake into my arms and we'd linger upon each other's lips for a good ten minutes before getting out of the vehicle with red, chapped lips.

Miranda teased us mercilessly, saying we might as well just eat each other's face. If I could have, I would have. Kissing Drake and tasting his sweet lips was like sucking on sugar. It gave me such a natural high, I practically floated through the halls.

The kids at school noticed the change in me. Instead of averting their eyes in fear, they'd smile and nod at me. Even stranger, I'd smile and nod back. Brandon wasn't pleased. He'd enjoyed our badass, don't-look-at-us reputations. He preferred having people fear him to trying to be friendly. He didn't know how to cope with kindness.

Simon and Eddie didn't seem bothered by the change in our status. They'd begun making friends outside of our small group. It was like they had been waiting their entire lives for the smallest amount of recognition. Now that they had it, they were eating it up.

After parking in front of Aunt Millie's house, I knocked on the door. A few moments later, she stood behind the open door, a smile breaking across her lips. Today she wore a long-sleeved, oversized white blouse with the top two buttons unfastened, which proudly displayed the emerald pendant Gerald Wa had given her before his death. "What's taken you so long?" she teased as she drew me into a hug. "I haven't seen you here for almost two hours."

"Just some family stuff," I answered. "But I'm leaving home tomorrow so that I can spend all my time here."

She chuckled and patted my back while lovingly stroking the smooth face of the green stone that hung around her neck. It obviously gave her great comfort. She seemed to touch it every chance she got. "You're welcome here anytime," she said.

"Don't encourage him, Aunt Millie." Drake leaned against the hall doorway with his left hip jutting out. He wore a white ribbed cut-off T-shirt that showed off the lean muscles on his arms. His khaki shorts hugged his groin, nicely lifting and presenting the package I most longed to open. "I'll never get rid of him that way."

I snorted. "As if you want to get rid of me. I'm quite the catch, right, Aunt Millie?"

Before she could answer, Drake chimed in, "If you mean like the cold or the flu, then yes. You're quite the catch."

"You two!" Aunt Millie said as she playfully swatted at me. "Anyone listening to you both would think you didn't like each other one bit."

"I don't," I protested, scrunching up my face in fake disgust.

"Yeah, me either." Drake turned up his nose and looked away.

"I don't know why I put up with you two." She sighed in exasperation.

"Because we're so darn cute," I answered with a cheesy grin.

She stared blankly at me before motioning to the front door. "Go on," she said. "I know you boys have plans, and I've got things I've got to get done. I can't spend all day doing nothing, like you two."

"Remember what your doctor said," Drake told her. "You have to take it easy."

"Easy smeasy," she spat. "Those doctors aren't God. They don't get to tell me what to do."

Drake sighed. "I doubt you'd even listen to God."

Aunt Millie tapped her chin for a few seconds. "You're right. I wouldn't. I've got my own mind, and I aim to use it." She opened the door and shooed us out. "Now you boys have fun."

Drake slid his hand in mine, and we walked to the car.

"Don't do anything I wouldn't," she called after us.

I turned around and waved. She still clutched her emerald pendant.

"Don't forget I know you, Aunt Millie," Drake said. "You were quite the pioneer in your day."

She snorted. "You're right. I was." She smiled and blew us a kiss. "Just have fun, boys. And be safe."

I got in the car with Drake.

"Where are we goin'?"

Before I answered, I put my arm around his shoulder and pulled him to me. Our lips molded together perfectly as he slid his tongue in my mouth. It wrapped around my tongue and coaxed it from my mouth to his, where I drank down the licorice flavor of his kiss. He'd obviously had a root beer before I arrived. My two favorite things combined—Drake and A&W.

His hand wound its way through my long dark hair, which he grabbed and passionately yanked backward. I moaned as he gazed down at me. "You're avoidin' my question."

I cupped his white cheeks in my hands and brought him back to my lips before kissing a soft trail to his neck, where I lightly nibbled. That always got him going. Drake groaned and dug his fingers into my shoulder. "Are you complaining?"

"Not right now, I ain't," he panted.

I sat up and stroked his cheek before flicking a stray blond strand from his forehead. "I didn't think so."

He twisted his lips. "Don't try and get cute with me. I'm immune to your charms."

"So you find me charming?" I asked. I pulled out of our embrace and started the car. Since Drake enjoyed nature so much, I aimed my car for the Ocean Avenue Bridge that would deposit us onto the peninsula that extended into Massachusetts Bay.

"I said no such thing. I said I'm immune to what you think is charmin'."

"Uh-huh," I replied before reaching over the console and grabbing his hand. I'd never held another guy's hand before, but whenever I was around Drake, I couldn't help myself. The weight and warmth of Drake's fingers interlaced with mine made me feel like I could cast any spell I put my mind to.

Drake seemed similarly affected. A sly grin turned up the left corner of his lips as he stared at our interlocking fingers.

We didn't say a word the rest of the drive. We relished the feel of each other's hand and the wind whipping through our hair.

Fifteen minutes later, we arrived in the parking lot of the Havenbridge Neck Audubon Wildlife Sanctuary, a state park home to rare birds, beautiful hiking trails, and a wonderful panoramic view of the ocean.

Drake smiled at the park sign and then beamed back at me.

"I figured we might see if we can find some more butterflies or something."

"You're full of surprises, Mason Blackmoor."

I shrugged. "Not really. What you see is what you get."

He turned in his seat to stare deeply into my soul. His turquoise eyes peered straight through me, breaking past the layers of bravado I'd carefully constructed around me. He was seeing the real me, the person no one else had ever gotten a chance to see. "That was what I first thought, but you proved me wrong. You keep doin' that, actually."

"I don't understand."

He glanced away and chewed on his lower lip.

"Just tell me," I said as I squeezed his hand. "I won't get mad."

"Well, if you want me to be perfectly honest." He stared intently at me to make sure I spoke the truth. After I nodded, he continued, "The reason I first walked up to you at school was that when I was lookin' for a place to sit down, I looked all around for someone who I felt might be just like me. When I saw you, my first impression was that there was somethin' about you—I don't know, familiar, I guess you could say. It didn't make no sense, but my daddy always told me to follow my gut, so I did. But after I went up to you, I regretted it because you were such a jerk."

I had no defense for the way I'd acted, so I nodded.

"And then in the woods, you couldn't stop starin' at me. But that cockiness that pissed me off was still there, and there was no way in heck I was gonna give you the time of day. But then when we ran into each other again—"

"You mean when you slid your ass across my car?"

Drake laughed. "Yeah. I'd had trouble sleepin' the night before. I tossed and turned somethin' dreadful, but when I woke up, I had this need to just run. As fast as I could. So I did, and I ran right into you. And when you chased after me, that was when I realized why you'd been such a jerk. You were a stupid dumbass guy who had a crush on someone and didn't know how to express it. But with your friends not around, you just went for it and chased me. I thought it was kinda cute."

That explained his devilish grin at the time. "So then why did you act like such an ass when you came up to me after all that?"

He rolled his eyes. "I don't just roll over because a hot guy chases me around town. I've got some self-respect, you know?"

I pulled Drake's hand to move him closer to me. "You think I'm hot?"

Drake's eyes fluttered, and he looked everywhere but at me. He evidently hadn't realized exactly how honest he was going to get.

"Don't worry about it." I rubbed my thumb across his light pink lips, which trembled beneath my touch. His response to me set free a tornado of butterflies within my soul. "I think you're pretty hot too."

He closed his eyes and tried to shake his mortification away. "So when you got confrontational again, I didn't know what the heck was goin' on. And then you saved my life, and I felt like I was on a carousel that was spinnin' out of control. That's why I went over to your house that night. I don't like not knowin' where I stand with someone. I've always been an up-front, in-your-face kinda guy. I tell it like I see it, and I am the way I am. I understand if you have problems with who you really are. I get that. Believe me. It can be a real ball twister havin' to hide who you are from everyone else."

No shit. Who could understand that better than a warlock and were?

"But it doesn't have to be that way, you know? One thing I've learned since I lost my parents was that I have to live life my way. By my rules. Life's too short for anythin' else."

He was right. Life was too short to give one flying fuck about the consequences of being with Drake. To hell with everyone else *and* the Conclave. They might not approve of a mixing of the species, but I wasn't going to live my life by what they wanted, so I pulled Drake all the way to me, nuzzled my forehead against his, and ran my fingers through his silky golden hair. A strong, earthy scent hung in the air between us, and it set my flesh on fire.

I bit my bottom lip as I leered down at Drake's delicate pink mouth. His lips called to me like a flower to a butterfly, and like the insect, my only desire was to settle upon them and drink till I was drunk.

So when I backed up, I surprised him.

"What's wrong?" he asked.

"Nothing," I said. "It's just time to go."

"I don't understand."

I grinned at him and opened my car door. "Maybe not now, but you will."

WE STROLLED down a boardwalk trail that cut through the dense woodlands and deep thickets that covered much of the area. Water from the nearby marshlands collected under the trail. Bees buzzed, and cheery birds sang in the trees all around us. Even without closing my eyes, I could see the magic all around me.

The green of the leaves glowed like emeralds, and the water shimmered like glass. The wildlife around me turned into a chorus, and our footsteps across the soggy wood thumped to its beat.

I'd never been this in tune with the wonder around me before. Had my feelings for Drake somehow unclogged whatever had been holding me back?

"It's beautiful out here," Drake said. He took in everything around him, and as he did, his eyes seemed to turn as blue as the sky around us. Did being out here in nature in relative peace call to his inner animal and make him want to shift? It was something I would certainly like to see.

"You can if you want to. It won't bother me."

He knitted his brows together. "Now just what are you givin' me permission to do?"

"You know. What you do."

"Oh," he said with a nod. He surveyed our surroundings, no doubt trying to verify if we were truly alone. When he returned his attention to me, he shook his head. "Nah. Not now. Not here."

It was hard to hide my disappointment. "How come?"

He laced his fingers with mine and smiled. "Because then I wouldn't be able to enjoy this with you."

That was a really good answer. "Okay. But you'll have to show me how you do what you do real soon."

He nodded. "I can teach you if you want."

Teach me to be a shifter? "What? How?"

"It's hard, but it's not impossible to pull off. With practice and dedication, anyone can get used to *parkouring*."

I scrunched up my nose. "Did you say park whoring?"

Drake scowled and bumped into me so hard he almost sent me flying off the boardwalk. Thankfully, he still held my hand and pulled me back. "Not park whorin'. *Parkouring*. It's a French word. You've never heard of it?"

So shifters used a French word to describe their shifting ability the way we used the derivation of the French word *grammaire* to refer to our book of spells. "Never," I answered. "But language isn't really my thing."

He chuckled. "I've noticed."

How the hell did a nonshifter learn to shift? Was it just a complicated, secret spell they somehow mastered? I was about to ask when the delighted squeal of a child caught our attention. We turned around to see a five-year-old tromping down the boardwalk to us with his parents, who were trying to catch up with their speeding kindergartener.

Drake crouched down in front of the little guy and smiled. "Where are you off to in such a hurry?"

"Birds!" he yelled as he pointed to the tree to our left. Two yellow-and-green birds sat on a branch, staring at us.

"And they're pretty birds too," Drake replied in exaggerated awe.

The boy tweeted at the pair just as his parents finally caught up to him.

"Jordy, what have we told you about running ahead of us?" his exasperated father asked.

"Birds, Daddy," little Jordy replied, as if that explained his actions.

His mother picked him up and held him in her arms. "He loves birds," she said as he struggled to get out of her grasp.

"Me too," Drake replied.

"I'm kinda partial to butterflies now," I added. Drake glanced at me and smiled.

"We actually saw some down toward the beach," the father said.

"Really?" Drake asked. He looked around as if he could see the beach from here.

Jordy's dad nodded and pointed down the path we were on. "Just keep going about another quarter mile and take a right at the fork in the path. It'll eventually drop you off by the beach. Hopefully those little guys are still there."

"Thanks," I said as we waved good-bye to Jordy and his family.

We trotted down the trail. How awesome would it be to run into the same swarm of butterflies I'd summoned the other day? I turned to say that to Drake and noticed his expression had changed.

Grief fell across his previously cheery blue eyes, and the smile he'd worn most of the day had become a thin line. It didn't take a genius to figure out why. Seeing a family together had reminded him of his family, the one he no longer had.

I'd tried bringing up his past before, but he always managed to either distract me with a hot make-out session or change the course of the conversation. He did that with most things about his past. It was why we still had yet to discuss being magical creatures.

Respecting Drake's boundaries had been difficult, but it was time to get around them.

I stopped and pulled him close, letting the strength of my fingers around his jaw and neck communicate what I hoped was the comfort of my presence. "It's okay to miss them and get sad when something reminds you of them."

"I know," he replied.

At least he wasn't denying it. Maybe he was finally ready. "Talk to me."

He studied me and then sighed in resignation. "Can we walk and do this at the same time?"

"I'm capable of multitasking."

He smirked as we resumed our walk. "So what do you want to know?"

"Anything you want to share."

He pondered in silence for a few moments. When the moments stretched into minutes, I figured Drake had decided not to say anything at all. When he finally spoke, I made sure he had my complete attention. "My parents owned and operated a ranch back home. We dealt in cattle mostly. We didn't live high on the hog like you do, but we were comfortable and happy. I was their only child, but they didn't want me spoiled or nothin'. They made me do chores before and after school, and I never got to sleep late on the weekends. There was always somethin' to be done. I hated it at first, gettin' up before the sun and workin' till long after it set. The friends I had didn't have to do that, and it made me real bitter for a while. But then my friends' parents started gettin' divorced. And my parents? Shoot! They were just as much in love with each other as I'd ever seen them. That told me they knew somethin' the rest of the world didn't. So instead of fightin' their ways, I went with it. I learned what they had to teach me, and they sure as hell taught me a lot." He closed his eyes to hold back the welling tears.

"So what happened to them?"

When his eyes opened, tears streamed down his creamy cheeks. I fought the desire to take him in my arms and tell him it was okay, but he had to cast the weight from his shoulders, or he'd never be free and he'd never stop running.

"Drunk driver," he mumbled. "Speedin' down the wrong side of a dark country road at eighty miles an hour without his headlights on."

Shit. At those speeds, his parents probably never knew what had hit them.

His tears suddenly dried, and a fury that rivaled my father's suddenly twisted his features. "And they never caught the fucker. He slammed into them and drove off." His eyes were wild with rage. "Can you fuckin' believe that?"

How the hell was that possible? At those speeds, both cars had to have suffered extensive damage. "That doesn't make sense."

He scoffed. "No shit! There was no wreckage from another car found at the accident site. It was like some phantom vehicle slammed into them and then disappeared. The police had nothing to go on."

Fuck. That was unacceptable. "Maybe I can do something."

He eyed me. "Like what? Use your power and influence to magically track down the bastard who did this?"

"Well, yes."

A small smile threatened to erase the scowl from his lips. "That's very sweet, but I can't ask you to do that."

"You're not. I'm offering."

Silence once again descended upon us, but Drake's mood had changed. He was still angry, hurt, sad, and a whole host of other emotions I probably would never understand, but those emotions didn't seem to hold him as tightly as they once did. Maybe now that he could talk to me, his pain wouldn't get the chance to drown him again.

That was when I decided I was going to do whatever I could to give Drake the closure he needed.

"You know," he said with my hand once again in his. "My parents taught me a whole heck of a lot, 'cause, ya know, that's what parents do. But why don't they ever teach us how to go on without them?"

"But we're not without them." I squeezed his hand and motioned to the natural beauty around us. "I believe your parents are with us now, just as my mother is. Their essences have become part of the world. They live and breathe all around us. We might not get to see them anymore, but they're here. I know it. On the breeze, in the songs of the birds, maybe even in the swarms of butterflies."

Drake's grin pressed pause on his grief. "There you go, surprisin' me again. I didn't expect you to be so sentimental and poetic. You're definitely not the tough guy you pretend to be." He leaned closer to me as we walked, and I wrapped my arm around his waist.

"I'm very tough," I said, jutting out my chin. "I'll deny otherwise."

Drake leaned his head against my shoulder. "Just so you know, you don't have to be tough for me."

"And neither do you," I added.

He gazed up at me and smiled. "I think I'd like that."

"Not being tough?"

He shook his head. "I'll always be tough. That's who my parents raised me to be. I just kinda like the thought of havin' someone that I don't have to be tough for."

So did I, and strangely enough, the idea didn't terrify me as much as I thought it would.

AN HOUR later we finally made it to the beach side of the park. Drake wore the biggest smile I'd seen all day. It practically split his face in two. "Like the beach?"

"Heck yeah!" he exclaimed. He kicked off his sneakers, flung off his socks, and dug his toes in the sand. "I've only been to a beach like once in my life. And I was ten or somethin'. My parents took me on a vacation down to Corpus on the Gulf Coast, and we spent the night on the beach in a tent. It was great. We had cookouts, ate s'mores, and even though we woke up to crabs in our tent, it was a pretty awesome time."

"So you've had crabs before?" I asked as I discarded my flip-flops. "That's good to know."

He frowned at me, but his playful anger couldn't completely wipe the grin from his lips. The wonderful childhood memory I'd unconsciously evoked refused to be cast aside. "Don't go smartin' off now and ruinin' our good time."

"I wouldn't dream of it." I walked a few steps past him before turning and walking backward. "How about we try something?" I asked after I ripped my shirt off and tossed it next to my shoes.

He put his hands on his hips and arched his eyebrow. "What?"

"Let's see how fast you can run in the sand," I said before taking off in a mad sprint.

"Cheater!" he called behind me. I took one quick glance over my shoulder. Drake was out of his shirt and barreling after me like a pistol shot. I wasn't exactly out of shape, but there was obviously no way I was going to be in the lead for long. His natural shifter speed made him more than a match for me.

A few seconds later, Drake caught up to me and made a surprising jump onto my back. The force of the collision upset my balance, and I crashed onto the beach. Drake landed half on my back and half in the sand, and his laughter echoed off the dunes around us.

I lay there for a while, spitting the sand from my lips while relishing the weight of Drake's body on mine. He made no immediate move to get off me. He giggled into my neck, his breath spreading across my flesh.

"I guess I win," he said.

We'd both won this one. He might have caught up to me, but Drake straddled my ass, and his groin pressed against my crack. How could that be counted as a loss? I closed my eyes, and I could see us in the privacy of my bedroom, our naked bodies entwined.

But Drake went and ruined it by getting off me. I reluctantly sat up and brushed both the disappointment and the granules of sand from my chest and face. "I think you like getting me dirty."

He pretended not to care, even though I could tell he did. For some reason, messing up my usually spot-on appearance made him happy. He certainly didn't seem to care that clumps of sand stuck to his bare flesh. He made no attempt to shake it off. "There's nothin' wrong with a little dirt in our lives," he said matter-of-factly. "Havin' fun means makin' a mess sometimes."

I smirked. "I like the way you think."

If Drake rolled his eyes any harder, they'd roll right out of his head. "You've got a nasty, one-track mind, you know that?"

I shrugged, mimicking his nonchalant attitude. "It's who I am. Take it or leave it."

He pondered the options in silence for a moment. Was he really making a decision whether to do just that?

"Just so you know, that's not a question you're supposed to actually answer."

He twisted his lips. "Pity," he said before standing.

"What does that mean?"

Drake grinned down at me and offered his hand. "Well, you'll never find out now, will you? I'm not supposed to answer."

I took his hand, and he pulled me up. I overexaggerated the strength of his assistance and used the gesture to fall into his embrace. Drake immediately wrapped his arms around my waist, supporting me as I leaned against him.

With our bare flesh once again in contact, our chests heaved in passion that exited our bodies in warm, panting plumes. The muscles in his arms twitched as he pulled me tighter against him until more than our chests made contact. His groin pressed into mine, and a lengthening hardness streaked across his thigh.

I reacted in kind. My cock snaked inside my briefs, reaching out for the desire uncoiling before me. I ached to feel every part of Drake touch every part of me. It was a yearning I'd never experienced before. I'd met boys who turned me on, but Drake appealed to me on a level beyond the physical.

It was almost magical. What else could it be but what I had suspected all along?

"What do you know about being spell bound?"

Confusion crouched in his eyes, but it wasn't from lack of understanding. He was searching for the words to explain what he obviously felt. "I guess I'd say it means meetin' someone you're so fascinated by that nothin' you do makes that go away." He hesitated for a breath before asking, "Why? What does it mean to you?"

"Do you want the honest, no-holds-barred answer?"

"That's always been my preference."

"It's right now," I said. I raced my fingertips up and down his back, following the dip and curve of his muscles. "What I feel when I'm in your arms and the fact that it happened so quickly. One minute I'm me, the guy I've always been, and then *bam!* There's you. You've been all I can think about since we met."

"Really?"

"Really."

Drake nuzzled his face into my neck and breathed deeply. "There you go again, surprisin' the fool outta me."

"I think I'm more surprised than you."

"I seriously doubt that," he added. He glanced up at me from my shoulder, and the last barrier existing between us finally fell away. Drake's expression turned soft and vulnerable instead of hard and distant. His lips quivered, and his body shook as whatever emotions were welling within him bubbled to the surface. "I never expected to actually like such a jerk."

I grinned. The feeling was definitely mutual. Drake was a shifter, someone I'd once believed to be the cause of whatever was going on in Havenbridge, but it wasn't true. I didn't need my magic to tell me that. Only my heart.

He peered over my left shoulder and let out a gasp. "Oh, Mason. Look," he said.

A group of butterflies flitted toward us. It wasn't quite the cloud that had visited us at Aunt Millie's, but it was definitely more than a dozen. "Wow!" I said. Even though I hadn't called to them, they'd come on their own, dancing and swirling around us.

"It's perfect," Drake said as he gazed up at me with his big blue eyes.

"Yes, it is."

I grasped both sides of his face, running my fingers across his smooth skin before hooking his chin with my thumb and forefinger and tilting his head up. I leaned closer, decreasing the distance between our lips until they brushed together as gently as the beating of a butterfly's wings.

And as the insects swirled around us, so did our heightening desire. I panted against him as he raked his fingernails down my chest and stomach. I pulled him tighter to me. I forced our bodies together while clutching his neck. I wanted my embrace to tell him that I wasn't letting him go, that from now on he was mine.

And Drake got the message. He went limp in my arms, abandoning the reservations that had previously clung to both of us, and he gave in to my unspoken request. I was his, so we savored the promise made sweet by our kisses. His warm, insistent tongue found its way into my mouth, and I swirled mine around his, enticing it deeper inside me.

I dipped my fingers beneath the waistband of his shorts. Drake gasped as I grabbed the swell of his ass, and he responded by clutching at my chest and dragging his fingers down my side.

When he reached the boundary of fabric, he hesitated. There was no doubt he wanted to dive in and take hold of my evident desire, and I didn't want to stop him. I had reached the limits of my restraint.

I pulled out of our embrace and surveyed the beach. We had the place to ourselves.

"What's wrong?"

"Nothing." I grabbed his hand and tugged him toward a huge sand dune. The sun had started to dip beneath the horizon, painting the sky a velvety purple. "I'm just moving us somewhere more private."

"Are you serious?" he asked as I took him in my arms. I kissed his neck and nibbled on his ear. His breath caught in his throat. "Out here?"

I placed my hands on either side of his face. His lips trembled in a mixture of obvious desire and fear. "I think it's perfect. We're on a beautiful beach, out here with the nature that you love. No one else is around. But if you don't want to, I'm okay with that."

Drake pressed his forehead against my lips. He clutched my back, then surfed his fingers down my spine. "I do want to," he said. He dipped his fingers below the fabric, fluttering across the swell of my ass.

"Then what's wrong?"

"I'm scared," he admitted before burying his face in my chest. "I've never—"

I tilted his head up until our gazes locked. "Me either."

"Really?"

I nodded.

"I don't know if I'm ready."

I kissed the tip of his nose. "Then we don't have to. Simple as that." I grabbed his hand and led him out from behind the dune.

"Where we goin'?"

"I don't know. Walk along the beach. If you're tired we can head back to the car."

Drake tugged me back into his arms. "Just because I'm not ready for sex doesn't mean I'm not ready for somethin'."

His lips immediately found mine, and the passion he'd kept reined in suddenly burst out the barn doors. He found the buttons of my shorts and undid the clasp. As our tongues dueled in our mouths, he grabbed my dick.

"Are you sure?" I panted. "There's no pressure."

His soft fingers wrapped around my shaft. I was wrong. There was tons of pressure, but it was in my balls, not between us. "Does this answer your question?" He tugged on my hardness, jacking me with evident glee. In response I slid down the dips and valleys of his muscular back, skimming along the border where flesh and fabric met before sliding to the front and undoing the buttons that kept his aching erection from my grasp.

I had trouble getting Drake's clothes off. Drake's slow, tight pulls on my dick had me seeing stars and my knees wobbling, but I finally managed to fumble his shorts open. I yanked down his shorts and underwear and was treated to a truly beautiful sight. Drake's seven-inch dick, which had a fat, hooded cockhead, jutted out of a thick bush of dark blond hair. My mouth watered. I grabbed him at the base of his prick. Heat I'd never experienced from another person's body rippled off his flesh in agonizing waves. A thin sheen of sweat coated his abdominals until tiny drops of perspiration slid slowly down his smooth stomach and disappeared in the blond thatch that surrounded his dick.

"Enjoyin' the view again?" This time there was no mocking in his question. Only desire.

"You're beautiful."

He traced along my nipple until it pebbled. I shivered in response. "And so are you."

Drake's gorgeous, naked body mesmerized me. I had to touch every inch of him, so I stroked his cock in a steady, slow rhythm that mimicked the rushing waves upon the shore.

"That feels real good." His grip around my cock grew tighter, and I pumped into his grasp.

I reached around and fondled his butt, running my fingers along the musky crevice before finding his center. Drake groaned when I brushed my index finger across his puckering middle, and he leaped onto my lips.

He let go of my cock, wrapping his arms around my neck. His tongue darted into my mouth as I traced slow, sensuous circles around his hole. Our thrusting pelvises crushed our cocks together as the sweat from our burning passion acted as the lube that allowed our dicks to slide easily against each other.

"I can't stop touching you," I panted. I moved from playing with his ass to gripping his waist, forcing our pricks even harder between us. I surfed my left hand up his back, across his shoulders, and down his chest.

Drake groaned and bit his lip as the friction of our slippery cocks grew more intense. "I need you on top of me," he said.

He didn't have to tell me twice. I kicked my shorts and briefs off from around my ankles, and Drake did the same. I took our clothes and made a narrow pallet on the sand for us. We'd still get sand all over us, just not in the really sensitive areas. Well, at least not much.

As Drake lay back on our clothes, I stared down at his beautiful body. The ripples of his muscles, the slight dusting of blond hair on his chest and legs, the hard cock pointing directly at me. How had I lived my whole life without ever seeing such perfection?

"You're doin' it again," he said. "Enjoyin' the view from over there when you could be down here." Passion painted the apples of his cheeks a fiery red. My gaze traveled down his strong, heaving chest and pink nipples, each nestled within a small circle of blond hair.

"You're right," I said, hovering over him. I ran my fingers along the ridges of his flat, muscular stomach and brushed across his dick, which pulsed against my touch.

"Please," he begged. He bit his bottom lip and reached up for me.

I slowly lowered myself on top of him. When our fully naked bodies met, we both gasped. Drake immediately wrapped his arms around me, and I held his face in my hands. If my brain had been a camera, I'd have been snapping mental photographs of this moment, of Drake's eyes half-closed in longing, of my darker skin pressed against his fair flesh, of his trembling body as I resumed thrusting my hardness against his.

"Damn, you feel good." My lips lighted upon his, and my tongue forced its way into his mouth. He moaned and trembled as our leaking cocks slid past each other.

"You too," he whimpered. "Too good."

I knew exactly what he meant. I wasn't going to last much longer. If we didn't put on the brakes, I was going to come. "Should we stop?" I asked, out of breath.

"Are you kiddin' me?" he asked. He grabbed my ass. He used the leverage to grind his throbbing cock harder and faster against mine. "I couldn't stop if I tried."

He smirked up at me before our lips molded together once again. As we kissed, our hard pricks thrust against each other, bringing us closer to the edge from which there was no return. Drake moved his hands from my butt to my waist, where he forced us into a harder, faster rhythm.

I braced myself with my arms, arching my body against his. Our hips moved in synch with each other until my already-hard cock turned to steel. This was it.

"Fuck!" I muttered as my dick spasmed, shooting streams of spunk and coating both of our cocks and our stomachs. With each jettison of sperm, I convulsed and moaned, and my reaction shoved Drake over the precipice.

"Holy shit!" he moaned as he bit down on my shoulder, adding his volleys of hot, wet liquid to the white mess I'd created.

When Drake's orgasm subsided, I lowered myself completely on top of him. He wrapped his legs around my waist as the fruits of our labors dribbled down his side. "That was awesome," I said.

"Tell me about it," he said. "If I'd known how good that would feel, I'd have done it sooner." I grimaced at him, and he laughed.

"You know what I mean," he said, brushing his lips against mine.

"I hope you're still okay with us doing this here."

He ran a finger through my dark locks and then kissed my nose. "This was perfect for our first time."

"First time?" I asked, my lips drawing into a huge smile. "Does that mean there's gonna be a second and a tenth?"

Drake chuckled and shook his head. "I swear. One-track mind."

I rested my forehead against his. "You haven't answered my question."

"Yes," he said, sighing. "Seconds. Tenths. And maybe even a one hundredth."

I grinned broadly. "Think we can get to a hundred by tomorrow?"

"Tomorrow?" he asked. "I was thinkin' tonight. You're such a slacker."

I pressed my lips against his, breathing in his scent and the emotions that seared the air around us. "And you say I have a one-track mind?"

He brushed his fingers through my hair before gently taking my lips between his teeth. He ran his hands across my back muscles, and I surfed mine down his flat stomach. "I'm a growin' boy too, you know?"

I did, and I couldn't have been happier about that.

CHAPTER 9

WE LAY on the beach for a few more hours, talking about nothing and everything at the same time. When the moon had trekked a quarter of the way across the sky, we realized it was time to head back. After we'd cleaned up and gotten dressed, we drove back to Aunt Millie's. The entire ride back to her house, we both looked like a couple of grinning idiots. I didn't typically appreciate couples who were so obviously into each other that they made everyone else around them diabetic, but here I was, with a big-ass smile on my face and Drake's hand in mine.

Drake wasn't any better. Every time our eyes met, he giggled and blew me a kiss. And damned if I didn't get another boner. I had half a mind to pull over and go for round two, but we had to get back to Aunt Millie. It was already approaching ten o'clock, and it was a school night.

I sure as hell didn't want to make Aunt Millie mad at me.

"It'll be fine," Drake said with a squeeze of my hand.

"What will be?"

"You're frettin' over Aunt Millie. As long as I'm home safely, she'll be fine. She's not your typical great-aunt. She knows boys will be boys, and she's okay with that."

My cheeks flushed. "You don't think she'll know, do you?"

He laughed. "You're so cute. Of course she will. We're both grinnin' like a possum eatin' a sweet potato, and we've still got sand everywhere!" He brushed some stray granules from my hair and smiled. "Besides, we probably smell like cum."

"That's hot," I said with an eyebrow wiggle.

"I know."

When I pulled up to Aunt Millie's, the house was completely dark. "Think she's asleep?"

Drake stared at the house and frowned. "Maybe. It's not like her, but her health hasn't been all that great, you know?"

I did. "Well, let's get you inside."

"First things first," he said.

He leaned over the console and delivered a soft kiss that quickly turned as passionate as the one on the beach. We breathed into each other's mouth, and my right hand caressed his cheek while my left went straight for the hardness tenting his shorts. "Looks like you're ready to go again."

Drake grabbed my crotch and stroked my shaft through the fabric. "And so are you."

"That's it," I said, starting the car again. "We're going somewhere else."

He laughed and turned off the ignition. "No. I have to get inside and check on Aunt Millie."

I grumbled. "I'd rather get inside you."

After delivering one final peck to my lips, he opened the car door. "Soon," he said. "I promise."

"I'm gonna hold you to that," I replied as I exited my car.

"You'd better."

We held hands as we walked up to the front door. I held Drake from behind, pushing my hard cock against his ass, and he reared back against it as he unlocked the door. When he swung it open, the interior of the house was even darker than the night sky.

"I can't see shit in here," Drake said, as he fumbled for the light switch. He clicked the tiny lever up and down without any result. "Aunt Millie?"

I immediately went on full alert. Something wasn't right. The air had a strange thickness, like I was wading through waist-high mud. I closed my eyes and opened myself up to the energy around me. Waves of ominous dread swept over me so quickly, I almost blacked out. I had to grasp the wall to my left to maintain my balance as an unseen gale chilled me to the bone.

Drake hadn't noticed. He proceeded into the shadow-shrouded house in pursuit of other lights. "Aunt Millie?" he called again as I heard the failed switch of the lamp on the hall table. "What the heck is up with the lights?"

I couldn't answer. My throat had closed. My magical senses were being assaulted by a sheer bombardment of supernatural currents that coursed around the room. They threatened to pull me under like a riptide from where I stood.

Drake's footsteps shuffled farther inside. I had to regain my human senses and shut down my magic. There was danger here Drake couldn't sense. How was that possible? Didn't shifters have better instincts than this?

"Is there a flashlight in your car?" Drake asked from somewhere in the darkness.

Yes, there was. That was what he needed to do. He needed to go out to my car for the flashlight and get the fuck out of this house. "Yes," I managed to force out.

"Well, can you go and get it? I'm kinda busy at the moment."

"Why don't you come with me?" I asked. I slowly pulled back, withdrawing ever so slightly from the chaotic energy that had almost done me in. With each even breath, I gained more control and was able to stand amid the crashing currents. "Before you hurt yourself."

"Maybe you're right. No sense breakin' somethin'," he said as he made his way back to me. "Besides, Aunt Millie's probably not here. I didn't see her car outside."

That was true. Her car hadn't been there when we arrived. I let out a huge sigh.

"What was that for?"

"Nothing," I said, trying to play off my evident relief. "Just glad you're listening to me instead of arguing like usual."

"Yeah, well, don't get used to that," he said. "Just because we— well, you know—doesn't mean I'm not gonna be as ornery as usual."

I wouldn't have him any other way. "What are you doing? It doesn't take that long to get from where you were to me."

"I'm fixin' to try one more light," he said. "The one in the livin' room, before we go on out to your car."

Oh, for crying out loud! "I thought you were going to listen?"

"I guess I changed my mind." I could hear the smile in his voice. He was intentionally being difficult at probably one of the worst times.

And that was when the unmistakable odor of bleach and pancakes made its way over to where I stood by the front door. I stiffened in response and widened my stance. "Drake, get over here. Now!"

"What's wrong?" He'd evidently noted the change in my tone. Fear crept into his previously playful pitch.

"Please. Just come to me. As fast as you can."

"You're kinda freakin' me out," he said as he once again drew closer.

I had to cover my nose and mouth. The stench had become overpowering: the acrid burn of bleach mixed with the sweetness of pancake batter. "Can you smell that?" I asked. He had to. He was a damn shifter!

Before he could answer, a low hiss filled the room.

"Mason, are you tryin' to scare me? Because that's not cool."

"That wasn't me," I said, piercing the black veil that kept me from Drake. I had to get to him before anything else in here with us did.

"Oh, there you are."

I stopped in my tracks. "Drake?"

"How are you doin' that?"

"Doing what?"

"Throwin' your voice over by the front door."

My hands clenched automatically, the way I'd so often witnessed Pierce do before summoning his active power. "Because I'm over by the front door," I replied, trying to home in on where Drake was standing. I would likely only have one shot, and I had to make it count.

"Then who...?" he asked.

Drake yelled as a loud hiss exploded in the room.

"Get down!" I hollered. I forced all my anger, all my emotions out of my outstretched hands, and a powerful force flew out of my fingertips. It wasn't the blue crackling of Pierce's electricity or the icy rush of Thad's frosty assault. No discernible light was visible, just a low, subtle rumble that preceded a loud explosion and the sound of a wall caving inward.

Whatever I hit screeched in pain before muttering, "You're too late."

"Drake!" I screamed as I forced whatever power I'd finally tapped into out of my hands again. I aimed in the direction of the scuttling beast I still could not see. "*Drake!*"

My enemy hissed at me again. It wasn't where it had last been. It had moved farther away. If I had to guess, it was in the kitchen, and it was trying to get away.

"Drake, will you answer me, dammit!"

Although I knew I was pushing my luck by casting another spell, I had to chance it. If I exposed magic I'd be in serious trouble, but I couldn't let that thing leave if it had Drake. I had to stop it. In order to do that, I had to see it.

"*Lucem*," I muttered, and three globes of light appeared in the middle of the room just as a shadow exited the broken back door and scurried into the night. I was about to charge after it when I saw Drake lying unconscious next to the living room wall. Pieces of plaster littered the floor around him, and a man-sized hole had been punctured clear through the kitchen wall. "Drake!" I was at his side in moments.

I felt for a pulse, and it was strong. There were no visible wounds. He'd evidently been knocked out cold. Again.

I sighed in relief, but then I remembered Aunt Millie. I surveyed the living room, but she wasn't there. A quick glance revealed a trail of blood down the hall. I choked back my emotions. No. This couldn't be happening. Not to Drake, not to Aunt Millie.

I followed the red path toward the last bedroom on the left and opened the door.

The moonlight from outside revealed Aunt Millie resting on her bed. Her hands had been neatly folded on top of her breast. When I saw her neck, I crumpled to my knees. Just like the corpse on the football field, there was no blood around her body.

Only the drops on the floor.

As I wept, I promised to find whoever had done this and make him pay.

With his life.

DRAKE SAT on the couch, shivering in my arms as police officers traveled in and out of the destroyed living room. Forensic crews worked in the bedroom while others dusted for fingerprints around the house. They wouldn't find any.

I wasn't exactly sure how I knew that, but I did. Every fiber of my being told me that what had been here was a being of immense power, more than capable of covering its tracks from humans.

But from my family and me there was no place to hide.

"So you didn't see him?" Officer Garrett asked. He and his partner Officer Fitzsimmons had been the first to respond after I called the authorities. When they arrived on the scene, Drake had just learned about his aunt and was in no shape to answer questions. I pointed, and when they entered the bedroom, I heard their call for backup.

Now that backup was here, though, it was time to get some answers.

"No," I replied. I pulled Drake to me, his tearstained face shoved into my chest. "The lights were off when we came in."

"And you didn't turn them on?" Officer Fitzsimmons asked from the front door. He flicked the lights on and off, and they flickered. "They seem to be working."

"I don't know what to tell you. Nothing was turning on. Drake tried the lamp over there and the light in the living room."

The cops exchanged meaningful glances. They couldn't understand how lights started working all of a sudden. Whatever had been here had obviously used its own magic to mess with the lights, but I couldn't very well admit that.

"And you knocked him through the wall?" Officer Garrett asked. "You had to touch him. How big was he? Tall like me or rounder like my partner?"

How the hell was I supposed to know? I hadn't laid one finger on him. It had been my active power, whatever the hell it was, that knocked him on his ass. "I don't know. I was disoriented."

"Come on, kid," Fitzsimmons said. "You've got to give us something here. You were in the same room, and you fought. You have to know something."

"Why are you houndin' him?" Drake yelled. "You should be out there findin' out who killed my aunt, not wastin' time with stupid-ass questions that we don't have the answers to."

Officer Garrett was about to respond when a voice stopped him. "Give it a rest, Garrett."

Both officers turned to stare at the man who stood in the front doorway. It was Charles Proctor. His gaze reflected sincerity and compassion, but his demeanor exuded a strength and confidence that instantly quieted his subordinates.

I would expect nothing else from the head of a white-magic coven.

"Why don't you give me a moment?"

The officers deferred to his presence and went outside. He surveyed the others in the room and inclined his head toward the front door. They understood the gesture and gave us some privacy.

"Thank you, Mr. Proctor," I said.

"It's Detective Proctor right now, Mason," he said after closing the door.

"Of course."

He sighed as he took a seat in the overstuffed chair across from where we sat. "I know you boys have been through the ringer tonight, but I want you to tell me everything that you can remember no matter how small or insignificant. Do you think you can do that?"

As he talked to us, his energy filled the room. He was evidently silently weaving a calming spell to ease Drake's anxiety enough for him to handle reliving the events. Drake collected himself and sat up straight, and then we did as he asked.

"So you didn't see him, but you heard him hiss?"

"Yes," I answered. Drake nodded.

"Like a snake or what?"

I shook my head. "Not really. It was the kind of hiss an angry animal makes, but it was none I'd ever heard before."

"Me either," Drake added. "And I'm from Texas. There are more critters than people on the farm." The effects of the spell had clearly worked their magic. Drake had settled down quite a bit, but it wasn't real. Underneath, he still bubbled with fear, anger, and worry, but Detective Proctor had given him the magical support he needed to be as clearheaded as possible.

"And you knocked him through that wall?" he asked me.

I raised my fingers to the side of my head hidden from Drake and wiggled my fingers as if I was casting a spell. "I did."

He nodded in understanding, and his half grin revealed he was impressed. Miranda had most likely filled her father in on my magical problems. "I see. Drake, is there anyone you can think of who would want to harm your aunt Millicent?"

He scoffed as if that was the most ridiculous question ever. "No! She was the sweetest woman in the world. She opened her home to me. To give me some semblance of family after what happened to mine. A woman with a heart like that can't be hated. She might not have always been the friendliest person in town, but she didn't speak ill of no one." Tears spilled down his cheeks. "She was the best."

Detective Proctor nodded. "Yes. She was." He looked around the house. "Can either of you tell if anything has been taken?"

Drake stood up and surveyed the room. "No, but I didn't think to look. Should I?"

"Not right now," he answered. "I only ask because you told us her car wasn't home when you got here. And neither of you heard it drive away after the assailant left the premises?"

We shook our heads. "What does that mean?" I asked.

He shrugged. "I don't know. Yet," he said. "But for now, let's get this scene cleared up, and then you can come back later to identify anything that might have been taken or that might point to some motive."

"Okay," Drake replied hesitantly.

"Do you have someplace to stay for the night?"

"He can stay with me," I said.

It didn't take a detective to figure out what was up between us. "Good."

"Are you sure?" Drake asked. "I don't wanna be a bother."

I pulled him back into my embrace and kissed the top of his head. "I wouldn't let you stay anywhere else but in my arms."

Drake held me close and nodded into the crook of my neck. I held Detective Proctor's gaze with my own. It was my way of telling him I had more information for him that I couldn't share at the moment. Whatever was here had come for something and had obviously left with it. His nod told me our families would be speaking later, and it couldn't be soon enough for me.

MY FATHER and brothers were waiting at the open front door of our house when I pulled up in the driveway. Pain etched its way across their faces, but it wasn't just for the tragedy Drake had suffered. The grief of losing our mother played through their minds. It was what happened to people whenever death unexpectedly called on those who had already suffered through a recent visit.

"I'm glad Mason brought you here," my father said as he opened the passenger-side door. Drake exited the car on automatic pilot. Since leaving his aunt Millie's, the effect of Mr. Proctor's calming spell had worn off. He hadn't spoken the entire drive, and his eyes had glazed over, as if he was slowly retreating from this cruel world.

A few hours before, we'd been happy, basking in the wonderful emotions we'd created together. Now pain gripped our hearts and souls.

"You can stay as long as you want," my father added.

Drake's manners kicked in enough for him to acknowledge the sentiment with a smile before Thad led him inside the house.

"He doesn't look too good," Pierce said after Thad and Drake had gone inside.

"His aunt was just murdered," I said. My tone was sharp. "What do you expect him to be doing? Somersaults?"

My brother threw up his arms and waved them in the universal sign that meant he'd been misunderstood. "Of course not. I'm just, well, I guess I'm stating the obvious because I don't know what else to say."

I grinned an apology. "I need to get to Drake."

My dad stopped me with his hand on my shoulder. "First I want you to tell me everything."

"Can't it wait, Dad? Drake needs me."

His even stare was my only reply. As much as I wanted to be there for Drake, he was right. I had to give my father all the information I could. He had to report to the Conclave, as if that would do any good. Lately all they'd done was sit on their asses.

Still, the faster I got this over with, the sooner I'd get to Drake, so I revealed everything that had happened.

"What do you think it took from Aunt Millie?" my father asked.

I shrugged. "Whatever it was, it's been looking for it this whole time."

"And it hissed like an animal?" Pierce asked.

I nodded. "But it wasn't one. It smelled like bleach and pancakes, and there are no animals I know of that smell like that."

"Agreed," my father said as he folded his arms across his chest and screwed up his face. "We thought we were dealing with a shadow weaver, but maybe we aren't. Perhaps it's a corrupted shifter? I haven't heard of one leaving Aeaea in at least a decade." *That* was the name I couldn't recall of the shifter island. "The return wasn't for any nefarious reason. She requested passage to visit a dying relative who hadn't made the pilgrimage to their safe haven."

"But shifters can't attack with shadows," I reminded him. Whatever attacked Elliot and me in the boys' restroom at Havenbridge High had not been a were. "If it's not a shifter or a shadow weaver, what else could it be?"

My father's brow wrinkled. "Something I don't even want to contemplate. That's why it's important for us to find out. We need to know exactly what we're dealing with."

Even though I didn't want to add to Drake's problems, I had to finally voice what I believed to be true. "There has to be a shifter involved."

Dad and Pierce traded glances. "Why do you say that?" my father asked. "You sound extremely certain."

I exhaled. Once I spoke the words, I'd never be able to take them back, and Drake's life would become even more complicated than it already was. He'd face interrogation by the Conclave, and I'd have to suffer through my family's wrath for keeping his identity a secret. "Because Drake is a shifter."

My father's mouth dropped open. I'd rarely seen him at a complete loss for words.

Pierce had no problem finding his voice. "What the fuck? And you're just telling us now?"

"I had to be sure," I explained. "I suspected by the way he jumped all over the place like I told you about. And when I was following him almost two weeks ago, he disappeared and a cat was suddenly in his place."

"That's not exactly hard proof," my father said. "Did you see him shift?"

I shook my head. "But he knew I was a warlock, and I figured he knew because he could smell the magic on me."

"*When* did he tell you this? Today?" The calmness in my father's tone rumbled in a wave of fury.

"Uh, a little over a week ago?"

"Fuck, Mason!" Pierce said. "That's information you're supposed to be giving us, not keeping between you and your boyfriend. This is serious shit we're dealing with. I can't believe you'd keep us in the dark."

"Your brother's right," my dad added. "It's obvious you like Drake, and I can certainly see why. But your first duty is to this family and to the Gate. Nothing else is more important."

They were right, but they were also wrong at the same time. Drake was extremely important to me. Just as much as my family or the Gate. I would do anything to protect him, and if it meant occasionally keeping something a secret, that was exactly what I was going to do.

"First thing we'll have to do is verify if he is a shifter or not," my dad said.

"How do we do that?" I asked.

"We could always ask," Pierce answered.

My father shook his head. "We wouldn't know for certain if he were telling the truth or not. Remember, shifters have the natural ability to camouflage themselves from humans and us. We need to search our Grimoire. It will have the answers we need."

"That's not going to happen tonight."

We turned to see Thad standing at the front door.

"Why not?" I asked.

Thad motioned for us to follow him inside, where he led us to the living room. Drake had passed out on the couch, his legs pulled up to his chest in a natural defensive posture; he was shivering.

"What happened?"

Thad nodded at the cup of tea sitting on the coffee table. "One of my special brews," he said. "I figured he'd need it if he was going to get some rest."

"I might need it too."

"No," my father said. "We need to keep clear heads. If Drake is a shifter being pursued by someone of his own kind, then he might be followed here. We have to be ready and waiting."

Pierce cracked his knuckles. "I'm always ready."

My family clicked on their active powers in a show of force. The hum of Pierce's electricity filled the air, and the temperature around Thad dropped a good twenty degrees. My father, who very rarely relied on his active power since his other magic was a force to be reckoned with on its own, gazed down at hands that had turned to big blocks of solid rock. Unlike Pierce and Thad, who projected their power, our father became his. He was the living embodiment of stone.

My family watched me, waiting for me to activate the power I'd yet to see. I concentrated with all my might, trying to force it to the surface. Nothing happened. "I'll be ready," I told them. "I promise."

"We know you will," my father replied. He patted my shoulder with a heavy earthen hand. It was like being tapped by a pile of bricks. "You get Drake upstairs to bed. Pierce and Thad, I want you to keep watch. I'm going to contact the Conclave."

While my family set off on their tasks, I scooped Drake off the couch and carried him in my arms. He instinctively held on to me, and I pressed my lips to his cheek to let him know that he was safe, that I would take care of him.

His deep sigh told me he understood.

CHAPTER 10

THAD SAT in the library, poring through our Grimoire. Wasn't he supposed to be walking the grounds like Pierce? I was about to chastise his apparent lack of concern for helping keep my boyfriend safe when the word stuck in my mind.

Boyfriend. Although we'd already accepted that, it meant even more right now.

Drake was the most special person in the world. Meeting him had triggered the inner warlock within me. I had more control over my spells, and my active power, whatever the fuck it was, had finally kicked in.

All of that had occurred because whatever magic sparked between Drake and me had jump-started my latent power. He was my own personal energy source. It was his strength and my feelings for him that made casting spells as easy as turning a faucet off and on.

And I would use that gift he'd given me to protect him. No matter what the cost.

"Is there a purpose to your lingering?" Thad asked. Whenever he was engrossed in his studies, his tone could cut through diamond.

"Just thinking," I replied.

"Can you do that elsewhere? You breathe like an inbred hillbilly when you're thinking. It's very distracting."

Instead of starting a fight, I inhaled three times before speaking. "What are you doing? I thought you were supposed to be—"

"Outside flexing my muscles?"

I nodded. "Well, yeah."

"That's not me," he said with a wave at the window. "That's Pierce's thing. I prefer to flex the strongest muscle I've got: my brain."

"So what have you come up with?"

Thad pulled his gaze from the yellowed pages of our leather-bound book of spells. "I'm not quite certain," he said. "I've gone over everything our family has ever learned about shifters, and it doesn't add up."

"What doesn't?"

He chewed on his lower lip. Whenever he did that, he was working through a particularly difficult problem. "Your deduction that Drake is a shifter."

"But I've seen what he can do. There's no way a regular human can do that."

"Not true. No matter how sluggish most humans are, some do possess great stamina and natural athletic ability. It could be possible that Drake's running and jumping is his means of exercise. How he lets off steam, not an indication that he is a were."

I was about to speak, but Thad stood up and paced. He scanned the floor in front of him and laced his hands behind his back. His posture indicated he was almost at a solution, and it was best not to interrupt. So I held my tongue and let him talk it out.

"If Drake was a shifter, how would he have gotten here unnoticed? The Conclave would have sensed his piercing of the spell that keeps their home safe."

"But Havenbridge has turned into a magical blind spot, remember?"

He nodded. "Correct. That could explain his unknown arrival. I've considered that. I've also taken into account that Drake's family could represent one of the few shifter families who chose this world over the relative safety of Aeaea. Only a handful of them stayed behind, and if they never utilized their abilities, they'd never blip on the Conclave's radar."

"And could stay hidden forever," I concluded.

"Correct." Thad walked faster. He resembled a caged lion ready to leap to freedom. The cogs of his mind were gearing toward some useful revelation. "In terms of circumstantial evidence, it can fit. But it's not right. It's like we're trying to force two pieces of a puzzle together that don't belong. We're missing something."

"Like what?"

"That's what I'm struggling to see." Thad paused, leaned against the fireplace mantle, and then gazed at me over his shoulder. "Are you sure you've told us everything?"

There was no judgment in his words. It was a sincere question without the venom-dipped tone he typically spoke with. It was a refreshing change. "I've told you everything I know and suspect about Drake. And about the attack tonight." And then I recalled Dad's reaction to the possibility of Drake being a shifter. He'd mentioned it could be something else, and that meant he had some idea what else we might be dealing with.

"What is it?" Thad crossed over to me. "You've thought of something else, haven't you?"

"Not about Drake," I said. "About Dad."

"Dad? What about him?"

"When you were inside taking care of Drake, he said that whatever might have attacked us tonight could be something else. Something that worried him. He didn't say what it was, but I could tell he really hoped it was shifters we were dealing with. The alternative wasn't something he wanted to think about."

Thad once again scanned the floor. He'd gone back into thinking mode. "He's keeping something from us. That's not good. He only does that if he's been ordered to or—"

"If he doesn't want us to worry."

He nodded. "Do you remember what you told him that made him think it might not be a corrupted shifter or a shadow weaver?"

"It was when I said whoever or whatever was in the house with us smelled like bleach and pancakes."

His gaze locked onto mine. "What did you say?" he asked, grasping my shoulders. A look of panic I'd never seen before twisted his usually stoic expression. "What did you say it smelled like?"

Thad's sudden change made me tremble. "Bleach and pancakes."

"Fuck!" he said and ran back to the Grimoire. He threw open the book and flipped through the pages.

"What does that mean?"

Thad didn't answer me. "Why am I just finding out about this now?"

"You were inside with Drake when I told Dad and Pierce."

"What smelled like bleach and pancakes was here?" he asked. His eyes had practically gone mad. "And Dad knew?" He turned from the book to study the air in front of him. He'd evidently been thrown for a loop. "He should have said something, but he obviously didn't want it to be true. He was trying to keep us safe."

Thad wasn't making sense, and his behavior was weirding me out. Thad was never flustered, but he could barely communicate. He regarded everything around him with suspicion, and anger smoldered on his normally pale cheeks.

He was giving me hysterics when what we needed were answers, so I crossed to Thad and shook him by the shoulders. "Will you get a grip already?"

He clutched my forearms and nodded. He took several deep breaths, and the crazed glimmer in his hazel eyes slowly subsided.

"Now tell me. What's got you so freaked out?"

"It's not a shifter," Thad said. "At least not in the traditional sense."

He returned to the Grimoire and found the page he'd been looking for. He turned the book around so I could see it.

The charcoal drawing on the parchment depicted a hideous monster with a long, forked tongue and a mouth filled with needle-sharp teeth. Its long black hair flew wildly about its menacing form and descended down most of its thin length. Freakishly long limbs, which ended in protracted black claws, extended from its body.

It was perhaps the vilest thing I'd ever seen in my life, but I had no clue what it was. The Latin word *Succo* had been written at the top of the page. "What the fuck is that?" I asked.

"A vampyre."

Fuck! Even I knew about them. They were the reason the *immortalitus* spell had been forbidden by the Conclave upon pain of death. It was the spell Bartram Kane had used to reanimate his son, Ebenezer, who was burned at the stake during the Salem witch trials. And Bartram's son *had* come back to life, but not as a warlock.

He'd returned as a vampyre, and not the sultry vampires most humans were obsessed with these days. They were monsters that had almost destroyed us all.

"DAD!" I screamed as we ran into his study, where he was supposed to be talking to the Conclave. The room was empty. Thad sprinted to the closed bathroom door and threw it open. He shook his head to let me know he wasn't in there. "Where is he?"

"I don't know," Thad replied. His face had drained of all its blood. "But this isn't good. We're no match for a vampyre."

He didn't have to tell me that. They were perverted, more powerful versions of all magical species combined. They represented the corruption of the Gate and how its gift could not only bless and create life but damn and destroy it as well.

Three hundred years ago, it had taken the combined magic of the Conclave to defeat and destroy the vampyren created as a result of Ebenezer Kane's mad rampage. That was why the *immortalitus* spell had been forbidden. The curse and the repercussions it carried tore through life itself.

Who had dared to cast that spell again? And how had it happened right underneath the Conclave's nose?

"We have to find Dad," I said. "And Pierce."

The two of us ran down the stairs and out the back door.

"Pierce!" Thad screamed.

"Dad!"

Only the silence of a deceptively peaceful night answered our calls.

"We need the other protector covens," Thad said. "It's here. It has to be."

"Fuck them!" I said. "We need the Conclave."

Thad motioned toward the house. "Make the calls. Get everyone here." He faced the darkness, which somehow grew thicker around us. "I'll give you as much time as I can."

"Thad, no."

"Just do it, Mason," he said. "We don't have time to argue."

He was right. If I wanted to save my family and Drake, I had to get to the house phone. My cell had died at the beach. I glanced one final time over my shoulder before I ran inside.

As I rocketed into the kitchen where the landline was, I heard a hiss outside, followed by a growl. Thad yelled a spell I didn't recognize. Instead of the vampyre hiss that had followed the attack at Aunt Millie's, Thad bellowed in pain.

I snapped around. I couldn't let my brother face that thing by himself. I had to do what I could to help him. Summoning reinforcements had to wait.

I ran back outside and immediately stopped in my tracks. Thad held his right arm, which was bleeding freely, to his chest. With the other he gestured at the vampyre, which had to be at least seven feet tall and was dressed in what looked like shimmering darkness. Ice crystallized around the creature, holding it fast from the waist down, and it howled in anger.

Its talons sliced away at its prison, and lines of black saliva dripped from its open mouth, from which dangled a six-inch tongue that waved around like a rattlesnake's tail. With each thundering strike of its nails against Thad's formation, the ground shook.

Thad wouldn't be able to hold it for long. I had to act before it freed itself and finished its midair leap toward my brother. I held my breath, concentrated, and then gestured at the crazy motherfucker before commanding it to stop with the word *desino*.

The vampyre's long, deadly limbs immediately ceased their incessant barrage against the ice, and its mouth hung open in a silent cry of fury. I'd done it. I'd stopped the damn thing.

I dashed over to Thad, who collapsed on the ground. His breathing was ragged. I fell onto the dirt, and he winced when I pulled him into my lap. "It's okay," I said. "It's not going anywhere."

"You're such a dumbass," he whispered through gritted teeth. "You were supposed to get help."

"Be nice. I just saved your life."

"Do you really think a simple holding spell is going to stop that thing longer than my ice?"

Well, yeah. But when I glanced back at the vampyre, its hands were inching forward once again. "I guess not."

Even in pain and freely bleeding, Thad couldn't stop his eyes from rolling. "Get help. Now. We don't have much time."

An exploding crackle filled the night, and a burst of white powder showered the area around us in flurries of falling ice. The vampyre was free, and it pulled its slithering tongue back into its mouth and snapped its rows of sharp teeth.

For once, Thad was wrong. We didn't have *any* time left.

"A SHADOW weaver," the vampyre whispered as its cold black eyes studied me. Was it talking about me? Obviously agitated, its tongue excitedly snaked in and out between its teeth. "How fortunate a find." It danced the tips of its long fingernails almost seductively across its chalk-white flesh.

"Desino!" I once again commanded with a gesture.

Instead of stopping as it had before, it continued forward, letting loose a series of booming, doom-laden laughs that made my ears hurt. "If I could so easily stop your family, what makes you think your weak baby-warlock spells hold any power over me?"

I clenched my jaw till the muscles popped. "What did you do with my father and Pierce?"

A menacing smile split its ashen lips. "Here. Let me show you." The dark clouds that bubbled like water around it gathered and popped. When they exploded, the rest of my family fell onto the grass at the monster's feet.

"Dad! Pierce!"

The vampyre fell into hysterics as it mocked me by repeating my cries. "Dad! Pierce!"

"Fuck you, you undead piece of shit!"

Its smile slid into a sneer. It opened its mouth and vomited a black tar-like substance straight at me. I grabbed Thad and rolled to the left, like I had with Drake a few weeks ago, and managed to evade the disgusting attack.

"You're fast. You've managed to escape me three times." It suddenly stood in front of me. It tore Thad from my arms and tossed him over to where the rest of my family lay crumpled. It wrapped its slender, bony hands around my throat and lifted me off the ground. "You won't do so again."

Three times? I ran through the close encounters in my head—the construction site, the boys' restroom, the woods, and Aunt Millie's house. I'd been attacked four times. Had it forgotten, or had one of those times been something else?

I wasn't going to get my answers at this moment. Right now I needed to get free.

Since the vampyre appeared thin and emaciated, I kicked it, hard. A physical attack might work where my magic had failed. But I might as well have been flailing against a petrified tree. Strong, steel-like muscles flexed beneath its deceptively fragile form. It responded to my attempt by laughing even more maniacally before gripping my neck with both hands. Its fingertips dug into my neck until warm lines of blood spilled forth.

That wasn't good.

Its eyes grew wide at the smell and sight of my blood. Its tongue coiled toward me, reaching for the crimson drops that it longed to sample.

A streak of lightning flashed between us, severing the tip of the vampyre's tongue. It howled, bringing its hand up to its wound and looking over its shoulder.

It was Pierce. He had awoken, and his grin told me he wasn't out for the count yet. The shadowy chains that restrained him couldn't prevent him from using his powers. "That's just fucking gross, you bloodsucker."

The vampyre bared its full set of teeth and dropped me to the ground, where I fell with a thud. It lunged for Pierce, but before it could touch him, my father rose from where he had been playing dead, turned his right fist into a chunk of solid rock, and slammed it into the vampyre's jaw.

It flew through the sliding glass door and crashed inside the house.

I scrambled over to my father. Blood dripped out of the corner of his mouth, and a monstrous purplish bruise sprouted on his right cheekbone. "Are you okay?"

"I will be," he muttered through clenched teeth, glancing over at Thad, who was licking his wounds. "When that fucking vamp is dead."

"Fuck yeah!" Pierce grumbled. He rose on unsteady feet and faced the shattered door, waiting for the vampyre to resume its attack. Streaks of electricity danced around his hands, arcing in lines of blue flame from him to the ground.

"We need to get out of here."

"I'm not running," Dad said. His tone told me he'd hear no more on the subject. The warlock temper reared its ugly head as he rose to stand next to Pierce. "That son of a bitch is going to pay for what it's done." Thad had been right. We were our own worst enemies.

"No," I said. I grabbed my dad by the shoulders and forced him to look at me. "That's not smart. We can't stand up against that thing without help."

"What the fuck do you think we are?" Pierce asked. He focused on the door.

"We're warlocks. Badass warlocks. But we're no match for a vampyre. You both know that."

Pierce took two steps toward the back door and snorted. "I sliced through that fucker's tongue with one blast," he said. "I'll fry his nuts with the next one."

"Will you two just listen for once?" It was Thad. He struggled to get up, but his legs didn't have the strength. "We can't beat it, but Mason can."

That got everyone's attention. I stared down at Thad, and even though he was in evident pain, a cautious smile lingered on his lips. It was one that told me he was proud of me and scared for me at the same time.

"You must've hit your head real hard," Pierce said. "Because you're not making a damn bit of sense."

I couldn't agree with Pierce more. How could someone like me, who had just started getting his spells right and who still had trouble summoning his active power, in any way defeat a vampyre?

"But I am," Thad answered. "I heard what the vampyre called you. You're a shadow weaver. That must be why it's after you. It sensed the power within you."

"Am I hearing this right?" my father asked as he switched his gaze between Thad and me. Like me, Pierce was only confused.

"Are you fucking kidding me?" I asked.

Thad shook his head. "That's why you couldn't see your shadow blast in the dark," Thad said.

And that was when chaos exploded once again in the backyard.

I NEVER saw what hit me.

One minute I was staring at Thad, trying to understand his words, and the next a cry of fury filled the night before all light vanished from my world.

Pain shot through every inch of my body as absolute darkness engulfed me. Its ebony tendrils wrapped around me, twisting my limbs. When they snaked across my chest, they squeezed. I struck whatever held me with my fists, pummeling it with all the strength I could muster. I even whispered a strengthening spell, but it made no difference.

No matter how hard I hit, the coiling arms didn't release. They tightened.

As I struggled for breath, more tentacles surrounded me. They slithered up my body until they lifted me off the ground and suspended me in midair.

From somewhere in the dark void behind me, the vampyre laughed.

But I wasn't alone. My father and brothers were with me.

"Stop him!" my father yelled as I heard the unmistakable *chunk* of his body turning entirely to stone. His feet thundered toward the vampyre as my brothers joined the fray.

Pierce howled, and his power sizzled. Its passage burned the air just as Thad's power chilled the night. A cacophony of magic erupted as my family fought to save me from whatever the vampyre had done.

Someone screamed, but I couldn't tell who it was. The familiar tone told me it might have been Pierce. He'd never cried out like that before. Nothing had ever hurt my brother, but this vampyre had.

It was killing him.

I twisted, trying to force myself free. I had to join them. Thad had said I was the only one who could stop the vampyre, but how? What did having darkness as my active power mean?

Thad obviously knew, and so did my father. But I'd never studied our books the way they had. My ignorance could mean death for us all.

"Dad, look out!" Thad cried out before his screams became muffled and faded away. My father bellowed, and the ground shook.

If I didn't do something fast, none of us were going to make it.

So I decided to do what Thad had so often accused me of not doing. Instead of going for the hammer, I turned inward to find the screwdriver that might do the trick.

I had to start with what I knew, which wasn't much.

Warlocks gained their powers from the five elements, just like witches, but our powers were a merging of two elements, not the manifestation of one. Each of the Proctors mastered either fire, earth, air, water, or spirit. It became their guiding force, their connection to the white magic energy that flowed from the Gate.

Warlocks harnessed the chaotic black magic. Our powers didn't give us mastery over one pure element. We couldn't directly influence one, but our ability to manipulate the chaotic forces of the Gate allowed us to bind two elements together and create a hybrid that was just as powerful.

Pierce and Thad's abilities came from the union of air and water. It manifested in both of them differently, as electricity and cold. If my brothers tapped into air and water, and my father's stone armor was a result of fire and earth, then what elements created darkness?

My father's cry of pain pierced my thoughts.

"You will die, Oliver Blackmoor," the vampyre said. It huffed and panted. My dad had obviously given the damn thing a run for its money. "But not before I force you to witness me feeding off your children. You'll watch as I rip their necks open and make their life's energy mine."

"Stay away from them," my father choked. "Take me."

The bastard laughed. "I will, but first I want to sample your oldest boy."

"Mason, where are you?" A groggy, familiar voice called from somewhere in the darkness.

I was hearing things. It couldn't be Drake. The potion Thad had given him to drink should have knocked him out until tomorrow afternoon.

"What's goin' on out there?" Drake asked again.

"Run!" my father screamed. "Get out of here."

I tensed. He had to listen. He couldn't come outside.

"Mr. Blackmoor?"

"Well, hello there," the vampyre said with a fiendish giggle.

"What the fuck are you?"

A swoosh of air followed a cry of terror from Drake. "You're about to find out. Just like your aunt Millie."

No!

I found the screwdriver I'd been searching for. It didn't matter right now what elements created darkness. If I could manipulate it, then darkness, any darkness, was at my command. Like the prison that held me.

Breaking free didn't require a hammer.

I reached out to the dark tentacles around me and commanded they release me. They twitched and fought against the order, refusing to obey. I dug my fingers into the rubbery flesh, clawing with a renewed sense of strength I'd never before possessed, and said, "Release me. Right. The fuck. Now."

The limbs relaxed, and I fell, dropping out of a cloud of darkness that hung about five feet from the ground. It resembled one of the billowy folds that bubbled around the vampyre, who now had Drake in its grasp.

Drake's blue eyes grew wider in fear. Not only did he have a monster about ready to devour him, but he'd just witnessed his boyfriend emerge from a floating cloud of black. "Mason?" His words were cut short as the vampyre wrapped one hand completely around his neck.

"Do you want him, Shadow Weaver?" it asked as it wiggled Drake from side to side.

I nodded. "And if you give him to me, I'll let you live."

It exploded with laughter. Its cackles thundered in the distance. "Far too much bravado from a boy with no bite." It snapped its jaws together, inches from Drake's neck.

"Oh, I bite," I said with a smirk. "Just not you." I pointed at the floating blackness above me and then gestured at the vampyre.

Its dead black eyes grew wide as the prison it had tried to kill me with sped straight back at it.

"*Illo dimitti*," I whispered with a quick flick of my wrist. In response to my release spell, Drake tumbled out of the vampyre's grasp just as the black cloud slammed into it.

It screamed and howled as the black cloud completely engulfed its form. It tried to scratch its way out, using its claws and powerful muscles to jettison itself from the crushing force that drew it in. "I'll kill you!" it screeched at me. The black holes that were its eyes blazed with fire as it fought a losing battle for its freedom.

"Go to hell," I muttered as the black cloud closed in on itself before disappearing altogether and taking the vampyre with it.

I surveyed the disaster around me. My brothers and father were badly bleeding and unconscious. It terrified me to see them like that, but what scared me the most was the look of fear that had darkened Drake's expression as he looked at me.

CHAPTER 11

PIERCE LAY on the couch, moaning like a little bitch, even though Thad had brewed a potion that took the edge off most of the pain we'd suffered fighting the vampyre. My father paced the hall, on the phone with Mr. Proctor. He'd just spoken to Mr. Stonewall, and soon all the protector covens would arrive. Then we could discuss events in person.

But I wasn't focused on any of that. I was worried about Drake.

He hadn't said one word to me since I'd defeated the vampyre. I'd gone over to help him up, but he wouldn't let me touch him. He brushed me off and walked away. He'd evidently needed space to process everything that had happened, from his aunt Millie to the vampyre he'd seen.

He sat in the farthest chair away from us, and I realized I'd been wrong this whole time. Drake wasn't a shifter at all, and now the family had to deal with the fact that for the first time in centuries, a human had become aware of our species's presence.

"They're on their way," my father said, shutting off his phone as he reentered the room.

My father's comment drew Drake's scrutiny. He sat up rigidly in his chair. Anger had replaced his earlier fear.

"Good," Thad replied. "We're going to need all the reinforcements we can muster."

"Fucking A!" Pierce moaned. "I feel like I've been run over by a semi after getting butt-fucked in a gang bang."

"Do you think we're still in danger?" Even though I asked my father the question, I focused on Drake. "I thought I killed it."

Thad shook his head. "I doubt it," he said. Drake balled his fists in response. "Your inexperience with your new power most likely trapped it long enough to save us. There's really only one way to kill a—"

"Are you sure?" I asked, cutting off the last part of Thad's question. Drake wasn't ready to hear it was a vampyre he'd seen. He'd dealt with enough already.

"Thad's right," my father said. "You saved our asses, but you didn't kill it."

Drake clutched the arms of the chair. He was clearly almost ready to voice the emotions that roared within.

"I still can't believe you're a shadow weaver," Thad commented. He sat in front of the open Grimoire. I couldn't believe it either. Having the power of darkness was pretty fucking awesome, but I couldn't help but remember what we'd talked about the other day. The power of darkness had corrupted every single warlock who'd previously wielded it.

"Am I going to go crazy like Bartram Kane?" My question caused silence to descend upon the room. Thad stared up from the Grimoire. He opened his mouth to speak but couldn't find the right words. My father couldn't even look at me. He stared at our family portrait, the one we sat for a year before my mother's diagnosis.

It was Pierce who broke the silence. "Who fucking cares?" he asked. "That's one badass power you've got, and it's on our side. That's the kind of muscle we need right now."

"Just what the fuck are all y'all?" Drake yelled as he stood. A tempest swept across his usually serene blue eyes.

Pierce glanced at Drake and regarded him as if he'd gone crazy. "What the fuck's the matter with you?" he asked. "Are shifters usually this touchy?"

"I don't even know what the hell that means," Drake said through pursed lips. "What the fuck *are* you?" This time he glowered at me.

Before I could answer, Pierce, as clueless as ever, did it for me. "We're warlocks. Duh!"

Drake switched his attention to Pierce, who once again rested his arm over his head and moaned. He clearly had no clue what he'd just done, but my father and Thad did.

"You're not a shifter, are you?" Thad asked.

Pierce uncovered his eyes and sat up. "What?" He regarded me with surprise. "I thought you said."

"I was wrong" was all I replied.

"Warlocks?" Drake whispered. He studied all of us, as if waiting for another attack.

"Take it easy, son," my father said. His voice had softened. He'd done the same thing when I was a kid, and I'd always found it soothing. It didn't have the same effect on Drake.

"Are you kiddin' me?" he asked. His Southern drawl was practically out of control. Whenever he was overly emotional, his twang made it difficult to understand him. "You're tellin' me that you're a bunch o' devil worshippers. Is that what that thing out there was? The devil?" He held his fingers up in the sign of the cross.

"Are you serious?" Pierce asked. "We just saved your ass from that vampyre."

"A what?" Drake asked.

Thad smacked Pierce across the head, which elicited a string of curse words from his older brother.

"Did you say vampire?"

I shook my head. "Vampyre."

"What the fuck's the difference?"

"A vampire is a creature of myth, found only in movies and books," Thad explained. "A vampyre is not, as you have recently experienced."

"Is this really happenin'?" Drake asked. He inspected the room, checking everything and everyone for signs this was a dream. He placed his hand against the wall and rubbed it. He then pinched his arm and slapped his face.

"You're not asleep," I told him as I drew closer. I spoke to him in the same whispers we'd used on the beach, when we'd been in each other's arms and delighting in our kiss. I had to get him to remember that I was still that person. That though his world might be spinning out of control right now, what he felt for me and what I felt for him had not changed. "This is real, and I know it's a lot to take in, especially considering everything else you have to deal with. But I'm here for you, and I would never hurt you."

Water pooled in the corners of his eyes. He evidently wanted to believe me. That was a start. "A warlock?" His voice trembled. "For real?"

"For real."

"I don't know what to do with this, Mason," Drake said when I stood in front of him. I placed my hands on his shoulders and rubbed them, trying to transfer some comfort into his confused and questioning soul.

"Neither do we," I said. "This is a first for us too. We've never dealt with anything quite like this before. That's why we've called the others."

He snapped his attention to the front door. "There's more of you?"

"Yes," my father said. "We are but one warlock family in the world."

That revelation practically made Drake's head spin. "And they're comin' here? Right now?"

I peered over my shoulder at my father, who glanced between Thad and Pierce. They nodded to each other and then to me. There was no point stopping now, but we would have to deal with the consequences later.

"Not quite," I replied. I grabbed his hands and held them in mine.

"Then who's headin' over here?"

"Two other magical families like us. But they aren't warlocks. They're witches and wizards."

Drake fell back into the chair behind him. I knelt in front of him, hoping my smile and the affection in my eyes would quell the rising tide of panic that surged within. I stroked his thigh while cupping his chin. "Don't freak out on me, Drake. I don't know what I'd do if you did."

Drake took a deep breath before looking around. He wouldn't stop fidgeting. "I don't know what to do with all this," he repeated once he'd looked again at me.

"Then we'll figure it out," I said. "Together."

My FATHER and brothers left the living room to give us some privacy. Drake had had a whole shitload of information heaped upon him, and we needed some time alone to sort through everything before the Stonewalls and the Proctors arrived.

"Talk to me," I said.

But he didn't respond. He paced the room, surveying every object, every picture. He studied our family portrait, his blond eyebrows arching as if he realized something, but instead of speaking, he moved on. He gnawed on his lower lip and resumed doing laps around the room.

"You can ask me anything. I promise to answer truthfully."

"Because you've been so truthful up until now?"

That hurt. "It's not like I could tell you what I was. We have laws, you know?"

"No," he said with a shake of his head. "I don't."

I told him about the rules that prevented us from revealing our true identities and why those laws were in place. We'd been hunted almost to extinction during the witch trials, and we were still hunted to this day. Our laws kept us safe. As long as we followed them, those who still wished to exterminate us wouldn't be able to find us.

"So you're sayin' there are modern-day witch hunters out there?"

I nodded.

"And they know about the existence of your kind and haven't told anyone?"

"Who would believe them?"

Drake chuckled, but it wasn't a sound that expressed joy. "I can't argue with that." He paused. He looked me up and down as if passing judgment.

"What?"

"If you're a warlock, does that mean you're evil?"

I winced. "What?"

"Well, aren't warlocks evil? Don't witches worship the devil? Isn't that why you're hunted?"

I took several deep breaths. I hated the stereotypes perpetuated by pop culture. "First of all, we were hunted because humans feared us. Their ignorance fed that fear. Nothing else. They don't like what we represent. They think we're evil because we can do things their gods say we shouldn't be able to do, but no, we're not evil, and witches don't worship the devil. We evolved from humans, the same way humans evolved from primates. Does that make you evil? Of course not. Are there bad warlocks among us? Sure, just as there are evil humans. Don't mistake types of magic for the people we are."

This wasn't going well. The force of my words added further distance between us, and whatever walls had previously fallen had gone right back up. Drake was rebuilding those barriers brick by brick, and the longer I stood there, the harder it was going to be to get around them again.

I crossed the room toward him, and he regarded me with suspicion. "I'm not going to hurt you," I said, drawing closer. "I could never do that. It's just, well, I know you've learned a lot of shit you probably never wanted to know about, but I'm still me. The boy you've been drawn to. The one who held you in his arms on the beach."

"That seems like a lifetime ago," he whispered. His anger stepped back for an instant as the boy I'd kissed, the one who'd pleaded with me to lie naked on top of him, came forward.

"I know it does," I said, taking his hands in mine. He tensed upon contact, but I wasn't going to give up. We'd given ourselves to each other, and that was a gift that wasn't so easily returned. "A lot of fucked-up shit has happened since then, but it doesn't change what I feel for you. From the moment I saw you, I knew you were special. I also knew you were a cocky motherfucker." A sly smile spread across his lips as the bricks he'd erected started to crumble. "But that's just who you are. That's what makes you Drake Carpenter, the boy I tried not to like but ended up falling in love with."

He inhaled sharply. "What did you say?"

I drew him into my arms and rested my forehead against his. "You heard me."

"Say it again."

"That you're a cocky motherfucker?"

He playfully swatted my chest. "You're such an asshole."

"Maybe," I said with a nod. "But I'm an asshole who loves you."

The smile that stretched across his lips might as well have been a wrecking ball, because it smashed through the barrier that had briefly come between us. "And I'm a cocky motherfucker who loves you too," he replied before pressing his lips against mine.

And when we kissed, the final remnants of Drake's fear and apprehension melted away.

We were going to be okay, and that was what I truly believed until the house went dark.

"IT'S BACK," my father said as he and my brothers charged into the dark room.

Drake held me tight, but it wasn't out of fear. Well, not completely. He trembled against me, so he was scared. Hell, I was too. But he wasn't holding me because he was terrified. His embrace communicated his love for me, his desire to protect me. It also told me we were in this together.

If a vampyre hadn't been about to attack us, I'd have been ripping off his clothes.

Thad muttered an illumination spell, and a dozen balls of light floated in the air above us. Pierce sneered, and streaks of blue electricity emanated from his clenched fists. A low rumble preceded my father encasing himself entirely in stone.

"Wow," Drake muttered as he saw my family prepare for battle. "That's fuckin' awesome."

Thad smirked as he gestured in a wide circle. Ice immediately started forming along the walls, covering up the windows and the entranceway to the room in solid blocks. "That'll slow the bastard down some."

My father nodded, his handsome face now only solid stone. "And alert us from where he's going to attack." As usual when he was in his rock form, his voice was low and gravelly.

"Why not just attack him?" Drake asked. "There's four of you and one of him."

"If only it was that easy," Thad answered. "A vampyre is pure power, capable of tearing through an entire coven all by itself. Our best chance right now is to hold it off until the rest of the protector covens get here. Then we might have a fighting chance."

"You have no chance against me," the vampyre said. Its voice didn't emanate from outside Thad's icy formation. It was in here with us, and we swept the room, searching for where it was hidden. I stepped in front of Drake, making sure that wherever I looked, he remained behind me, but Drake, stubborn as usual, stepped out from behind me and stood at my side.

"We're in this together, remember?"

I was about to remind him he was human and had no powers to fight off an attack—but his steely gaze told me he'd hear none of that. There was only one acceptable answer. "I do."

The vampyre laughed. "How touching! The human thinks it stands a chance against me. Does it not realize I could rip it in two before it even saw me coming?"

Its threat sparked my anger. I used it to fuel my magic. I still had no clue how to call forth my active power the way my family did, but I felt it bubbling to the surface the same way it had when the vampyre had attacked Drake at Aunt Millie's. "If you lay one pasty finger on him, I'll kill you."

The vampyre's cocky laughter echoed off the ice around us, making it sound as if a dozen vampyren surrounded us. "You can't kill me. You already tried. And failed. There's nothing you or anyone can do to stop me and my mission."

"And what mission is that?" I asked as my father and brothers continued to search the room. Perhaps if I kept it distracted, one of them would either find where it lurked or come up with a plan to stop this motherfucker.

"*Tsk-tsk,*" it said, as if I were a silly child. "I'm not about to give away all our secrets."

Our? Was there more than one vampyre or did this thing have an accomplice?

"But I will tell you this," it said. "Mostly because it involves you."

Drake tensed. I gripped his hand, hoping my touch gave him the comfort his gave me. "Me? What about me?"

"Nothing is going to change what is coming. It's inevitable, but I can offer you this. One of the things I was sent to retrieve was you, Shadow Weaver, and if you come with me, your family and your human will be spared. For now."

My brothers and my father stared at me, shaking their heads. They realized I was considering the offer. I loved them and Drake. If I could buy them a few more hours or days, they might be able to find a way to stop the vampyre and whatever schemes it had concocted with its friends.

"I don't think so," Drake answered for me. He gripped my face in his hands and forced my attention away from the threat that surrounded us. "There's no way I'm lettin' you sacrifice yourself."

"It might be the only way."

"Mason, no," he said. He wrapped his arms around my neck and held me tight. "There's always another way."

"He's right," my father said. Pierce and Thad nodded in agreement. "We stand together. Like always."

What else could I say? My family and my boyfriend had my back. What more did I need? I looked about the room. "Go fuck yourself."

An angry wail filled the room as the vampyre leaped out of the shadow cast across the wooden floor. Its sudden appearance startled all of us. We'd been prepared for it to be in the room, but none of us expected it to jump out of a shadow as if it were an open window. Just how powerful was this vampyre?

Pierce was the first to respond. He unleashed a powerful lightning bolt that struck the vampyre in the chest. Thunder reverberated in the room as it flew back into Thad's ice wall. Thad seized the opportunity. He gestured toward his creation, and the ice started to crystallize around the vampyre. It thrashed and cursed as the ice formed around its limbs. My father stomped over to where it was held fast. His massive, rocky fists pummeled the monster's stomach.

Even though I wasn't the most educated among us in terms of vampyren, even I knew their efforts were in vain. They were only pissing it off.

Black spittle flew from its lips as my father continued his assault and Pierce unleashed another barrage of electricity. It strained against Thad's formation. Its superhuman strength caused the ice to crack, and no matter how quickly Thad reformed the prison, he wasn't going to maintain it for long.

Only a stake through the vampyre's heart would end this.

"We've got to do somethin'," Drake said.

"I will." I turned to the wooden coffee table that sat in the middle of the room. It was the only piece of furniture sturdy enough to have what we needed. "Pierce."

My brother glanced at me and then at where I pointed. He nodded in understanding and fired a volley of electricity at it. I shielded Drake with my body as my brother's assault caused the coffee table to explode into a shower of splintered wood.

"No!" the vampyre screamed. It vomited a stream of black tar at Pierce, which coated him from head to toe. He gasped and clawed at the substance as it clogged his nose and throat. If we didn't get it off him, he was going to die.

"I'll help Pierce," Drake said as he ran to my brother's side. "You do what you need to do."

I nodded as Drake began wiping the oily substance from Pierce's breathing passages. I searched the splintered mess for a piece big and sturdy enough to kill that fucker.

A huge explosion tore through the room. One glance over my shoulder revealed the vampyre had freed itself and was leaping through the air at me. My father grabbed its foot and slammed it into the ground.

When it landed, boiling black shadows erupted around its form. It was the same darkness it had tried to kill me with earlier. Was the vampyre also a shadow weaver? The black clouds quickly engulfed my father and Thad. They screamed in pain as the tentacled creatures that lived within squeezed the life out of them as they had tried to do to me.

I returned to the broken remains of the coffee table. There was nothing in the mess that would help.

"Watch out!"

Drake's warning came at just the right time. I managed to move out of the way just as the vampyre crashed down upon where I'd previously stood. It hissed and snarled as it lunged at me again, but this time I was ready.

The shadows around us bent to my command. They lifted from where they were cast and solidified after wrapping around the vampyre. Some anchored it to the floor, while others coiled around its neck. It pulled against the shadowy restraint.

I'd stopped it, but not for long. It would be free soon, and I had to get Drake out of here. I pointed my hands to the ice wall that covered the exit to the room, and a stream of black energy flew out of me. It collided with the barrier, causing it to explode in a shower of ice. "Get out of here!" I told Drake. He'd managed to remove the black tar from Pierce, who'd passed out from lack of oxygen.

"I'm not leavin' you," he said.

The vampyre snapped free of the shadow ropes and leaped upon me. We fell to the floor in a heap. It hissed, and its claws sliced through my skin. "Please, Drake," I said as its tongue darted through its sharp teeth at me. I didn't have much time left, but I had enough to keep it distracted while he escaped.

Drake stopped arguing. He realized we'd lost, so why was he smirking? He sprinted at top speed out the exit I'd made. When he was gone, I sighed in relief.

"I'll hunt him down," the vampyre said. Its tongue lapped at my face before moving to my neck. It couldn't wait to tear me open and drink. "But first, you die."

"*Stamató.*"

The vampyre's eyes grew wide at the sound of the voice emanating from the shadows around us.

"But he refused," it told the darkness.

A silhouette lifted off the wall and formed a giant pumpkin head similar to the one that had attacked Elliot and me at school. So there were two—a vampyre *and* a shadow weaver. Its hollow eyes regarded me before settling its gaze on the vampyre. *"Ton se ména férei."*

The vampyre snarled at the command but eased his stranglehold around my throat. "Fine. I'll bring him to you."

The pumpkin head didn't say another word. Its form flattened against the wall and merged with the other shadows.

"Today's your lucky day," it hissed.

"Yeah, well, it's not yours."

The vampyre spun around. Drake jammed a sharp wooden slat from the garden fence in the backyard into the vampyre's chest.

Its scream pierced through the house, and it took one step toward Drake before falling on its knees. It gripped the wood protruding from its chest. Black blood poured from its wound and bubbled out of its mouth. It stared in disbelief at my boyfriend. It couldn't believe that a human, not a warlock, had been the one to defeat it.

Its body burst into flame. When the fire had subsided, all that remained was a pile of ashes.

"You killed it?"

He nodded and knelt beside me. "It was either him or you."

I struggled to rise, but Drake pushed me back down. He sat on the floor and gathered me into his arms. "How did you know what to do?"

"Duh. It's a vampyre," he said. "Everyone knows a stake to their heart will take them out."

"I wish you hadn't done that," I said. Now that Drake had killed the vampyre, he'd officially made himself a part of this conflict and an enemy of the shadow weaver, who had obviously been the vampyre's master.

What did it want? But more importantly, where the hell did the shadow weaver go?

"What was I supposed to do?" Drake's question pulled me out of my thoughts. He ran his fingers through my hair and smiled at me. "Let you die? You've saved my life three times. This was the least I could do."

Except now he was in more danger than before. "I don't want anything to happen to you. I love you."

"I'm glad," he said before pressing his lips to mine. "Because I don't kill vampyres for just anyone. Only for the boy I love."

As Drake held me tight, I surveyed the disaster. Pierce lay passed out with black gook all over him, and my father and Thad had fallen out of the black clouds that had disappeared when Drake killed the vampyre.

We were safe for now, but the shadows were everywhere.

CHAPTER 12

I SAT behind Drake on the leather sectional, my arms wrapped around his waist as the Stonewalls and the Proctors, minus Mr. Proctor, who was no doubt still working the crime scene at Aunt Millie's, made their way into our living room. They eyed the shattered coffee table, the melting ice, our tattered clothes, and our bruised and bloodied bodies.

"What happened here?" Mrs. Stonewall asked.

"A vampyre," my father replied.

They tensed and surveyed the room, looking for the next attack.

"Don't worry," I said. "It's dead."

They all visibly relaxed, but their gazes settled on Drake.

When he'd seen Miranda, Elliot, and Edith—other kids from our school—enter, his grip on my arms had relaxed a tiny bit, but now that everyone kept staring at us, the tension had returned. I ran my hand up and down his back in comfort.

He didn't have anything to fear. I was here, and he got the message. He exhaled and leaned against me, propping his head on my shoulder.

"Who is this?" Mr. Stonewall asked. As was usual, his tone was flat. Wizards didn't beat around the bush. They got straight to the point.

"Lawrence, this is Drake Carpenter," my father answered with a reassuring smile at Drake. "He's the one who killed the vampyre."

They gaped, almost as if their actions were synchronized. If this hadn't been such a serious situation, I'd have been laughing.

"How is he even involved in this?" It was Mrs. Stonewall's turn to ask a question, in an even tone that mimicked her husband's.

"His aunt Millie was—" My father stopped, searching for a gentler word than the one that dangled from his tongue.

"Killed," Mrs. Stonewall answered.

My father sighed as the eyes of everyone once again settled upon Drake. "Yes, Rachel. That would be correct."

Everyone regarded Drake with sad skepticism. The only ones with different expressions were the Proctor kids. The overly sympathetic Charlotte had distrust in her eyes, while Adam, who typically only scowled at Drake, nodded. He obviously no longer had problems with seeing the two of us together. Miranda's usual resting bitch face had relaxed into one of sympathy and regret. What the hell was going on with that family?

Their mother Camille, however, remained true to her ways. She was always a mother first and a powerful witch second. "I'm so sorry, dear." She crossed to where we sat and plopped down next to us. A comforting, maternal smile parted her lips as she rubbed Drake's back. "I can't imagine what you've been through tonight."

"It's been awful, ma'am," Drake replied.

"Where's Charles?" my father asked.

"He's on his way," she said. "He was still at the station working the case."

Drake pulled out of our embrace and scooted closer to Mrs. Proctor. "Wait a minute. Detective Proctor is your husband?"

When she nodded, he turned to me. "That detective is a warlock too?"

Pierce and Adam snorted in unison. They glared at each other before Mrs. Proctor answered. "No, honey. My husband is a witch. Just like my children and me." She motioned to the Stonewalls, who stood behind the couch in an orderly line from Mr. Stonewall all the way down to the youngest pair of twins. "And the Stonewalls are wizards."

"I'm sorry," Drake said. "I didn't mean to offend. I'm new to all this."

"Well, I am deeply offended," Mr. Stonewall said. "Why we are revealing ourselves to this human?"

"We didn't," my father said. "It was the vampyre. It attacked him and us."

"So that means we spill generations of secrets to him?" Mrs. Stonewall asked. "That's unacceptable. Just spell him and get this over with."

Wait, what?

Drake glanced at me and then at everyone else. Even though Mrs. Proctor still smiled at him, she nodded in agreement with Mrs. Stonewall. "It's the only way."

"We're not spelling him, and that's final." I stood and pulled Drake up after me. There was no way I was letting anyone use magic to alter Drake's memories. Even the most powerful among us couldn't control the consequences of such actions.

"That's not your decision," Mr. Stonewall said. "You're not head of this family."

"Neither are you," my father replied.

As usual, the bitter rivalry among our families erupted.

The Stonewalls berated my father for delaying what they logically believed the Conclave would order anyway. Camille took a gentler but no less firm approach. She mentioned only the tragic history of our species the last time humans had knowledge of our existence. What we had to do was for the good of our race and our children.

I wasn't going to listen to it anymore.

"That's enough!" Mrs. Proctor and Mr. and Mrs. Stonewall glared at me. Their children stood in the background, glancing back and forth from me to their parents. "No one is spelling the boy I love. You got that?"

"What the hell does that even mean?" Drake asked.

"They want to erase your memories," I told him. "Make you forget everything you've learned."

He shook in anger. "Who the fuck do you think you are? You can't make a decision like that for me. It's my life. My memories. Don't I have some say?"

"Ordinarily, yes," Mrs. Stonewall answered. "But according to our laws, no. The only surefire way to protect our secret is to wipe your mind clean."

What she wasn't sharing was the potential loss of all Drake was and could be. To her, it was obviously a small price to pay to protect our species.

"Yeah, well, I'm not going to let it happen. The only reason my family isn't dead right now is because of him. If the vampyre had killed us, it'd have come after each and every one of you, and you know it. We'd all be dead."

"Nonsense," Mr. Stonewall said. "Your thinking is illogical."

"Bite me!"

Mrs. Proctor stood. She clasped her hands in front of her and offered us a tense smile. Though she appeared small and nonthreatening, her power could have brought this entire house down around our ears. "Mason, I understand that you have an emotional attachment to this boy, but that doesn't change the fact that he is aware of our existence. That will not be allowed. We know this. Your family knows this. You know this. We can stand here and debate until the end of time, but the conclusion will remain the same. The Conclave will order us to spell him."

Of course she was right. I'd known that from the moment I realized Drake wasn't a shifter. And now that he'd killed the vampyre, taking away his memories might be a way to keep him safe.

"Mason?" Drake asked. He'd clearly seen the shift in my thinking.

I held his hands and forced him to look only at me. "They're right," I said. He took one step back and glared at me as if I was a stranger. "The Conclave won't let you walk around with what you know, and now that you've killed the vampyre, well, you're on the shadow weaver's shit list. You aren't safe."

"I can take care of myself. You know that."

I nodded and ran my fingers through his hair before hooking his chin with my thumb and forefinger. I loved him so much, and sometimes when you loved someone, you had to do what was best for them whether you liked it or not. "I do, but I don't want you to live life looking over your shoulder. You deserve to be free from all this."

Drake clutched at my shoulders, his lower lip trembling. "No, don't let them do this," he pleaded. "I won't remember you. Or us." He kissed my lips while he moved his hand from my shoulders to my face. He gently caressed me before locking eyes. "I don't want to forget you."

I didn't want that either. We had a chance at creating something great together, but we'd never be given that opportunity. "I'll never forget you, Drake," I said before stepping out of his embrace. "You'll live forever in my heart."

"Mason!" he said. "This isn't your decision."

I turned to my father and brothers and nodded. Profound sadness cast their eyes downward. Their hearts were breaking for me.

"*Per singulos dies...*" Mrs. Proctor chanted the spell that would make him forget.

Drake held on to me, sobbing. Tears spilled down my cheeks as well. This was the first time I remembered crying since my mother's death.

"*...Defluxerant...*"

"I love you, Mason," he sobbed. "Even though I'm so pissed off at you right now."

I swallowed hard, trying my damnedest to speak around the sobs lodged in my throat. "I know you are, but I'd rather have you angry with me than the alternative, because I love you too, Drake." I stared deeply into the cornflower-blue eyes that had spelled me since I first looked into them. They were so beautiful and pure. I'd give anything to look into them for the rest of my life.

"...*Et quia memoriam nostri omnes evanescent...*"

His eyes grew heavy, and he had trouble keeping them open. "What's happenin'? I feel funny."

Through the tears and snot that streaked my face, and despite the heart that broke in my chest, I smiled. He might not remember me when he woke up, but I didn't want him to go to sleep without seeing me grin at him one more time. "Nothing bad, I promise. When you wake up, all will be good."

"...*Sic erit et generationi.*"

When Mrs. Proctor finished the spell, I waited for Drake to go limp and pass out. But he didn't. His eyes snapped open, and he looked around at everyone, who stared at him with open mouths.

"What happened?" he asked.

"How is this possible?" Mrs. Proctor asked. She scanned the shocked faces around her.

"I don't know," my father answered. "This has never happened before."

"What's never happened before?" Drake asked.

I couldn't stop the smile that cracked across my face. "It didn't work," I told him. "The spell didn't work."

"Let me try it," Mr. Stonewall said. "We all should."

"No," I protested. I stood in front of Drake, a scowl on my lips. They'd tried to make him forget, but for some reason, his memories refused to go. I had no clue why, but I wasn't about to let them continue to use their magic on him. There was no telling what repeated failed spells could do to a human. "You could kill him, and you know it. And killing a human who is not actively trying to harm us is another law we're honor bound not to break."

That shut them all up. That rule was as sacred as keeping our existence a secret and not casting the *immortalitus* spell.

"He's right," my father said. He stepped between us and the other covens, and my brothers joined him. "Drake Carpenter has proven himself a friend to our species. We have followed the rules, and for whatever reason, his memory remains. I therefore place him under the protection of the Blackmoor coven."

What had my father just done? That statement basically made Drake an honorary member of our family. Any move made against him would be considered an attack against our coven.

Everyone immediately understood. If they persisted, they'd ignite a war among our covens that would not be in the best interest of our species.

"Fine," Mr. Stonewall said. Even though he was obviously pissed, his voice never rose. "But you have also officially made him your problem. If anything bad happens because of this, it will be your coven that pays the price."

"I'm well aware of that," Dad responded. "And I embrace that as openly as I do my sons."

I'd never wanted to hug my father so hard in my life.

"It's been a long night, and there's nothing more that can be done today. We can discuss everything tomorrow," my father said as he gestured to the front door. "So if you wouldn't mind...."

Before he could finish his thought, the Stonewalls and the Proctors turned and filed out of the house. When they closed the door behind them, we all let out a collective sigh.

"What the hell just happened?" Drake asked.

My father shook his head. "I'm unsure, but it's a mystery we'll solve another day."

"Damn straight!" Pierce said. "We just kicked vampyre ass and threw those fuckers out of our house. I just *love* being a warlock."

Thad shook his head and patted Pierce on the back. "I'll investigate all this tomorrow. There's got to be a reason why the spell didn't work. But right now, I need sleep."

"Amen," my father said as he and my brothers turned to leave the room. But before he did, he glanced back over his shoulder. "And Drake?"

"Sir?"

"Welcome to the family."

Drake smiled at my father, but when he looked at me, the smile grew even bigger. He settled into my arms and rested his head against my chest. My father was right. Drake was home, and wherever he was, I was home too.

A WEEK later, after we'd buried Aunt Millie, we invited all her friends to our house to celebrate her life. Blackmoor Manor was packed with people who couldn't say enough good things to Drake about her. They shared stories about his aunt during her youth and how enterprising she had been with her business.

It was a beautiful way to honor the life of a strong, independent woman who had been taken from us much too soon.

The only uninvited guest was Charles Proctor. Even though we knew what had ultimately been responsible for the string of deaths in town, the investigation continued. The case would be unsolved in the eyes of humans, but for us it was closed.

What we still didn't know was what the vampyre had been after at Aunt Millie's, and Detective Proctor had figured it out. Something had been taken from her house on the night of her murder. Drake had given the police an inventory of most of his aunt's prized possessions, and the one item that was missing was the necklace with the green pendant given to her by Gerald Wa.

"That's bizarre," my father said. "Wizards don't normally purchase such extravagant gifts."

"Perhaps it was a magical charm of protection," Thad said.

"It could have been," Detective Proctor admitted. "That could be why the vampyre took it. It might have believed it would somehow give it added protection from us."

It made sense, but I didn't buy it. If it was a protective charm, it hadn't exactly worked for Aunt Millie or the vampyre. "But it didn't, did it?"

Everyone had to agree.

"I can research charms," Thad said. "See if I can find something in our Grimoire that might help us make heads or tails of this. I'm also hoping my research will turn up some clues as to why the shadow weaver is after Mason in the first place."

"Good idea," Detective Proctor said. "I'll also have Lawrence go through his Magus. Since Gerald was a wizard, there might be something in his book."

After that, he left us to finish celebrating Aunt Millie's life. Although I was supposed to tell Drake what I'd learned, now was not the time. He needed to stay focused on what was truly important, and right now that was only Aunt Millie's life, not anything having to deal with her death.

I made my way through the crowd, talking to people who praised my family for giving Drake a place to live. It was nothing, I told each and every one. As far as I was concerned, Drake Carpenter would live with me for the rest of our lives.

WHEN THE last guest left the house, it was almost ten. My father and brothers told us to go to bed. They would take care of cleanup. I didn't argue. We headed upstairs to the bedroom we'd been sharing ever since the first night Drake moved in.

We still hadn't had sex. Everything was still too new, too raw. But we did enjoy sleeping next to each other. We cuddled and held each other tight, and sleeping with Drake in my arms was far more magical to me than any spell I might whip up.

Drake sat on the edge of the bed and kicked his shoes off with a sigh.

"What's wrong?"

He gave me a small grin before saying, "I'm just sad. I miss her somethin' awful."

I walked over and sat next to him, taking his hand in mine. "I know you do. I do too, but it was a beautiful ceremony, and there were so many people saying so many great things."

His small grin drew into a big smile. "I know. It was great to hear all those wonderful things about her. She was truly loved, even though she was a bit crotchety at times."

I chuckled. "She could be a bit crabby. I remember this one time when I was like ten or so. Pierce and I went into her store to get some candy, I think. She didn't really like Pierce, because he's always been a pain in the ass, and she followed us around that store, watching us like a hawk. Pierce said something shitty to her, and before I knew it, she had him by the ear and tossed him out of her store. It was one of the few times I ever actually heard Pierce cry. He was so embarrassed."

"That's priceless," he said as he undid his pants and shoved them to the floor. He unbuttoned his dress shirt and tossed it in the dirty clothes hamper. As he walked around in his boxer briefs, telling more stories about Aunt Millie, I didn't hear a word he said. How could I? His perky butt and nice package, proudly displayed in his black briefs, deserved my full attention. "You're not listenin', are you?"

His question snapped me out of my lustful thoughts. I'd been imagining Drake sliding his briefs off and bending over the bed, begging me to take him. "Um, yeah. You were talking about Aunt Millie."

He glared at me. "And what did I say?"

I stammered, "Something about how much you loved her." It was a complete guess.

"Nice try," he said as he pushed me back on the bed. He straddled me and pinned my arms to my side.

"Are you going to spank me?"

"You wish," he said before brushing his lips against mine.

I craned my head forward, trying to drink as many of his sweet kisses as possible. When he pulled away, I groaned.

"I think it's time."

I grimaced. That was Drake's way of telling me it was time to go to sleep. "Okay. Let me just brush my teeth, and I'll be right back." I tried to get up, but Drake placed his hand on my chest and gently pushed me back onto the mattress.

"Not for sleep," he said. "For bed."

My eyes grew wide, and my cock immediately responded. I'd been doing my best to not bring up sex even though we'd been sharing a bed. The timing wasn't right. Drake needed to grieve, and the past week had been about Aunt Millie, not my desires. "Are you serious?"

He nodded. "I appreciate how patient you've been with me. I can't tell you how much that means to me. You've given me the time I needed to work through everythin'. And it's been a lot. A whole hell of a lot. But Aunt Millie wouldn't want me to stop livin'. She'd want me to embrace life, to embrace you. And that's what I intend to do. If you'll have me."

Was he kidding? "Of course I will. I've wanted you since the first day you pissed me off in the cafeteria."

He smirked. "I know you have." He rubbed his hardening cock against my erection. "I've felt it, and I feel it really well right now."

I smirked and rolled over, pinning Drake underneath me. He parted his legs and wrapped them around my waist as our tongues found each other's mouth. I drank in his candy kisses as I explored the peaks and valleys of his lean muscles and slid my fingers across his smooth flesh.

Drake moaned and nipped at my chin as I licked a fiery trail to his neck. "You have too many clothes on," he said.

He didn't need to tell me anything else. I stood and was out of my clothes by the time Drake had slid off his underwear.

"Damn, that was fast," he said with a smile. "I hope that's not a sign of things to come."

I rolled my eyes, but I couldn't respond. His nakedness left me speechless. I followed the lines of his body, from the golden hair that trailed along his upper thigh to the lines of muscle that outlined his legs and biceps. His hard, throbbing cock pulsed amid the nest of golden fur, and his big cum-filled balls rested between his powerful legs. "You're so beautiful."

"Not as beautiful as you," he said. He reached out to me, and I crawled back onto the bed. I hovered above him. Even though I longed to feel his flesh against mine once more, I didn't want this moment to end. If it lasted until the end of time, I'd be perfectly happy. Perhaps there was a spell for that.

"Come here." He wrapped his arms around my neck, bringing me down to him, and when our bodies made contact, we both gasped. The pressure of his lean body, hard cock, and muscled legs against me drove me wild. It scared me how much I loved and wanted him. It made me vulnerable in ways warlocks didn't enjoy. We were about strength and power, but against Drake I had none.

My heart belonged to him, and even though it terrified me, it couldn't have made me happier.

"Mason, I want you inside me," he said.

I wanted it too, and even though I understood the mechanics, I'd never done it before. I didn't want to hurt him. That was why I had to prepare him first.

After delivering long, wet kisses to his soft lips, I nibbled and licked a winding path down his chin to his chest. I ran my tongue in lazy circles around his nipple, flicking across his sensitive flesh until it stiffened. Drake moaned and thrust his hips against me as I tweaked the pebbled flesh with my fingers while enticing the other nipple to attention.

"Holy shit," he said. "That feels good."

"Let's see what you think about this," I said before nibbling my way down his rippled abs. I followed the ridge of each muscle, which made him whimper and thrash. He tangled his fingers in my hair, guiding me down to where we both wanted me to go.

When I arrived at his hard, throbbing cock, I took it in my hands. His shaft pulsed, and Drake inhaled sharply as I slowly teased the flesh with slow strokes. Drops of precum slid out from the hooded cock slit, and I wiped my tongue across the sweet liquid.

"Fuck!" Drake cried out. He gazed down at me with wild eyes. "That feels good."

"And you taste good." I then ran my tongue along the ridge of his fat cockhead. More precum leaked out, and with each pass of my tongue across the opening, Drake shivered and trembled.

"Oh, Mason," he mumbled.

I took that as a sign I was doing well, and if that was making him happy, what I was going to do next was going to make him fucking ecstatic.

I placed the head of his cock in my mouth and suckled. Drake arched his back, forcing more of his dick inside my hot mouth. I slobbered up and down his shaft, cradling his balls in my hands. He grabbed a handful of my hair and guided me farther onto his prick. His slack jaw and dreamy eyes told me he enjoyed the sensation. I increased suction and pace, bobbing up and down his shaft as he thrust his hips.

When his cock slid into my throat, I gagged.

"Sorry," he said. A sheepish grin slunk across his face.

I wiped the spittle from my lips and kissed the shaft of his cock and the inside of his thigh. "Don't apologize. I liked it."

"Liked it? It's fuckin' great."

"You think so?"

He nodded vigorously.

I lifted his legs to my shoulders and said, "Then tell me what you think about this." I then parted his white cheeks and gazed at his pink center. I drew small circles around the edges of his hole, and Drake's head fell back against the mattress. He moaned and drove his ass harder against my finger.

"Oh yeah," he said. "That feels fuckin' great too."

I replaced my finger with my tongue, and Drake inhaled so sharply, I had to look up to make sure he was still breathing. His chest heaved and his legs trembled. He was so lost in the pleasure of my mouth against his ass, he looked like he'd been transported someplace far away, so I continued what I was doing. I licked around his center before piercing his puckered flesh.

"Shit! Oh shit!" he exclaimed, as my tongue wormed farther up his ass. I wiggled it side to side, delighting in the muskiness of his butt as I ground my hips into the mattress. I was so hard, my cock was in danger of tearing a hole in the bedding.

I withdrew my tongue and replaced it with a finger. He immediately tensed.

"Am I hurting you?"

He shook his head. "I just need to get used to it. Your finger's bigger than your tongue, you know?"

"And my cock is wider than three of my fingers."

Apprehension briefly crouched in his eyes before he blinked it away. "I know, but I want you inside," he said. "I love you."

I drew circles inside his butt with my finger before inserting two. Drake gasped and bit his tongue. The passion in his eyes had turned from a flickering desire to a blazing inferno. "And I love you too."

I inserted a third finger. After a few minutes, his muscles finally relaxed.

"It's time," I told him, to which he nodded eagerly.

"Thank God," he panted. "I need to feel you in me. On top of me. All over me."

I reached into the nightstand and pulled out a bottle of lube and a condom. He eyed the rubber and asked, "Um, you haven't had sex before, right?"

"No. Why?"

"Well, since I haven't either, I figure it's safe without. Well, you know." An embarrassed smirk slid across his lips as he nodded to the condom.

"Only if you're sure," I said.

"I am. For my first time, I just want to feel you. Nothin' else."

I put the rubber back in the drawer. "Sounds perfect. So how do you want to do this?"

"I've heard it's easier if I'm on my stomach. That okay?"

"Since I love looking at your ass, I'd say that's fine with me."

Drake turned onto his stomach, and I got behind him and between his legs. I squirted a generous amount of lube on my dick and then on his hole.

"It's cold," he said, looking over his shoulder.

"Don't worry," I replied as I kissed the back of his neck. "I'll warm it up real soon."

I stroked my cock and aimed it straight for the place it had wanted to go for so long. His pink hole shuddered as I placed my bare cock against his entrance.

"I'm ready," he said. He gripped the sheets, no doubt in anticipation of the pain.

"Me too," I replied before I nudged myself against him. When the head of my seven-inch cock pierced his flesh, Drake yelped and arched on the bed.

"Holy shit, that hurts!"

I stopped and hovered above him. "Should I get out?"

"No," he said. "Just give me time to get used to you."

I braced myself with my left arm and leaned over his back. I swept my lips across his neck and nibbled at his ear. With each kiss and bite, Drake relaxed and his body opened up more. His muscles slowly dragged me farther inside before stopping once again.

Sweat beaded across his back and a low moan escaped his throat. I ran a hand across his back, gliding across his flesh while I massaged the tension out of his body.

Drake relaxed and took in more of my shaft until I was buried all the way to the hilt.

"Just stay there," he mumbled. "Don't move."

"I won't," I said, lowering myself until my full weight rested on top of him. Being inside him, feeling his flesh wrapped around mine, was the most intimate and special moment I'd ever experienced in my life. The fact that I was in love with Drake made it that much more wonderful. I couldn't have been happier that I'd saved my first time for a boy like him.

I kissed his neck while I roamed my hand down his side, clutching at his muscles and his ass. Drake responded by lifting his head and turning to the left, giving me access to the lips I loved to kiss.

Our mouths found each other, and our impatient tongues were reunited. Drake pushed his tongue into my mouth, and I delighted in the fact that I was inside him and he was inside me, just the way we were always meant to be.

"I'm ready," he said after he broke the kiss.

"Are you sure?"

Drake's response was to push back against my cock. I moaned and thrust into him. Our bodies locked into a rhythm both frenzied and sensual. Every time I shoved myself into him, Drake grunted and pushed back against me when I pulled back my hips. We panted and groaned as our bodies collided.

I grabbed his head and turned it back to the side, so I could kiss him while we made love, and we stayed that way for several minutes until my balls drew up tight and my dick became hard as steel.

I got up on my knees and pulled Drake onto all fours. With my hands on his waist, I slammed into him. He moaned and grunted from the force of my thrusts, and a wet *thwack* emanated from our bodies every time his ass crashed against my groin.

"Damn, you're so hard," Drake moaned as he palmed his cock, furiously jacking himself to the same beat I fucked his ass to.

Sweat poured off me and dripped onto Drake. I slid my hand through the perspiration until I reached his shoulder. With one hand on his shoulder and one on his waist, I had the perfect leverage to thrust into him even harder and faster.

Drake clearly liked the change. He whimpered and moaned, his head thrashing backward and forward. My thrusts grew wilder as the cum churned up from my balls.

"Shit," I muttered. "I'm gonna come."

"Yes," Drake muttered. He rested his chest on the bed, his ass in the air and still jerking his cock. "Come in me. I want to feel it."

He didn't have to ask twice. My cock spasmed deep inside his ass as I flooded his hole with half a dozen forceful jets of spunk. Drake shivered as I unloaded in his butt. The sensation of my orgasm inside his ass must have brought him over the edge. He cried out and went rigid. His sphincter tightened around my dick as he came hard. He trembled, and when he was done, he collapsed on the bed.

I fell on top of him, my semihard prick still lodged inside him. Even though I was spent, I had no intention of pulling out.

"You can stay there all night if you want," he said.

I wrapped my arms around him and buried my head in his neck. "I was planning on staying here a little longer than just tonight. If that's okay with you."

"Fine by me," Drake said, glancing at me over his shoulder. Sweat matted blond locks to his forehead, and he had to blow some strands out of his eyes. "At least until it's my turn to fuck you."

I wiggled my eyebrows at him. "Didn't I tell you? I'm a total top."

"Not with me, you're not."

And I liked that. Before Drake, I'd fashioned myself based on what I thought my family or the other covens thought I should be—strong and powerful. And while I was still those things, probably even more so now, I'd also found strength in being vulnerable and just being me. Because after all, that was what being in love was about.

It was like magic. We could harness it and use its power, but it was at its most powerful when we simply let it be.

And even though we had a long, rocky road ahead of us, my gut told me that in the end, nothing could ever come between us.

We were spell bound, and that was a bond that could never be broken.

Coming Soon to Dreamspinner Press

Blood Tied

The Warlock Brothers of Havenbridge: Book Two

By Jacob Z. Flores

Thad Blackmoor's heart is as cold as his icy magical abilities. He considers emotions a waste of his time and prefers to study the arcane, using the sacred books of his coven to grow in his craft. He aspires to supersede his father and elder brother Pierce in power, and now that his younger brother Mason has tapped into the rare warlock power of darkness, he needs to work harder than ever.

But Thad's ambitions are halted when he saves Aiden Teine, a fire fairy, from a banshee. Thad's immediate attraction to Aiden catches him off guard and thaws his cold heart for the first time. As Thad, Aiden, and his brothers investigate the connection between the banshee attack and the vampyre and shadow weaver who almost killed them, Thad tries to dodge Ben, a sexy warlock who won't let him be after a one-night stand.

Their search leads them to the Otherworld, where something even more insidious is at work—something Thad will need more than logic to stand against.

JACOB Z. FLORES lives a double life. During the day, he is a respected college English professor and midlevel administrator. At night and during his summer vacation, he loosens the tie and tosses aside the trendy sports coat to write man on man fiction, where the hardass assessor of freshmen-level composition turns his attention to the firm posteriors and other rigid appendages of the characters in his fictional world.

Summers in Provincetown, Massachusetts, provide Jacob with inspiration for his fiction. The abundance of barely clothed man flesh and daily debauchery stimulates his personal muse. When he isn't stroking the keyboard, Jacob spends time with his daughter. They both represent a bright blue blip in an otherwise predominantly red swath in south Texas.

Blog: http://jacobzflores.com
Facebook: http://www.facebook.com/jacob.flores2
Twitter: @JacobZFlores
Pinterest: https://www.pinterest.com/jacobflores2/
Goodreads:
https://www.goodreads.com/author/show/5142501.Jacob_Z_Flores
Google Plus: https://plus.google.com/u/0/+JacobFlores9595/posts

3

By Jacob Z. Flores

Justin Jimenez has loved his partner, Spencer Harrison, for ten years. He'll do anything for him—including bury his feelings for a man he met while he and Spencer were separated last year. Justin never planned to fall in love, and he certainly never planned to tell Spencer about it—but when a phone call wakes them in the middle of the night to inform Justin that his former lover, Dutch Keller, has been in an accident, he doesn't have a choice.

Justin's revelation shatters the fragile relationship he and Spencer were trying to rebuild. The weight of his guilt—both for hurting Spencer and for leaving a heartbroken Dutch to find solace in a bottle—crushes him. But what Justin doesn't know is that Spencer and Dutch guard an explosive secret of their own. All three men are tangled in a communal web of lies, and unless they find the events in their lives that ultimately led them to friendship, passion, and betrayal, they won't see the love at the heart of the pain.

http://www.dreamspinnerpress.com

Being True

By Jacob Z. Flores

Truman L. Cobbler has not had an easy life. It's bad enough people say he looks like Donkey from Shrek, but he's also suffered the death of his policeman father and his mother's remarriage to a professional swindler, who cost them everything. Now dirt poor, they live in the barrio of San Antonio, Texas. When Tru transfers to an inner-city high school halfway through his senior year, he meets Javi Castillo, a popular and hot high school jock. Javi takes an immediate liking to Tru, and the two become friends. The odd pairing, however, rocks the school and sets the cliquish social circles askew. No one knows how to act or what to think when Mr. Popular takes a stand for Mr. Donkey. Will the cliques rise up to maintain status quo and lead Tru and Javi to heartbreak and disaster or will being true to who they are rule the day?

http://www.dreamspinnerpress.com

The Gifted One

By Jacob Z. Flores

As his birthday approaches, Matthew Westlake fears more than just growing a year older. He fears never seeing another year at all. Each birthday brings a close call with death, leaving holes in his memory, recurring nightmares, and one more glimpse of his guardian angel. This birthday Matt must stand against ancient evils that have hounded him since birth, because he is a Gifted One—a seventh son of a seventh son.

Within Matt rests the unlocked potential of a force for good, but it also makes him a target. Being the Gifted One and dodging demonic attacks aren't Matt's only problems, though. He's fallen in love with his protector, the Archangel Gabriel, and Heaven will condemn that love to save Matt's soul. But Heaven doesn't count on Gabriel loving Matt in return, defying divine law and placing them in danger from demons and angels alike.

http://www.dreamspinnerpress.com

Please Remember Me

By Jacob Z. Flores

Successful lawyer Santi Herrera couldn't be happier with the direction his life is taking. Not only is he on track to becoming a partner in his law firm, but he's planning his wedding to Hank Burton, a south Texas contractor who has made a name for himself despite his humble beginnings. The introverted lone wolf Santi and the friendly, outgoing Hank complement each other perfectly. From the moment they laid eyes on each other, they were hooked, and as far as Santi and Hank are concerned, a happily ever after is their destiny.

But fate deals them a devastating new hand.

A construction accident leaves Hank with severe head trauma and brings him precariously close to death. When he finally awakens, Hank doesn't remember Santi or the love they shared for the past three years. Santi faces the greatest challenge of his life. Can he respark a flame his lover can't recall? And can he stop the diverging paths that fickle fate charts between them?

Santi has faith in the love he and Hank shared and in the words his father once spoke to him: "It's never too late to fall in love. All over again."

http://www.dreamspinnerpress.com

When Love Takes Over

Provincetown: Book One

By Jacob Z. Flores

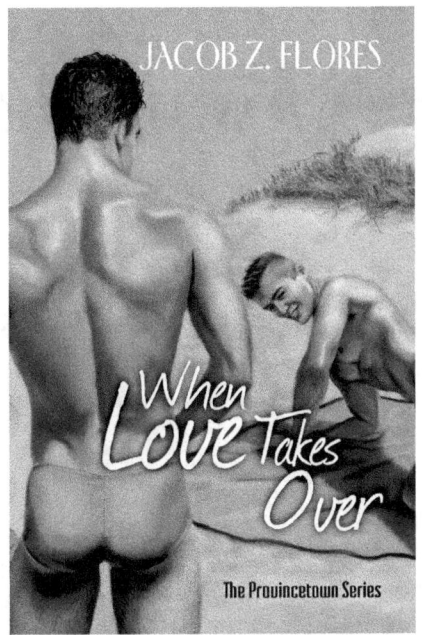

Zach Kelly's life is a shambles. His boyfriend of three years dumped him, and his writing career is going nowhere. On a whim, he heads to Provincetown, Massachusetts, to nurse his broken heart and figure out his next step. He's expecting to find rest and relaxation on the sandy beaches of Cape Cod. Instead, Zach meets a hunky porn star during a chance encounter at a leather shop he mistakes as a place to buy a belt that is definitely *not* for whipping.

Van Pierce is smitten when shy and inexperienced Zach crashes through a shelf of fetish gear. Though Van's got an insatiable appetite for men on and off the set, his porn persona, Hart Throb, hides a broken heart. He's struggling to find the reality the porno set doesn't offer, and Zach is fighting to find the fantasy that will set his writing on fire. The odd goofball and the suave beefcake may either find love amid Provincetown's colorful pageantry where summer never seems to end—or more heartbreak than either can imagine.

http://www.dreamspinnerpress.com

Chasing the Sun

Provincetown: Book Two

By Jacob Z. Flores

As a physician and prominent citizen of Victoria, Texas, Dr. Gil Kelly took a hard fall when his vengeful wife revealed his infidelity with other men. Closing ranks around her, the town's elite ostracized him, and his relationship with his children was nearly destroyed.

After spending his life focused on living for others, he has no idea how to live for himself. He wants to find love but now settles for anonymous sex that only further clouds his world with shame and guilt. Gil believes finding true love is an unobtainable dream, what his father used to call "chasing the sun."

Then he runs into Tom Martinez, his son's childhood best friend, who returned to town a grown man and offers everything Gil needs. But Gil hesitates to fall into Tom's arms, because after his high-profile divorce, the potential scandal of loving a younger man could separate him from his children permanently.

http://www.dreamspinnerpress.com

When Love Gets Hairy

Provincetown: Book Three

By Jacob Z. Flores

As vain as he is beautiful, Nino Santos happily lives life waiting for the next ferry full of fairies to bring him new conquests. As long as they aren't hirsute, he's all in. So he's shocked to wake up after a beach party he cannot remember with a hairy naked man lying next to him.

Teddy Miller doesn't remember the "Bear Week" party either, much less the Abercrombie & Fitch model wannabe next to him. Teddy doesn't give two cents about appearances, but guys like Abercrombie don't return the favor. That's why he prefers men with extra fur and padding over carbon copy clones of perfection—a type of man Teddy is far too familiar with.

When Nino and Teddy glimpse each other the next morning, it's loathing at first sight. Instead of exchanging phone numbers, they exchange insults and vow never to see each other again. In Provincetown, however, escaping a trick best forgotten isn't easy. Mutual friends and chance circumstances keep Nino and Teddy in each other's orbit. But are they fighting each other or the attraction growing between them? The answer lies amid Provincetown's windswept dunes and the night neither of them can recall.

http://www.dreamspinnerpress.com

When Love Comes to Town

Provincetown: Book Four

By Jacob Z. Flores

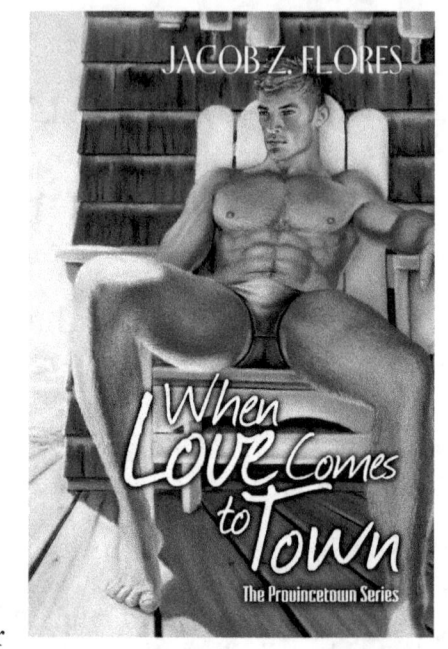

Brody O'Shea isn't looking for much, just a hot guy with a decent job, who is sane and doesn't have kids. The son of a former rock star, Brody has lived through the pain of bankruptcy and bad parenting, and he doesn't want to experience it again. As a reformed horndog, he wants the security and stability of a relationship. But almost every guy he meets seems satisfied with Mr. Right Now, and he wants to find Mr. Right—now!

The only men Eric Vasquez chases are criminals. As a deputy and single father, he has no need for a relationship after his last one ended disastrously. He lives for and through Maddie, his nine-year-old daughter. Everything else is a needless distraction, but distraction is what Eric gets when he comes to Provincetown to attend the wedding between his cousin Van and the man of his dreams.

When Brody and Eric meet, what they want and what they find conflict. An ocean of expectations separates them. If they cannot move past their reservations to reach each other's shores, they might miss the boat when love comes to town.

http://www.dreamspinnerpress.com

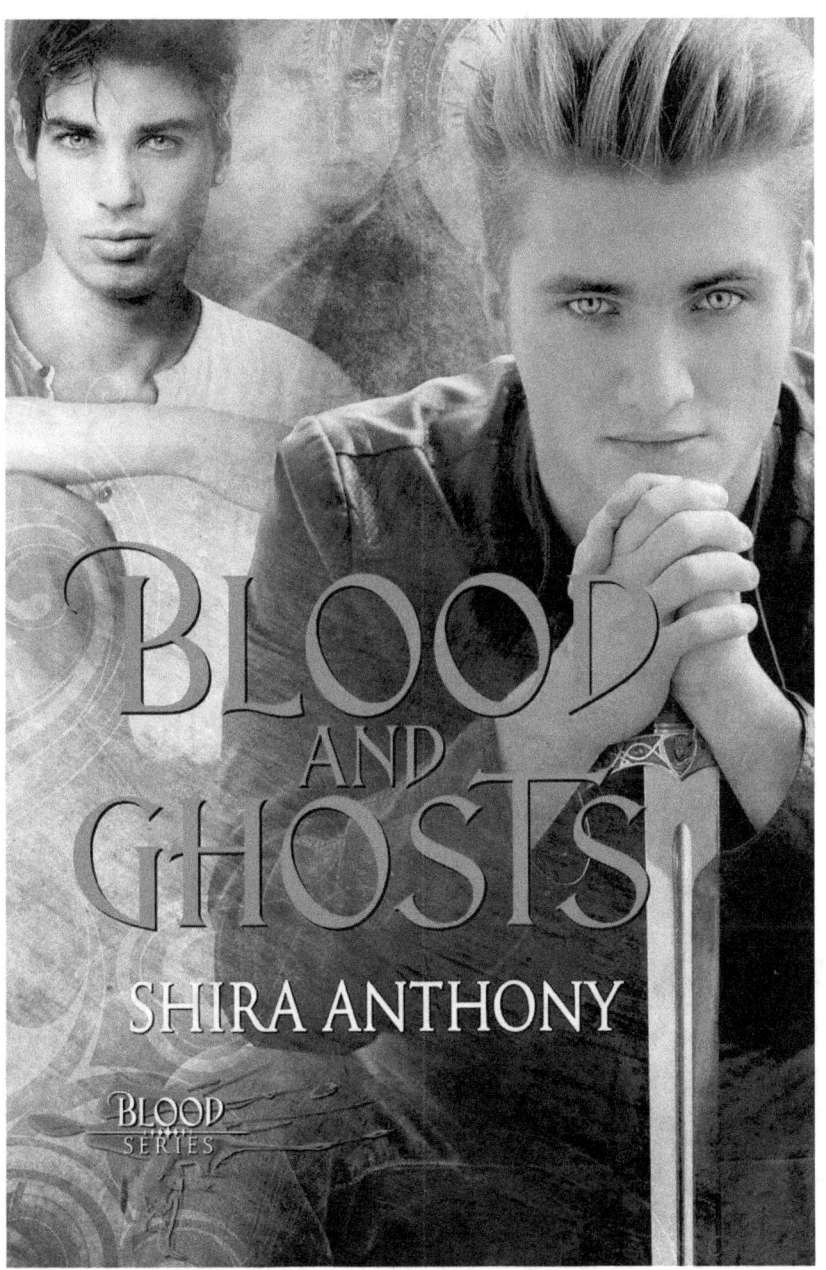

BLOOD AND GHOSTS

SHIRA ANTHONY

BLOOD
SERIES

http://www.dreamspinnerpress.com

LIV OLTEANO

A
counselor
AMONG
wolves

LEADER MURDERS: CASE TWO

http://www.dreamspinnerpress.com

THEY COME BY NIGHT

TINNEAN

www.ingramcontent.com/pod-product-compliance
Lightning Source LLC
Chambersburg PA
CBHW070117260626
47160CB00004B/1509